Soul of Light and Shadow

Lords of the Underworld
Series Book 1

Maggie White

The following text is a work of fiction. All the characters, organizations, businesses, and events portrayed in this novel are products of the author's imagination or used fictitiously.

Soul of Light and Shadow by Maggie White
Book 1 of the Lords of the Underworld Series
Story Copyright 2023 Maggie White
Editing by Jenny Raden
Map by B.C. FaJohn Books

All rights reserved.

Identifiers
Paperback: 979-8-9876093-1-6
Hardback:: 979-8-9876093-2-3

All rights reserved. No part of this book may be reproduced, stored in, or introduced into a retrieval system, or transmitted in any form or by any means (electronic, mechanical, photocopying, recording or otherwise) without the prior written permission. Any reproduction of this publication without prior consent from the publisher is an infringement of copyright law.

Content Warning

The book you're about to read includes the death of a parent, moments of tension or danger, mature language and situations. For a full list of possible triggers, please visit www.maggiewhitebooks.com.

Contents

PROLOGUE	11
CHAPTER 1	14
CHAPTER 2	33
CHAPTER 3	47
CHAPTER 4	68
CHAPTER 5	75
CHAPTER 6	84
CHAPTER 7	101
CHAPTER 8	119
CHAPTER 9	132
CHAPTER 10	147
CHAPTER 11	160
CHAPTER 12	170
CHAPTER 13	178
CHAPTER 14	192
CHAPTER 15	202
CHAPTER 16	214
CHAPTER 17	223
CHAPTER 18	228
CHAPTER 19	237
CHAPTER 20	248
CHAPTER 21	261

CHAPTER 22	270
CHAPTER 23	280
CHAPTER 24	292
CHAPTER 25	303
CHAPTER 26	315
CHAPTER 27	324
CHAPTER 28	330
CHAPTER 29	348
CHAPTER 30	359
CHAPTER 31	368
CHAPTER 32	378
EPILOGUE	380
THE END	384

There are thousands of books published every day, I'm so honored you chose one of mine to share your time with. Without our readers, authors are merely daydreamers and story-spinners. You are what makes this all real.

To my mother and her unwavering support, you can never know what it means to have you on my team every single day. To my kids, who interrupted this book a thousand times to ask me to play, please never stop. Being your Mom is the best part of my life.

Prologue

Lucia

When I was six years old, Molly from first grade's mom hit me with her car. I should've waited in the designated pick-up line. I should've followed the teacher's directions, but I didn't. I couldn't wait to see my mother. She'd been working long hours, and I was relieved to spend the night together, just the two of us, no babysitters, no day care. No interruptions.

One minute I'd been skipping across yellow-striped pavement. The next I was skidding backward across cool cement after a large, dark vehicle slammed to a halt, breaks squealing. A frantic crowd had instantly descended on me, a hundred eager hands looking for injuries.

And yet, nothing. Not a single scratch on my little body.

It seemed even after the squealing impact of the oversize SUV, I remained completely unharmed. Well, except for the tongue lashing I received from my mother as she held me against her body and cried with relief.

I never walked home again. We never even discussed the event. My mother simply switched her shift and was the first car in the pick-up line each day. Her love for me was deeper than anything I'd ever felt before and since. I knew even then how hard it was for her, a single mom in an old-fashioned neighborhood. I didn't want her to worry any more than she already did.

Perhaps that's why I never told her when Molly's enormous car had borne down on me, there had never been an impact. Because in the moment directly before the metal should've broken my skin, a figure had appeared, in white and gold armor, bracing himself between the car and my body.

I'd skipped across the pavement, sure, but it hadn't been a backpack that kept me from road rash. It was an iron-strong arm that had swept me up against that white armor, and for an instant there was a luminous pair of ice blue eyes staring back at me.

A blink later and he was gone, my invisible protector. Leaving me on the ground, a dent in the front bumper and a thousand questions I couldn't answer. In the end, I vowed to never explain his presence to my mother. Not when she was already so frantic.

But I couldn't keep him a secret forever. I caught sight of him when I was in the hospital at age ten. This time he appeared with two others at his side, dressed in the same strange, body-fitting white tunics and layered leather armor. I had had pneumonia and fever dreams for days. But my eyes found him easily. Standing outside my curtained-off area, his blue eyes glowing under the fluorescent lights of the hospital. A flash of gold over each shoulder and across his chest.

An emblem perhaps? But my eyes wouldn't focus enough to tell what it was. When I woke up next, insisting to my nurse I'd seen someone here visiting, she'd hushed me, promising me no one had been there for hours. When I mentioned the pair of dark, curving horns and the soft gray tone of his skin, the nurse laughed aloud.

She claimed I'd only imagined it during the worst of the fever.

But it had been him again, the same creature who had saved me from the car wreck then vanished into shadows and light. I knew for sure I'd seen him. But again, the more I insisted, the more worried and anxious my mother became.

After some time, I gave up trying to explain. And then high school, friends, boys all cluttered my mind in the years following.

It wasn't until the day after my twenty-first birthday that I would finally find out what the creature in white was. And why he was following me.

And it was something I never, ever could've imagined.

1

Lucia

The morning sun blazed into my room, sending the shadows and swells of the morning darkness back into hiding. I lay completely still, basking in the comfort of bed and the strange longing that always followed waking up.

Stretching languidly, I stared around the small but familiar space. It was mine for now, until I left for college again in a few months. I loved being home. I loved the way it smelled. I loved the way that my mother insisted that each and every trophy, prize, and drawing I'd ever done be hanging somewhere around the two-bedroom apartment we'd spent the last few years in.

It was home.

I rolled over, grinning as I noticed the single white rose bud lying on the pillow beside my face. Picking it up, I touched the delicate petals that were only now beginning to bloom.

"Beautiful," I whispered into the quiet morning.

Heart lighter than before, I dashed down the hall, still in pajamas with no interest in changing, and found my mother sitting grumpily in the kitchen. Her usually smiling face was drawn, and when I appeared there, she jumped in her chair, her fair skin even paler than usual.

"Is my hair that bad? You look like you've seen a ghost," I teased, grabbing the orange juice from a top shelf in the refrigerator and pouring myself a glass.

"No, no ghosts." She fixed her smile, pushing more of her usually sunny disposition back to the surface. "How did you sleep? Too much birthday cake yesterday?"

I laughed, letting my hip bump against the countertop as I went back through my night. I didn't dream often, a fact my mother always considered fascinating, but last night there was something there, lingering just out of reach. Probably brought on by the confetti cake coma that I had spent most of the evening in. Slowly the images took shape, a familiar form in my mind, ever present, ever familiar.

Him.

The shadowed form of a male, my protector and constant companion.

Sipping the sweet citrus drink down, I considered my mother's face. I had to be careful with this subject. It was...sensitive. "Do you remember when I had that invisible friend all those years ago?"

Mom's knuckles were white as she gripped the table. Disappointed by her reaction but unwilling to stop my thoughts, I pushed onward. "I dreamed about him last night. We were sitting together at a table like this. He had this armor on, covered in dirt and looking like he was fresh from war. But as soon as I tried to focus on what we were saying, he lifted a hand and began to take his helmet off—"

"The shadow devil. That's what you always called him. Did you see him?" My mother's voice was strained as she interrupted me.

"Like...around the house? No, of course not." I chuckled, my humor deflating when she didn't join in. "No, Mom, it was just a dream. He is just a dream." I put a hand over hers. Her eyes, glazed with fear, made me uneasy. "Hey, are you okay? You don't look so great."

Clammy fingers found mine, and I barely resisted the urge to pull them away from her grip. "Do you dream of him often?" Her words tumbled over each other as she pulled me even closer.

"Not really." I scrunched my nose, "I used to see him more when I was a kid. It's been years though, since I don't know..."

I broke off, thinking about when the last time I'd seen him was. Suddenly, little memories trickled in, bits and pieces of my own history. But just as I tried to focus on the answer, my head throbbed hard, and I couldn't seem to pinpoint the exact instances.

Taking a breath, I tugged my hands free and pressed the heel of my hands against my eyes, the white rose still in my fingers.

"Where did you get that?" Her voice was dark and low and cut straight through my thoughts. I glanced down at the rose, my headache temporarily easing.

"It was on my pillow; did you forget you'd left it?" I waved a hand in front of her blank blue eyes. She stared at the rose in my fingers, jaw loose and sagging. The juice was sour in my belly. Something was very wrong.

"Mom?" I didn't bother to hide the quiver in my voice.

She stood quickly and moved past me without answering, an odd, frozen look still on her face. Her long, slender form paused in the doorway. "I need to go lie down. Can you stay around here if I need you?"

I reached over to squeeze her arm, surprised when she pulled away from my touch. "Of course. Sorry if I upset you." And I meant it. Whatever I had said, whatever my dreams had brought up for her, it had rattled my mother. Deep in my gut, my nerves still roiled.

She staggered out, her shoulders slumped as she moved down the short hall. I popped the rose into the smallest vase I could find, which ended up being one of our few glass ones, and promptly set up shop by the television. I had books to read, phones to scroll… I was happy to be here to hold the fort while my mother rested.

I grinned to myself, remembering my birthday yesterday. We'd done manicures, movies, and finished it off with a taco feast with a handful of my closest friends from school.

Only a few moments later, I heard the distinct sound of my mother's voice. Wondering if she needed me, I carefully made my way down the narrow hall to her room.

The door was cracked, and I leaned against the frame, pressing my ear as close to the threshold as I could. Inside, the words were falling fast and frantic from Mom's lips. So quickly it took me a moment to catch on to what she was saying.

"You don't understand. I didn't tell her anything. I was so wrong; she's going to be terrified." There was a pause as if she was waiting for someone to respond. Then a soft, nearly muffled sob. "I need more time."

I pulled back a little, panic simmering in my veins as my mother's strange words made my heart race. Through the opening, I could see her, but instead of providing reassurance, dread continued to fill my chest. From here, most of her room was visible, and there was no one else there. My mother was standing completely still, looking intently at the shadow between her dresser and the beige-painted wall of our apartment.

Trying to remain calm, I searched her form, considering that she could be on a call or was rehearsing something. One glance at the bedspread ruined that theory. Her phone was there, lit up but clearly not in use.

Before I could push in, Mom started speaking again, this time harsher. "Yes, I know the rules, but so do you. You have to bring her back if she asks. You have to. I don't care what realm you rip in two to make it happen. She's my baby. I can't bear to see her hurt."

There was a shorter pause. "You say you won't hurt her? Then why have you been showing up all these years? You think I didn't notice the flowers? You said you'd stay away. You promised."

She stiffened, her back completely straight. "I understand." There was a finality that snapped through the air and made the hair on the back of my neck stand up.

I backed away from the door, my slippered feet silent as I shuffled quickly back out to our living room. My heart was pounding hard enough that I could barely hear my own thoughts, but what I knew deep in my chest that something was very, very wrong, and I didn't like any of it. I sat stiffly on the sofa, my phone in my hand but unable to focus.

I'd never seen my mother do that before. Speak to something like there was a person there. I choked back a sob that bubbled up in my throat. Confusion and fear tumbled around in my chest until a single tear escaped and slid down my cheek. I swiped at it, angry at the show of weakness and my desire to curl into a ball and let a thousand more follow it.

Because now I knew, more than ever before, that something was very wrong.

When my mother came in later, her face pale but less strained, I pretended none of it happened. She sat on the couch beside me and tangled our fingers together in a tight hold. Perhaps she too felt the void between us, the fear and confusion that had suddenly become impassable.

I forced my head to bend, to drop until I pressed my nose against the softness of her shirt. I breathed her in, my heartbeat slowing as I focused on the warmth and comfort of the woman beside me. She had never led me astray. It had always been the two of us, just making our way in the world. And that's how it would stay.

Maybe that was because I liked it.

But maybe it was because right now I couldn't bear to find out what my mother had been talking about. Because if I knew, I had a feeling it was something that changed you forever.

I wasn't ready for that.

***

Weeks and months passed, and I had found myself forgetting, purposefully I'm sure, as my mother seemed to grow happier, brighter over the course of the time. I let my mind trick me into thinking things were good. School was out for the summer; my college classes were off my schedule so that I could spend my days making a little extra money at the sandwich shop down the road. The work was monotonous, but I loved being able to contribute to the family like an adult.

It gave me another reason to insist, for the hundredth time, that we couldn't move again. I had responsibilities here, if not roots. I saw the potential though, the chance to belong somewhere for the first time in my nomadic life.

Mom obsessed over my education, worried constantly that I had chosen to go into historical literature. She couldn't understand how I would make a living this way. What I wanted to explain to her is that I couldn't ever see myself sitting in a cubicle somewhere or even working in the diner like my mom had. I wanted to learn—I wanted to spend my days learning.

Which I was bound and determined to explain to her someday. Or better yet, show her when I finished up my schooling next year and decided what I wanted to do next.

All of those plans changed one summer afternoon, when my mother called, her voice gentle and quiet over the line. "Lucia, my love, I need you to come down to Saint Peter."

"The hospital?" I froze, my shoes squeaking against the cheap tile of the sandwich shop. "Mom?"

"Yes, the hospital." Her voice was fading. "Now."

I didn't even bother saying goodbye or clocking out. The soles of my feet ached as I sprinted across the parking lot. The sound of horns and squealing of tires meant I wasn't paying enough attention to what was happening around me.

I threw my car into gear and flew down the highway, a million prayers and wishes and wants flying through my mind. As I grew closer, I turned on the windshield wipers, surprised at the rain on such a sunny day, and it wasn't until I had turned off on the ramp to the hospital that I realized that it was tears blurring my vision, not rain.

They continued as I walked woodenly into the emergency room, my mother's name a ghost on my lips as I passed into the fluorescent lights and glaring white walls all around me. A kind-faced nurse led the way, her sedate steps forcing me to collect myself, to wait and walk with poise rather than all out sprint I craved.

"She's right here, Miss Walker," the nurse said, pulling back a curtain to reveal my mother with a barrel-chested doctor who looked to be in deep discussion. As soon as my face appeared, my mother's changed, relaxed, loosened even until there was a small smile on her lips. It was worse, I think, seeing that smile.

Because it was the same one she'd given me every time we'd had to pack up and move. Each time she'd left me at a new day care, a new school, a new job, a new apartment. She would kiss my forehead, brush the hair from my face, and tell me "straighten your crown, princess, there's work to be done."

It was a goodbye smile.

My heart lurched, and even as the doctor turned to me, a practiced and well-schooled expression of greeting on his face, I was completely sure this goodbye would be something else altogether.

"Mom?"

"Lovey, come here," she said, her sharp blue eyes, exactly the same color as mine, darting between the doctor and the nurse. Neither moved. After a moment, the doctor sighed and shifted on his feet.

"Good-bye, Juliette."

At that, I rushed across the space, my throat burning and hot as I took her cool fingers in my own and squeezed.

"What's going on? You're scaring me." I had to clear my throat, my voice tight enough it ached in my chest.

"Come here, baby." My mother opened her arms. "It's time."

"Time for what?"

Goosebumps raced along my flesh as the doctor spoke again. "I'll be right outside whenever you are ready, Miss Walker."

My mother nodded, and I moved closer, settling between her legs, hovering over her. For a moment, perhaps the first in my life, our roles were reversed, and with a sigh, my mother leaned her cheek against my shirt, her breath warming my skin even through the cotton.

"Mom, you're freaking me out. What's happening?"

The silence grew taut between us, until finally, she pulled back, her eyes rising to mine, guilt and pain evident.

"I've been keeping something from you."

The place where her breath had just been warming chilled against my skin. Panic made my mind clear, every muscle drawing up as I clutched her hands in mine. "Mom." I hated how whiny my voice had become, the pitch rising.

"I'm sick, baby." She pressed our combined hands to her cheek for a moment. It was cool against my shaking fingers. "Really sick."

I blinked, and the world shifted. I breathed sharply, and the world seemed to shift again. "Sick? Well then, let's get you some medicine. I'm sure they—"

"They've already done everything that can be done."

"What? You just got here."

Her face dropped again, a sign of her betrayal, of the untruth I'd just uttered.

"You've been sick for a long time, haven't you?" The words were bitter on my tongue, but not from anger. Just more of that panic, piling onto me and turning my stomach sour.

Mom's face turned back to mine, her eyes shimmering with tears. The sight of them was more terrifying than everything else. "I was granted more time, more than I should've ever asked for. But now my time is up."

My knees threatened to buckle, and I stared down at her. "No, no, no. That's not possible."

"I'm sorry, baby, but that's how it is."

"No," I pleaded, my voice ragged now. "We need more time."

She looked at me with such acute longing for a moment, my words sputtered off. I simply stared, holding her gaze with mine as I attempted to sort this out. There was hurt, such deep hurt that I could feel it in my bones. But more than that, there had to be something. I could find a way; I could do something.

I realized then I was whispering, it must've seemed like nonsense, just words and pleas tumbling over and over each other as they filled the cold room. Mom let me mumble, her trademark good-bye smile firmly in place. When there were no more words, the tears came, and I finally relinquished my position over her, letting her tuck me in close, holding me, stroking my face and back as wave after wave of tears slipped from my body.

Exhaustion came just as the tears dried. Resolution settled over my heart, and I pushed away from her to stand.

"We can fight this."

"Oh baby, I've been fighting, but that time has passed."

"I don't accept that."

"You have to. I have so much I have to tell you and not much time." Oddly, my mother glanced at the clock ticking away on the wall behind me. "I need you to listen."

"Listen? Now?"

"Yes, now." Mom swallowed hard, pulling me so we were facing each other on the uncomfortable hospital bed. "I wanted to tell you this three years ago when you turned eighteen, but I couldn't bring myself to do it then. I wanted so badly to keep you for myself. I should've known that by now. But you are the best of both worlds. I know you will be okay."

"Mom..."

"You're special, Lucia, my beautiful light, more special than even I realized." Her laugh was sad.

I leaned back, taking in her face. "Did they give you something, Mom? You're talking nonsense."

"I carried you, loved you, knew you from the beginning as my own, but you were never destined to be here. You are destined for so much more. And I know you will be everything they need and more."

Her arms were tight on mine, forcing me to listen, to hold still, even as my body recoiled from her strange words. "Momma, stop, you're scaring me."

A cool hand stroked my forearm. "You and I both know you've felt them. Maybe not seen them, but they've always been there. *He has always been there.*"

Time seemed to stop as we stared at each other. Her lips quirked a little. "I'll admit at first, I was offended by him stepping in all the time. Kings are not easy to keep as company, but I got used to him. Maybe because what he was doing kept us alive. He and his soldiers, they will take care of you now, I know it. You just need to give them more time."

I swallowed, more tears filling the corners of my eyes as I watched my mother push on, her voice growing ragged and dry.

"There are ten days until the full moon. That's the easiest time, when the veil between worlds is loose, easy to shift and move within. He will come for you then. And only then. He will come from the shadows, but don't be afraid, baby. Don't ever be afraid."

"He?"

Her face changed. "You've met him before. I wish I'd asked to meet him face to face, but I couldn't. His people, though, they can travel more easily. The boundaries apply to their souls less. But I know he would never hurt you. None of them would. The Others, though, will do anything to keep you from him. To keep you from fulfilling your birthright."

"What do I do? Mom, you're not making sense."

Her fingers pinched my skin. "Run, Lucia. Run fast and hard, and don't stop until he's there."

Adrenaline flooded my bloodstream. "What?"

"They will come for you, the Others. You have to run."

"But this man, will he save me? How will I know him?"

Her smile grew, bright and shining. "He is your other half; you will know him like one star knows another." She reached out to stroke my face. "The moment I'm gone, his spell hiding you from the Others will be broken. You have to hide."

"Mom, no, you're not going anywhere."

That sad smile again. I swallowed down the panic.

"I'm going to go get the doctor, and when I get back, we will get you some water and then get you home again. I'll take care of you, we can order pizza, watch *The Mummy* a few hundred more times, and all of this will be behind us."

Her fingers stroked across my cheekbone, tucking a stray strand of my dark hair behind my ears. "My beautiful Lucia, I love you so much."

I captured her hand, pressing it against my face as I pushed off the mattress "I'll be right back. Don't go anywhere." Rising from her hold, I moved to the door just beyond the curtain.

Desperate for help, I hurried toward the nurses' station and the doctor I'd seen earlier. Behind me, I heard her whisper something, and I took a steadying breath.

The doctor was only a few steps away, talking to the same nurse as before.

"Excuse me, Doctor?""

"Miss Walker." He slid his glasses from his nose, face serious. "I'm so very sorry for your loss."

I tilted my head, staring at him. "What?"

"Do you need more time with her?" He put a gentle hand on my shoulder, but it felt like a thousand-pound weight. "I know you're an adult, but there's a social worker on-site who can discuss your next options with you. Provide any support you may need."

I stepped away from him quickly, making his hand drop between us. Breathing hard, I pressed a hand against my chest, my eyes blinking rapidly. "Doctor, I'm not sure what you're talking about."

I felt the sting of tears again but didn't break his stare, even as his eyes grew dark and worried.

"I'm so sorry for your loss. I know she was so worried to tell you, but your mother has been in and out of the hospital for months now. The cancer was extremely aggressive."

"The cancer? Aggressive? What are you talking about?" I knew I was shouting, the sound echoing around me, but I couldn't stop myself. I stared around, eyes focusing in on the kind nurse from earlier. She was standing to the side, her eyes wide and rimmed in thick, glossy tears.

"What's wrong with all of you? I just came out here to see if you could help her!" I stormed back into the room, ready to shout at Mom for not telling me, to scream at her for hiding this, and then I saw her.

She was lying on the bed, near to where we'd been just a moment ago, but her face was pale, smooth, and opaque as granite. Someone had tucked the sheets up around her arms and her eyes were closed. Had I done that? I didn't remember doing that. I stepped closer, my heartbeat a throbbing reminder in my ear of what my mother now lacked. I knew it in an instant, but denial kept me staring.

"Mom?"

There was no movement. Of course there wasn't.

Because my mother was gone.

Pain like a lance flew through me. And then panic. Because I'd just been talking to her. I hadn't left her like this. Chills covered my arms and legs as I moved closer. My eyes inevitably drew to the chart next to her bed. There, in bold black ink, the following note was scrawled.

Time of death: 3:12 p.m.

I looked at the clock on the wall. It was 3:24.

My mother had been dead for twelve minutes. I slipped my hand into hers, unafraid of the cool skin on mine.

"Momma, how?"

Was I hallucinating? Had I imagined our entire conversation? Something deep in my gut resisted the idea, twisted at the idea entirely.

Because as much as my rationality resisted the idea of the creature who protected me from harm and who visited me in my dreams, my entire being wrapped around the truths of the idea. Of the possibility that all of this really did make sense. My memories were filled with the strange occurrences in my life, the things I couldn't explain or understand.

I leaned my head against her shoulder, pain and grief slicing me to my core.

"Good-bye, Mom." Shaking, I reached for her hand, wanting to knit my fingers into hers. But my fingers encountered a piece of paper instead, folded and tucked into her palm.

I unfolded it, my hands swiping angrily at the tears that kept me from seeing her message more clearly. In a long, sloping script, the message appeared hastily written.

She has been mine since before she took a breath. Of course I will come for her. Stay safe and keep to the shadows. Lucia will know safety soon.

I stopped reading, barely containing my scream as I looked up to find someone else in the room with us. In front of me stood an angel. My mind froze at the improbability, but every other part of me was shrieking at the embodiment of something that shouldn't exist being so close.

He was dressed in a dark robe, his immense figure human-like but too tall, too wide to be a human man. Above his dark, short-cropped hair curled immense white horns, the ends of them adorned with a variety of charms that dangled and chimed in the silence of the room.

"Who are you?" I whispered, my throat working as I flung an arm out over my mother's body.

He met my gaze head on, his eyes completely white and glowing in the light. Slowly, as if to answer my question, dark, mahogany-colored wings rose from behind him, spreading until most of the room was encompassed in his wingspan.

"Move aside," he said, voice deep enough I felt it in my chest as I stiffened. "Her time has come."

I gasped, sliding away from my mother until I could press myself to the wall, shock and fear replaced by awe as his charms shook and moved on his head as if by an invisible wind. He stared at me intently, or at least I believed he did, the whites of his eyes making it difficult to tell. Deep in my chest, something twisted painfully, and I winced, pressing a hand to the spot.

"Who are you?" I repeated, dropping onto my haunches in an effort to avoid the power thundering through the room.

Was he one of the Others that Mom had mentioned? "What are you going to do to her?"

A creature moved toward her; his wings still held high. A stride away, he slowed, reaching his fingers toward me. Just before he reached my skin, he jolted, his head tilting as if listening to something. The room was eerily silent, as if the rest of the world held its breath in this instant.

"Not mine," he said finally, his voice making my ears ring. To my surprise, his lips curled in what might've been a smile. "I am merely a guardian, soul bound."

"What? For me?"

His horned head bowed then shook slowly. "For her."

I panted, staring up as he moved quickly to the bedside, his wings tucking in close. One hand reached out, laying across my mother's hand as if to give her a hand up. And then she did, or at least some version of her did—a misty image of her, as if painted by watercolor instead of reality, rose from the bed. It was vibrant and beautiful and so utterly shocking that I did nothing but stare at this thing the creature had guided from my mother.

I knew what it was.

Her soul.

"Momma," I whimpered, and to my surprise both creature and soul turned my direction. Her features may have been a blur, but I recognized her movements in an instant. That sarcastic tilt of her head, the way her body swayed toward me.

The soul, my mom's soul, glanced at the creature beside her, her hands moving toward him. Then a soft voice, familiar and gentle, spoke in my ear. "There was never enough time. Go, Lucia. Be loved and be whole."

And then the soul of my mother let the creature touch her again and they were gone.

I hit the tile hard, the floor biting into my knees as I crumbled in pain, my mind consumed by the thought of not just losing my mother, but of never knowing her at all.

2

Lucia

I was exhausted. I'd been walking all day, crisscrossing the heavily crowded city center in an effort to both keep moving but stay within sight of another human. Something deep in my chest told me I shouldn't be alone right now. Not since I had just lost the only person I'd ever counted on.

I knew the sun was dying though, and with it my idea of what to do. I still had my credit cards, plenty of cash in my bank account, but I was terrified. Afraid of what I could or could not do. These "Others" my mother had said, they wanted to stop me from fulfilling my birthright.

But I didn't even know what that meant.

If you'd told me any of this this morning, I would've screamed in laughter. But things were different. I had a full-on conversation with my mother *after* she passed away. And then I saw someone, something, tug her soul free, walk her away from the body that had failed her. It was horrifying and beautiful all at the same time.

But now, I was here, alone. I sat at a vacant table and pressed my fingers to my eyelids, begging my mind to cooperate.

She said I'd seen them or felt them.

And I had. But I didn't know what to make of that. I was nearly eight when I realized that no one else my age still had imaginary friends. Or if they did, they were nothing like the shadowy warriors that slipped in and out of my life. The few times I'd confessed seeing them to my mother, she begged me to ask them to leave, to tell them we were safe without them and didn't need them.

Holy shit. I groaned. These imaginary friends were distant, misty memories, flashes of white robes and shining metal. And warmth, instant comfort, like being surrounded by blankets fresh out of the dryer.

None of those things were going to keep me safe.

Not in this world.

A hand landed on my shoulder, and I leaped up, staring wide-eyed and gasping at a young man around my age. He raised his hand in defense, a white apron at his waist staking him as a waiter. "I didn't mean to scare you. Do you want to order anything?"

I dragged air into my lungs, hoping to calm down my racing heartbeat. I offered him what I could, a wane smile, I was sure. "I'm fine, thanks."

He moved away, but I understood the message. I needed to either order or get out of here. I stood, stretching my legs, and a deep thump of pain and grief struck me like a blow.

I had to go home. I was being ridiculous, taking the rantings of my mother's final moments this far. She must've been hurting; she must've been lost. And I was only making things worse by hiding out here.

I needed a whole load of therapy and a ton of medication. But first, I needed to get home. I should check on the apartment, I needed to check Mom's paperwork, to figure out what was next. I swallowed the throbbing in my throat as tears threatened once more. And when I sat in my car, I leaned back and let them flow until I had nothing left.

I was empty, exactly like my world was.

I only made it a few steps into the apartment before I curled up on the couch, holding the pillows, smelling like home and her and safety, close.

And cried myself to sleep.

***

My eyes took a long time to adjust to the light. I recognized that I was still on the couch, even after a week, and my face and heart still ached with a ferocity that made it hard to breathe. Crying oneself to sleep was not conducive to beautiful wake-up calls, but I was grateful for the sleep. The past week had been a blur of decisions I'd never imagined making. At least never having to make them alone.

Suspicion grew as I pushed the blankets down my legs. I didn't remember pulling them over myself. As I swung my legs over the side of the couch, I stared out around our living room. It looked exactly like it had every day we'd lived here. No sign of my invisible friends, as I had called them as a child.

In the week since my mother had died, there had been no magic. No king of my dreams who was going to swoop in and save me from a world that now seemed dull and pointless.

There was only pain here, coupled with the hollow feeling of being adrift in the world once more.

"Anyone there?" I whispered. And for a moment, I swore there was movement to the shadow in the corner of the room, but when I turned my head, there was nothing. Goosebumps raised along my arms, and I paused. Waiting.

At least I'd gone completely crazy. First, I'd lost my mind at the hospital, and now I was talking to walls. I shook my head, giving in to a tear-filled laugh as I pushed myself into a standing position. I closed my eyes, pressing the lids tight, and counted down from ten then forced my brain to slow. I needed a plan. I would shower, then get dressed in real clothes, and then open the folder the hospital had sent home.

Where there was a process, there would be comfort.

Blinking, I let the tears flow as I made my way to the bathroom and turned on the showerhead. The water mixed with my tears, and by the time I got out, there was a certain resolute weight in my stomach that my world had forever changed. But life was carrying on. Even if I was barely able to.

I dried my hair, threw on my favorite pair of clean black leggings and a T-shirt I found, and had just made it back to the couch when the doorbell rang.

I glanced through the peephole, not surprised at all to see the neighbor from a few doors down, Susan. She'd been good friends with my mother. My heart sank, and I hesitated at the door. I pressed my forehead to the cool surface before swallowing twice and jerking the lock open.

Susan stood on the small stoop, her soft gray eyes worried.

"Lucia, thank the Lord below." She pressed a hand against the door, assuring I didn't shut it.

A chill ran down my spine. I shoved it away; everything made me nervous these days. It must be the impending insanity I kept waiting to finally take over.

"Susan." I cleared my throat. "What are you doing here?"

"Are you alone?" Her eyes were already over my shoulders, searching frantically around the dimly lit interior of our—my— home. I stepped toward Susan and closed the door slightly. Her eyes darted back to mine and held me in place.

"I'm afraid I have bad news."

"Your mother passed, I know." Susan's words were callous, shocking.

I stared, pain growing in my chest and creating another whirlwind of nausea I had barely gotten hold of. "How? How do you know?"

"She wanted me to make sure you didn't stay here; she was worried you wouldn't understand and you might come back."

I rubbed my forehead, stifling a groan. "Susan, this is my home."

Her rebuttal was quick and brutal. "It isn't. It never has been."

"What?" I'd lived in a lot of places, but this woman, commanding me on where I could call home, was a little over the top. Heat warmed my cheeks as my temper joined the fray of emotions circulating through my body.

Susan clearly didn't pick up on my emotions or didn't care, because she was pushing on. "Her protection will be wearing off. Even I could sense you. We have to get you out of here."

My back snapped tight. "I'm not going anywhere."

"You have to. Please." Susan reached for my hand again and tugged it into hers. "Just until Sunday."

"Sunday?"

"The full moon. That's when he can..." Susan trailed off, turning her head slowly to stare at a man walking his dog down the street.

Caught off guard and irritated at her disjointed invasion into my grief, I pulled my hand free of her grip and began to step back into the apartment.

She was frozen in place, her usually warm brown eyes sharp and narrow as she looked across the parking lot.

"Good-bye, Susan. I'm not really in the mood for..." My words drifted to silence as I followed her stare. The dog walker. She was still staring at him, harder and more obsessive than before. My irritation was replaced by some modicum of instinctive fear. Like the moment one deer sights a predator, so the entire herd freezes.

I'd always thought of humans, or myself, as the predator.

But then, staring across the parking lot, I realized just how much I was actually the prey.

His features were wrong. They were too even, too symmetrical, as if someone had drawn half a face then simply duplicated it to the other half. And while I scolded myself for judging someone so severely, my mind was suddenly distracted by something else. The dog on his leash was some kind of black and brown hound, but it was staring back at me.

The dog... But it was all wrong. The eyes, the colors, the man's face. Goosebumps erupted across my flesh.

Susan's voice was barely a whisper. "Go, Lucia, now."

My brows dropped, shock freezing me as the man suddenly changed path, his dull eyes boring into mine. Chills crept over my skin again, but this time they were powerful, making my muscles shake, my body coil in on itself. There was a wrongness about this man, the way he was moving as he stepped onto my side of the street. Our apartment was the first line next to the parking lot, and he was only a few moments from us.

"Run." This time Susan's voice was loud, rasping and so unlike her that I jumped, startling into the door and slamming it into the wall behind me.

"Susan?" I looked to her, only to see her eyes were bright white, no iris, no color, no pupil, just a glowing white that sent me straight into survival mode. I grabbed my phone, watching as Susan—kind, warm, pie-baking Susan—let out a shrieking war cry and launched herself at the approaching man.

Shock slowed me down, but I felt my feet moving, instinct taking me away, the chills on my arms racing over my skin, making my body move.

The man released his dog as Susan took him to the concrete, and instead of running away or barking, it simply stared at me with humanlike focus, and then it slowly, purposefully tilted its head. The movement was so eerie that adrenaline poured through me. The terrifying scrape of canine claws against the concrete made me realize that the dog had given chase as well.

I ran as fast as I could, my feet and lungs aching as I got farther and farther from Susan and the man rolling around in the parking lot. My thought was to find more people, but now, seeing that man, the way he had turned to me, I didn't trust anyone.

But I couldn't stop. Something in my skin, in my mind screamed for me to keep going. There was a neighborhood park ahead, and without hesitation, I knew that was where I needed to go. I launched across a yard, trees throwing shade across my skin as I came to a slow, panting halt. My legs were shaking, the muscles inside quivering with exhaustion.

"My lady." A deep voice, familiar and warm, filled my ears, and I turned. There, standing under the shade of the largest tree, was a man in a white tunic. A slash of gold fabric across his shoulders caught my eye, along with a crest there, metallic and embossed with the shape of a crescent moon.

"Stay away from me." My voice shook as I spoke, betraying the fear that pulsed through my body. I had had enough with strange people, and I struggled to get away when his ham-like hands settled on my shoulders, pulling me tight to him.

I retaliated, flailing and punching at any part of him I could find.

Huffing, the man dodged my hits. "Calm down, my lady," he murmured, voice low and deep.

I wasn't convinced, yanking hard and trying to free myself from his grip, but he was frustratingly solid.

"Easy. It's all right now; he set me up to protect you."

"What? Who?" I was still panting, breathing hard from my run and the need to put more distance between that thing chasing me.

Just then the dog turned the corner, trotting with its head held high and casting a wide glance across the park. There was nothing dog-like in his movements now, and my entire body recoiled at the way he moved.

"Fucking devil dogs," the man holding me said, his voice a low grunt. Then, as if I weighed nothing at all, he scooped me up in his arms, bridal style. "Time to go."

"Time to go where? Put me down!" I wiggled in his grip, not that it did anything. The man was sturdier than anything I'd ever felt before. Ignoring me, he broke into a run, jostling me against his leather armor as we moved.

"Paran! Did you secure the house?" my captor, or protector, shouted.

A lean, powerful-looking man with close-cropped hair stepped out from behind a stone-walled park bathroom, dressed in the same loose white tunic and gold adornments across the chest. He gave my captor a hard look then turned to the dog, and its owner reappeared at its side, his face blank and strange in the morning light.

"Of course I did, ye of little faith." The new man's voice was as sharp as a blade and cut through the air between us, and suddenly my giant seemed to be the better of my options.

As the new man, Paran, approached, his face changed, softening as he looked down at me. And as soon as he was close enough, my body prickled with awareness. I knew this man.

It had been the same with the giant who was now jogging purposefully across the park lawn with me in his arms. I'd never seen them, but they were so familiar—the smell and the way their auras merged with mine.

"I know you, don't I," I whispered.

The giant's head turned a little, curly hair falling into kind brown eyes. I could see the edge of his lips curl in a smile.

"You do, my lady. And we are happy to explain things more when we get you somewhere safe." The giant cut across behind the playground, putting more and more space between my eerie walking pursuers.

"Where would I possibly be safe?"

Bracing myself on the giant's' shoulders, I peered back at the park. The man, or whatever he was, had disappeared again, his dog too. And instead of soothing my fears, my terror only grew. I curled in on myself, feeling the giant's muscles stretch and contract as he moved quickly.

Paran strode back up beside us, and for the first time since we started walking, I noticed the silver metal gauntlets on both wrists. He jerks his wrists, and long, slender blades drop down from the metal glove, shining in the shadows. They reached just below his fingertips, and when he curled his fists, it reminded me briefly of Wolverine from the superhero movies.

"For now, you're safest with us. " He looked at the giant, a strained smile on his lips. I noticed a scar there, across his bottom lip. "Arafel will have all heads if anything happens to you."

The giant grunted. "Can you blame him? Almost twenty years, and now these things are coming—"

Paran gave a jerk of his head, cutting off the man carrying me, and then shot me a grin. "Don't worry so much, Sim. We know this girl. She's tough as nails."

My heart was pounding in my chest, and my mind was a whirl of information and fear and grief so deep that I could only stare between them, these two men who I felt like I'd always known.

But they were still so unfamiliar.

And clearly dangerous.

That much was as obvious as the danger I was in. It was in the way they moved, the careful lift and placement of each of their feet. They were warriors. We had reached the end of the park, the trees overhead turning to houses as the sun blazed over them.

My protectors halted there. "Gatam has the house. Let's go," said Paran.

The giant shifted me, putting me down on the ground between him and Paran. A lifetime of fear of strangers rose in my gut, outweighing that strange, deep knowledge that I felt so comfortable around them.

I tried to step back, but they caged me in, both looking slightly uncomfortable as their bodies pressed against mine.

"I'm sorry, my lady."

"Simeon, focus, let's go."

Simeon. That's what my large friend was named. He grimaced a little, interlocking his fingers with Paran for a moment before Simeon simply breathed out. In the next instant, we were standing in a strange living room, shaggy carpet under my feet and peeling floral wallpaper all around us. It was, in a word, the last place I would've expected to be. Especially since a moment ago, I had been in a park, sandwiched between two not-strangers.

Yet, here we were, standing in a living room that was typical of a grandmother, a wealth of delicately crafted doilies on every surface.

Both Paran and Simeon stepped back immediately, and I took in a deep, shuddering breath. "Who are you? How did you do that?"

Both men looked down at me, and I covered my face with my hands. "Oh my God, am I crazy?"

This time, Paran cracked a smile. "No, not crazy. There's just a lot you don't know."

I plunked down on the sofa, staring at the both of them. "Then you better start talking, or I'm going to call you in and report you for kidnapping."

I was only sitting a moment before I realized that I needed to call help for poor Susan. "Oh my God! Susan... She needs help." My voice broke as I remembered who or what she'd been, turning to sprint across that concrete in a way that no woman her age should've been able to.

The men glanced at each other. "Susan Smith, as you know her, is gone. She's served your family well, and the Brotherhood as well. She knew the risk associated. ``

"Susan is...gone?"

Paran nodded, dropping to his haunches in front of me. "She was trained and entrusted with the protection of you and your mother. Her passing was with great honor. She will be deeply rewarded in her next life."

"The Brotherhood?" I raked my hands over my hair, the braids still tight and wet from my shower this morning. "Oh my God, what is happening to me?"

Paran glanced over his shoulders to Simeon. The larger man broadened his stance and then looked down at me.

"Your mother and the Brotherhood have spent our whole lives making sure you were safe, Lucia. We tried to keep our distance, but it was hard." Paran looked back up. "You were such an injury-prone little thing, always falling, always sick. It was quite difficult to guard you all this time and not want to protect you from everything. Simeon here nearly had a heart attack when you learned to ride a bike."

"You...were there?"

Simeon chuckled. "Not always, but a lot. Arafel would insist upon it, even when his father and brothers pushed back. He knew what would be coming for you."

"Arafel? And who's coming for me? This is all so insane. I'm nothing special."

Paran chuckled this time, dropping a knee as if to be more comfortable. "You are incredibly special, Lucia. That's what we're trying to tell you."

Simeon stepped forward. "Have you heard of the phrase *move heaven and hell*?"

"Yeah?"

"That should've been based on your life, my lady."

3

Lucia

"I'm going crazy." I pressed the heels of my hands to my eyes again, begging the darkness to take me, to tell me this was some kind of insane dream. "Completely crazy. I'm probably already in some padded room somewhere and you are all figments of my imagination."

"You aren't."

Paran's voice lost its edge. "You are soul bound to a Lord of the Underworld. The King of Dreams to be more exact."

I pulled my hands down to stare at Simeon. "Soul bound? That's what the winged guy at the hospital said."

The two men traded glances, and then Paran cleared his throat. "Arafel can explain. Did you say there was a winged male at the hospital?"

I nodded. "He came and…" I swallowed. "He took my mother."

"Did he say anything to you?" Simeon's voice was gentle, but I could see the tension on his face.

"He called me a soul bound but said 'not mine' or something. Then he told me he was my mother's guardian." My head snapped up. "Oh my God, does he mean guardian angel or something?"

"Not quite an angel, but something similar." Paran looked to his comrade. "Kadmiel must've been tasked with her soul because of the deal."

"The deal?" I asked, but neither male acted like they heard me. When I opened my mouth to repeat myself, Paran cut me off.

"What you have to know is you've just walked into a millennia-long war between the Others and the Underworld. And there is nothing they won't do to get to you."

I opened my eyes and my mouth to beg for my explanation, and maybe just a bit more proof, when I glanced up and noticed a second version of Paran standing in the doorway. I couldn't help it. I screamed.

"Gatam, dammit," Paran said, rising to cover my mouth with his hand. "We don't need her bringing half the Corrupted here with her screams. Not to mention Arafel. You and I both know he's already tearing at the boundaries."

The new man, the duplicate of Paran, moved into the room. And now that he was closer, I could see the slight difference in hair length, the absence of the scar across the new man's chin.

"My twin, Gatam."

I nodded at him, his aura washing over me. Now there were three. Three of the most unreal, inhuman men I'd ever imagined.

I had to get out of there.

And soon.

"Gatam." I forced the unfamiliar words through my lips. "Paran, Simeon. I'm grateful for you rescuing me, saving me from that creature, but I can't stay here."

I swallowed hard. "My mother died last week. There's so much I have to do. So many things she would need me to do."

Gatam cocked his head and then glanced at his brother, who had stood to be by his side. Paran nodded solemnly, as if they'd been having a silent conversation. "Gatam and I have already seen to her arrangements."

"What?"

"Time is of the essence, Lucia. We have an entire twenty-four hours still to keep the Other away from you. To keep you safe until Arafel can get here."

I dropped my head into my fists. "I don't even know this person. You cannot possibly tell me I have to change my entire life waiting for him to come here. What if he turns me away? You say he's some kind of royalty in your world? I am no queen."

"You aren't being forced to marry him or anything like that. If it makes you more comfortable, you can look at it as an elaborate merger. And honestly, Arafel would claim he was the worst king his role has ever seen," Paran said calmly. "If that makes you feel better."

Simeon snorted.

"It doesn't. Can I please just have some time? To soak this in?"

All three males nodded solemnly.

"I'll reach out to Castle Fel, see how they are faring."

"I'll be at the front, Gatam at the back," Simeon stated, moving away with a ripple of white and gold fabric.

And then I was alone.

My chest ached. Fear may have clouded my grief, but it hadn't removed it. And now it could sweep back. Along with a strange sort of anger. My mother had waited until the day of her death, after the moment of her death, to tell me the truth about who and what I was. If I wanted to believe these males, my soul was only half human. Maybe not even that. And I was bound to this male, Arafel, and he was going to defend me from the creatures who were coming to take me?

It was too much.

I loved reading fantasy books, but I never wanted to live them.

Maybe it was because I knew the main characters were often more miserable at the end than they ever were at the beginning.

I wanted to live in a nice romantic comedy or even some women's chick lit. I didn't want this.

Dragging heavy, knitted blankets over my body, I let my body sag in the cushions once again.

It only took a breath for exhaustion and stress to tug my body back into sleep.

***

I felt rested, my brain finally pulling itself from the bottomless well that had been my exhaustion.

Phantom hands brushed against my forehead—hot, silky touches, but so light they could've been made by a feather. A kiss, I realized, my mind still pulling itself from sleep.

"I'm glad you're safe, Lucia," he said then, the sound coming from within my own mind, not from the surroundings. It was as familiar as my own voice, filling me with inexplicable joy and comfort as I felt another touch this time, a phantom hand that smoothed over my cheekbone and across my ear.

"I'm coming for you," the deep voice rumbled. "I will always come for you."

And then he was gone from me, the air around me suddenly thin and cool. I threw back the covers, swinging my legs to the floor. I glanced at my phone, noticing I had been asleep for several hours. Hunger gnawed at my stomach, but I wasn't sure what these soldiers ate. *If* they ate. I stretched, rising to my feet and moving through the house, my eyes looking everywhere for a kitchen, or a bathroom for that matter. Because I could use both at this point.

I found the bathroom first and used it quickly, and then I continued my exploration of the house. I glanced into a bedroom, surprised to see Simeon sitting on the edge of the bed, his eyes closed, arms crossed over his broad chest. He may have been asleep, if not for the slender older man who sat on the bed next to him, his eyes filled with a glowing milky white instead of the normal eyes. Like Susan's had been. Almost like the male at the hospital.

I didn't scream this time, mostly because I wasn't sure whether it would make things better or worse. The older man didn't even move, didn't change his stare at the blank wall in front of him. He merely sat there, his eyes glowing.

"Simeon," I whispered, my voice strained and horrified.

The big man's warm brown eyes found me instantly. Unruffled, he grinned at me. "Did you sleep well?"

I couldn't speak, so I held a hand out to him, finger quivering in the air. "What did you do to him?"

Simeon glanced over. "Oh, Tim? He's completely fine. When we identified where you were, we knew we needed a place to hide out. We simply knocked on the door, and Tim let us in."

"And now he's like this?"

Simeon looked between Tim and me. "It's not what you think." He sighed. "I'm holding him in a sort of trance. The moment we walk out of here, Tim will get up and go about his business, never knowing we were ever here, save some missing groceries."

I crept closer, my pulse thrumming. "It doesn't hurt him?"

Simeon shook his head. "It's similar to a very vivid dream. In fact, our friend Tim here is currently riding the Ferris wheel at the carnival from the small town he grew up in."

"Can you make him do that?"

"I simply led him to dreamland; the rest was up to him." The soldier cast me a sidelong look. "I hate Ferris wheels, so that would've never been my choice."

I blinked at him, and then to my surprise, a corner of my lip curled. This man, his biceps the size of my body, was afraid of

Ferris wheels. The idea was comical. But then, so was the idea that I was some kind of hybrid soul keeper for a king of dreams.

Tim smiled a little in his dream, and for a moment, I sorely wished I could swap our realities.

"I reached out to Arafel." Simeon's voice was gentle but firm. "He wants us to stay here. He said he will be here as soon as he can leave without causing a cosmic break in time and space."

I stared at him until my eyes burned and forced me to blink. "Oh, well then, no rush."

Simeon laughed a little. "You get the point."

"I do." I fiddled with the edge of my shirt. I loved naps, but I always woke up feeling rumpled, and today was no different.

"Why don't you grab something to eat, and then we will look into finding something to do while we bide our time?"

I nodded, still tugging at my shirt. "Simeon..."

"Yes?"

"What do you call yourselves? Are you human?"

His face was warm, unjudging. Somewhere in the back of my mind, I remembered it again, but the focus wasn't clear. Like the reflection on a rippling pond, both vivid and distorted all at once.

"We have human-like features, but that is only to better serve you. I was born an angel, and upon my death, I volunteered my soul to the Brotherhood so I could continue to serve the Underworld."

"Are you saying you're dead?" My voice dropped to a hushed gasp. "Is that what happened to my mother? Is she one of you?"

"I'm not dead, not really. Arafel selected my soul for the Brotherhood, and this body was made to serve me as such." Simeon pinned me with a serious look. "What do you mean about your mother?"

I shifted, still distracted and way freaked out by Tim and his glowing white stare. "She was talking to me, having a whole discussion with me, but they told me she'd been dead for ten minutes. I thought I was crazy. They thought I was mad with grief. But I saw him."

Simeon's face didn't move. "Him? You mean the winged male."

"You said his name earlier right, when I first told you about him."

The big man rose to his feet, shaking out his hands as if to stretch his back muscles. "You're not crazy. That was Kadmiel, one of Arafel's brothers. As for the part about you talking to her, I imagine there's a certain quality of power about you, since you hold a Lord of the Underworld's soul inside of you. It wouldn't be unheard of that you kept her tethered there until Kadmiel came for her."

"I did that?"

"It appears you did. Otherwise, I'm not sure how to explain it." Simeon moved to stand directly in front of me, brotherly affection crossing his gaze. "I'm glad she was granted the chance to see you, to say goodbye. But that was a gift none of the Brotherhood could've managed. That's a lord's gift."

I scrubbed my face. "So many things I don't understand."

His crooked smile made his eyes wrinkle in the corners. "There is so much more you have to learn, my lady. And the first is a very important lesson."

"What's that?"

Simeon leaned down, bringing his face closer to mine. "That the world is so much bigger than you could've ever imagined."

"I'm not sure I'm ready for that." I sighed a little, looking down to my bare feet.

Simeon slung an arm around my shoulder. "I'm not sure you have much of a choice, my lady, but if you were to ask me, I think you're going to love it."

"Love what?"

He raised an eyebrow. "You'll see."

I breathed out hard. "Honestly, anywhere but here sounds pretty good right now. No offense meant, Tim."

The sleeping man didn't move, but Simeon let out a gusty laugh, steering me back to the door. "A wise observation. Now, to the kitchen."

I followed him down the hall to the kitchen, where Gatam sat, a wide array of food out on the table.

"Are you hungry?" Paran asked from behind us, making me jump. He smirked, but the expression was less aggressive. Or perhaps I was growing used to him.

"I am."

"Gatam is the best cook between us three, but don't let that fool you. It's still not much." A blade, quick as lightning, flew past us and embedded itself into the wall over Paran's shoulder. The chatty twin didn't even blink. And Gatam continued on as if nothing had changed.

Simeon grunted a short laugh and then pulled Paran into the other room, leaving me with the newest of my guardians.

"Thank you for helping me."

Gatam shot me a quick look then went back to chopping. Clearly not a big talker, but I didn't mind. I picked up a banana, wondering if we could leave some kind of reimbursement for Tim when we left. Guilt warred in my mind, but in the end, my stomach won out and I peeled it free and began to munch. The sweet fruit soothed my empty belly.

Gatam had thrown together some kind of vegetable pasta with a thin but delicious sauce on top of it. I ate it all standing by the table, oddly disinterested in sitting down. I wasn't ready to relax or even to let my brain settle for a minute.

If I did, I might be forced to recognize just how insane my life had become. And that this was, inevitably, the end of everything I'd known before. The things I'd seen, I couldn't unsee. The gaps in my life that were slowly coming to light.

And that I was thrust into this world, completely alone.

And I still wasn't sure this wasn't a trauma response from my mother dying. There was always that.

That was a problem for another day. Perhaps one in which there weren't a bunch of evil inhuman creatures coming to kidnap me from the kind inhuman creatures already here.

I chuckled, drawing Gatam's eyes for a second. When the laughter finally worked itself out of my system, I was left feeling a little haggard and leaning on the back of one of Tim's kitchen chairs.

"I hope you get paid extra for this."

Gatam offered me a small, close-lipped smile.

"Hey, Gatam, let's chat for a minute," Simeon called from the living room.

Gatam moved past me, patting me on my shoulder as he did. And while I knew instantly that the move made him nervous, I was glad to have it.

These were the good guys. I may not understand what was happening all around me, but I knew that every move they made, every word they had said, seemed to be in honor of me, to keep me safe. Their intentions were obvious, if not a bit confusing.

And Arafel? This demon lord they served, they claimed he was the King of Dreams. And he was connected to me, bound to protect me and keep me safe.

I paused at the back door, staring blindly out at the small backyard. I would meet him tomorrow, give him whatever he needed, and then be on my way. A lump lodged itself deep in my throat. Then I would take care of my mother. I would close our life here. Maybe even go home to Kansas, the last place I could remember being happy.

There was a soft rap on the glass of the window in front of me, and I blinked back tears, squinting out in the afternoon clouds. It looked like rain again, and it matched my mood perfectly. For a moment, I swore there was a small dark shadow at the back of the yard, by the wooden fence. But then I blinked again, and it was gone.

Replaced by my mother.

Juliette Walker stood in the middle of the yard, her body dressed in her same casual look from that last morning. She looked whole, her smile bright and wide.

She was alive.

My heart nearly choked me as I pressed my face up against the glass, barely able to comprehend what I was seeing.

It had been easy to explain to Simeon, to try to explain away those strange minutes after her life had left her and she had lingered to explain things to me. I was explaining this to a man who seemed to travel through shadows and was stronger than any human I'd ever met.

But now, standing here alone in the kitchen, staring out at my mother's face as she smiled at me, everything in my belly overturned. I pressed a hand up and against the glass, tempted to wipe at the pane, as if trying to see if she had an imprint or fingerprint left from before. My mind scrambled to catch up, even as my other hand reached for the knob.

"Mom?" My lips were shaking so hard I could barely form the word.

She cocked her head and then turned, motioning over her shoulder. There was a school behind her, a wide field there, sprinkled with playground equipment and heavily leafed trees. In the distance was a parking lot. Nothing special, an average neighborhood school.

Why did she want me there? Did she mean for me to go to her?

My brow lowered as I slipped the door open. Mom motioned again, pointing at the school as if it meant something. I had to go to her. She had talked to me, even in death. She had claimed I was special. Maybe she was something special too. It was the only thing that made sense.

I stepped out into the sun, blinking rapidly as I moved toward her. But she was already halfway across the yard, moving to the fence line at the edge and hopping over it as if it were nothing. I did the same, my nerves scraped raw.

"Mom, wait. What are you doing?" My voice was a gasp. "Mom, wait. Mom!"

And then I was tearing across the yard, the door slamming back against the house as fear laced through my veins. I couldn't let her get away. Not this time. I was across the yard in a breath. At the low fence, I paused and then, with a grunt, hurled my bare feet over it, landing in the cool fallen leaves on the other side.

It wasn't until I stared around did I realize the gravity of my situation. I swallowed hard. Not my situation. My mistake.

And it wasn't subtle. A ripple of tangible power washed over me as I stepped onto the property. My mother stopped instantly, turning to face me before crossing her arms and tilting her head at me. Nausea roiled in my gut. It was the exact expression the man and his demon dog had given me only this morning.

I had messed up.

Badly.

A sob crawled up my chest. But I couldn't stop the desperate words as they slipped out. "Mom?"

The creature who looked like my mother paused. Then, slowly, a hand reached out and her fingers snapped together. Instantly, there was a creature in her place, only a few feet tall but staring up at me with a depth of knowledge and violence that it set my blood pounding once again.

What was this? My fear and surprise must've shown, because the creature smiled up at me, its sharp, dagger-like teeth shining in the light.

"Good afternoon, my lady," it said, still grinning up at me.

Horror turned my blood to ice. "What are you? Where's my mother?"

"Not very smart, are you?" It slid a long, black tongue over its teeth after it spoke, and my eyes couldn't help but follow the motion. Not human. Not an animal. It was…something else. I needed to run, needed to get as far away from this thing as I could. But my feet remained rooted to the earth. I blinked at it, terror making my limbs heavy. Too heavy.

Why couldn't I move, I screamed at myself. I needed to move.

"What are you?" I took one heavy step back, forcing my knees to bend, my legs to cooperate. But still, it felt like moving through cement.

Its grin spread wider. "I'm a messenger." It glanced at its claws and then clacked them together as it moved a step closer. "And a lure."

Run, I screamed at my legs. Run away.

"For what? I don't know what you want." Even my tongue felt sluggish now, the words slurring together.

"It doesn't matter what I want." The creature stared me up and down, yellow eyes glowing. "It's what they want. And they want you."

His sharp, bony shoulders straightened as he rose to the full extent of his height, and he flashed his teeth again. "Time to go to sleep, light walker."

It worked its fingers in my direction, and instantly I felt it, the heavy weight of sleepiness that took over my limbs, growing ever heavier, until I went to a knee in the cool grass, my body unable to fight. I jerked my chin up by sheer will, horror making me gasp as a dozen more of those dark creatures moved into the clearing. Panic and fear seeped into something else entirely.

Acceptance.

Because I was tired, so very, very tired. It was easier than I wanted to admit to myself that I could simply lie down here. The inevitable destruction of my life ending here was cruel, but an ending all the same.

My fingers curled, the cold dirt digging into my nails as my ears were filled with the sounds of my death bringers. Under the fear, my heart throbbed with recognition that this was the end. It had to be. But maybe, if there was more to life, then I would see my mother again.

I could picture the lovely lines of her face as she smiled at me, the kind strokes of her hands against my cheeks.

She had fought so hard for us. For me.

That thought soared through my mind like a spear, shocking me back to wakefulness for a moment. I grappled in the dirt, the creatures hissing and taking a few steps back as I shoved up onto my elbows.

She had fought for me. And all I could give her was a single day of fighting on my own. Tears filled my eyes. She would be so disappointed. With a groan, I dug my fingers into the earth again, forcing myself up.

How insane for my mother to have fought for so long to keep us together? For the woman who had raised me on her own, I could feel her grip on me now. Growing stronger as my vision grew dark.

What would she say if she saw me now? Only a week alone in the world, and I had failed.

I was weak.

The thought drove off the darkness for one moment then another. Fury, laced with a grit I hadn't believed I had, made my mind whirl.

But the bottom line was this:

I wasn't raised to be weak.

I slammed my palms into the damp, chilled foliage. "No." Anger poured through my system, and the shadow of the trees above me seemed to expand and grow around me.

"No?" There was a cackling of laughter all around as the sky seemed to darken. Or maybe that was my vision, getting darker and darker as I sat back on my haunches. I would face them. Even on the brink of death.

"You don't want to do this. Arafel," I said, surprising myself with the ease his name rolled off my tongue. "Arafel will make you pay."

The creatures laughed again, and darkness pounded in my head, my body begging for sleep while my mind fought.

"As I said before, goodnight, dearest."

I screamed, my eyes sliding shut at the pull of the darkness, the sleep that lurked just beyond. I focused every part of me on that thick, pulsing power that slid over me, focused on pushing it away, focusing on the smell and taste of the life around me. I wasn't going anywhere. My fingers plunged deeper into the cool dirt, my nails digging in.

And with that, I threw my shoulders back, hands fisting as I rested on my knees. "You. Can't. Have. Me."

A bitter, cool wind swirled around me, making me flinch for a moment, and my entire body began shaking. A crack sounded from behind me, and then a steady buffet of warmth came over me in waves. It was like stepping into a warm bath, starting at my toes and moving up my body as if my blood itself was carrying this heat upwards.

I knew this warmth. To some degree, it was the same thing I felt with Paran and Simeon and even Gatam. Yet, at the same time, it was different all together. It felt like I'd swallowed the sun, my body vibrating with energy and consumed by light.

It was something I'd craved, a sense of completion and comfort. I didn't need to turn to know who had brought this feeling with them. There was only one answer. Only one being who had ever given me even a sliver of feeling.

"Arafel," I rasped, my lips dry.

His shadow fell over me, but instead of the chill of shadow, there was only heat that made my hair stand on end.

He was here.

The creature in front of me hissed, his fingers spreading wide as narrowed eyes swept back to me.

"She's right, you know." His deep voice was like thunder over the horizon, ominous and foreboding. "You can't have her."

The noises coming from the creatures were no longer English, the syllables tumbling over each other as they scurried back into the shelter of the trees. Many of them seemed to vanish into pockets of air that appeared before them.

"You believe that you will leave so easily?" Arafel's voice was so low, it rumbled in his chest. He was behind me; I could feel the warmth of him against my shoulder as I kneeled in the dirt. But I was afraid to look. There was a snap, like the snap of fingers, and every remaining creature but the original one suddenly disappeared, leaving a small cloud of dark dust in their wake.

I swayed, half-horrified, half-awed at the singular destruction. One moment they had all been there. The second, they hadn't. My chest burned as whatever control…or spell or whatever they'd placed on me began to lift, and I managed to struggle to my feet, turning to stare at my rescuer.

He was exactly what I pictured and, at the same time, nothing like him. I'd had dreams about my protectors in the shadows after all. The white tunic they all wore, the gold sash. This male, he wore the same, but it was different.

He was different.

I'd always considered myself tall. I was five feet eight in my bare feet, and he towered over me. Not only because of his height, but because curling from his forehead were a pair of shining black horns. They curled slightly toward the end, making his height with horns very close to seven feet.

Instinct warred with that warmth that still burrowed deep into my chest. Instinct was telling me to run, that again, I was the prey in this situation because he was and always had been an ultimate predator. But the look he was giving me, it was so strange that it held me in place, every muscle on edge, every particle in my body ready to flee.

"You called, Lucia."

For some reason, a choked laugh escaped. "I did." I stared up at him. "And you came."

"I always have, little one, and I always will."

His words were a balm, making my heartbeat thrum in my chest. "Arafel," I started, but this time the word was on a cry. The magnetism took me as I stepped toward him once, twice, a third time.

He stayed completely still, obsidian eyes watching me closely. The eyes, I thought in wonder. I know those eyes.

The Brotherhood had said he was irrevocably tied to my soul. But they hadn't explained this, this need to be closer, this desire to be with him. All those things I had missed, all the things I had never felt, it was like they were suddenly waiting, screaming for me to press myself closer to him. Because something in my body and mind was clamoring that he was the solution to everything. That he would fill in those gaps, he would make me whole. Instinctively, I could feel it.

But fear still filled my belly.

Not enough, though, to stop when he moved forward a step, leaning down from his height to wrap an arm around me and slowly tug me against his form. Instinctively, I pressed closer, turning my face against the black fabric of his tunic. He smelled like a warm, sun-kissed male and something spicy that made my mouth water. As soon as my face was against his clothing, his body sagged and his powerful arms tightened around me, heaving me upwards until my arms were crawling over his chest so that I could knit my fingers around his neck, pressing my face into the hot flesh there, my legs dangling in the air.

"Always?" I couldn't stop myself from asking.

His head turned, and I felt his breath brush over my ear. "Always." To the creature who struggled within Arafel's hold, my protector turned. "I have a message for your master."

The creature hissed, choked syllables which might have been another language filling the air.

"This woman and all others like her are under my protection. Do not try me again, mahr, or I will drag you back to the world from whence you came."

There was a beat of silence where the mahr's eyes met Arafel's, and then he vanished into a sliver of darkness. The moment he was gone, the birds above began to chirp, I could hear the distant sounds of cars driving down the road, and somewhere, someone had a radio blaring.

The world raced onward.

But without me. I blinked up at Arafel. I was permanently and completely removed from the normal world. I knew that for sure. As I stared up at him, his sharp features under the soft gray-toned skin illuminated even more in the light of day, I couldn't find it in me to be scared.

I was tired of being scared and sad and broken.

My mother hadn't raised me for that.

She had said I was meant for more. I swallowed hard. I would prove to her that she was right, if it were the last thing I ever did.

His eyes glowed a bright blue as they met mine.

"Take me away from here, please."

Arafel's rumbling agreement soothed my ragged emotions. "Of course." And he turned, stepping into the shadows and out of the world I'd always known.

4

Arafel

I had thought about this day, every day, for most of my existence. Ever since my father had explained what they had done. What they had been forced to do. He and my mother had severed our souls, implanting half of my soul, of all my brothers' souls, into unsuspecting humans. We would survive, they promised, but with only part of our power and even less of our hearts. Not to mention we would be bound to the caregiver of our soul to a degree none of us could even understand.

At first, we boasted we didn't need our souls, that we were better than that. Stronger than that. But over time, over hundreds of years, I felt the wear and tear on myself. Not my body—it remained as strong and diligent as always. But something deep inside had shifted.

That all changed the day I first heard her call. It was nothing, a child's tummy ache on a stormy night, but I was there. The pull in my chest was strong enough to drag me through from the dream realm to the human one. I'd held her little hand, staring into the wide, unafraid eyes of the one I was bound to, and knew that I was forever changed.

From then on, the need to be close to Lucia, to protect her above all else, ruled my every thought and action.

I didn't know what to expect. I was not the first of my brothers to be affected by the human who was soul bound to me. But my eldest brother, Nephesh, and I were not exactly on casual speaking terms. What I knew of Nephesh's time with his soul bound was that she had welcomed him, loved him even. But all had come to a crashing end only a few weeks after they met.

Nephesh hadn't been able to protect his soul bound.

I would not let that happen to Lucia.

Lucia was a child when she had mastered calling for me, after which there was a stint in time where I spent most of my nights lying in her room, spread out on the floor listening to her chatter about school, her mom, and her favorite books.

And while the warrior in me wanted to be frustrated, or even mad, I couldn't be. Maybe it was the bond between us, maybe it was something else, but she was special to me. The most important person in my world, in the entire world. Every aspect of her trivial world was now a part of mine.

In time, I allowed more and more members of the Brotherhood to assist her. Going back and forth between the Underworld and living world was a strain on my magic, and I was forced to get creative in order to keep things moving. My abilities grew even more strained when I extended protection to Lucia's mother, tying another piece of my magic to the living world in an effort to protect my soul bound.

When it became too much, I had asked my trusted advisor, Simeon, for the job of managing my young half-soul because of his kindness and gentle demeanor. After some time, the twins approached me, Paran first, asking if they could be assigned to Lucia's care as well.

It was not the human world that interested them, but the child herself. They had heard my stories, heard Simeon's stories. In a world where order was life and there was only darkness most days, the days spent by Lucia's side were full of joy, peace.

They were not held to the same rules as I was, so they came and went from the Underworld with more ease. Lucia took to them in a moment, wrapping all of them around her fingers in a matter of months.

She adored them, and they took her protection seriously. Most days I envied them, but the dream realm deserved my attention, even as my soul cried out for its missing part.

We were immortals, our bodies and minds molded from the minds of good and evil to create a perfect warrior, a perfect ruler. But in that way, over the years, we had been infused with human ways, human emotions courtesy of our human mother. Father had hoped that they would make us better caretakers to the souls we managed in the Underworld.

I glanced down at the woman in my arms, my heart pounding as I curled her closer. She felt like nothing to me, her slender form sagging into mine as she moved through the shadows and into my kingdom for the first time.

She was home.

I'd dreamed of this day for years. Ever since I'd confronted her mother, begging her assistance in protecting Lucia. Juliette had been confused at first, fearful even. But it hadn't taken long for her to take me up on my offerings of protection. And in return, I had agreed that she needed to grow, to mature alongside the humans whose design she'd been based on.

But she was not human. Not completely.

"Lucia," I whispered, leaning my head over hers. For a moment, I considered shifting into my human form, glamouring into something might be less shocking to her. The Brotherhood was more human-looking than me, and while she had accepted them easily, my true form was more of an acquired taste.

I had appeared ready for battle, my heart pounding as I considered what my bound might have gotten into for her to be able to reach into the shadows to call me to her.

I glanced down at her body, the peace on her face calming my own raging thoughts. In the end, I didn't bother. She had already seen my true face, my true appearance. There was no reason to hide from her.

She groaned, her fingers tightening on my arms as she woke slowly from her sleep. Moving between the realm of the living and the dead wasn't easy.

"Lucia, you are safe. Open your eyes."

"Arafel? Where are we?"

I looked down and saw her eyes were wide, the beautiful golden iris so full of surprise and wonder as I followed her gaze around us.

And then I smiled too, for the first time in a very long time. "You are in my home, Lucia. It is safe for you here." I carefully neglected calling this place what her people might've.

Hell was not the right word. It was so much more, and I would show her.

"This is your home?"

I gently bent over, releasing her legs so she slid down to stand on her own feet. And while she wavered for a moment, her spine was ramrod straight as she looked around us. "It is."

Her hands slowly rose to press over her mouth. "I had no idea." She spun to face me. "We aren't on Earth anymore, are we?"

Head cocked, I wondered how much more she could handle today. "We have not left the planet. We are in a concurrent realm, my realm. We exist together but separate."

Lucia blinks rapidly, head swiveling. "This place, it looks exactly like..." Her brows furrowed, and she took a small step away from me. "What is it called?"

"It has plenty of names. The realms my brothers and I rule are within the Underworld. This"—I gestured around us—"is where I have been placed to lead, the dream realm."

This time her words came out in a rush. "Why does it look like something out of the English countryside?"

A smirk tugged at my lips. "I'm afraid you're the one to blame for that. My dominion is a chameleon, constantly changing and altering itself to please those who have sought counsel with me."

Her eyes bulged and she took another step away from me, and then she slowly knelt to brush shaking fingertips against the grass. "It's real. This is real?"

I laughed this time. "It is a state of stasis, awaiting your command to stay or go." I looked up, inspecting the sprawling brick manor with its cobblestone brick drive, bubbling fountain. The hills swept up behind it, a green swell against the gray and blue mottled sky that was more familiar to me.

Usually where we stood was nothing but dead, pale grasses, weaving back and forth in a nameless wind that always blew. Unalive. Uninteresting.

And now, gone. Something in my chest roiled; I had no idea how she had done this.

Lucia straightened, looking up at the sky of my world, her freckles stark and bright on the bridge of her nose. I longed to trace them someday, to know exactly how many she had. Tilting my head, I thought to myself, What an odd compulsion.

"And if I want it to stay?" Her voice was soft, but I heard the resolution in it. She'd already decided, my soul bound.

I nodded to her. "Then it stays. The doorways look plenty tall enough for my horns to pass through."

She grinned then pressed her hand over her mouth again. "You must think me a horrible monster, laughing after what happened to all those people."

My emotions grew somber as her expression did the same. I held out my hand to her. "There is so much to talk about, Lucia. But you don't have to explain yourself to me."

She nodded, watching me closely as she tangled her fingers with my much larger ones. She felt delicate against my skin, her flesh pumping with life and warmth. I wondered what I felt like to her.

"Thank you." She shuffled a little. "I want to know everything. I want to know why this is all happening. I want to know why I'm here." Her eyes met mine, shining and deep. "I want to understand."

I nodded. "I know you do. Let's go in. We will start at the beginning."

We didn't get far before one of my creatures emerged from the freshly created manor. This one another mahr, but a loyal one, not one the Drude had gotten his claws into.

Lucia stilled, her entire body frozen as the young alp continued on their path, surveying the land beyond Lucia's manor. Then with one quick shout, she turned and leaped against my body, her tight, shockingly strong arms around my neck in an instant.

5

Lucia

They'd come back for me. I stared down at the waist-high creature, nearly identical to the horde of them that had swarmed me in the woods. Black skin. Thin, tight facial features stretched over a too big skull. I shook, my entire being screaming at me to get to safety. And in this world, this strange, terrible, beautiful world, my only safe space was the enormous demon behind me.

Arafel.

Yes, he looked exactly like demons were depicted in my books and in the TV shows I'd watched growing up. He was larger than life, towering over me with his swirling horns and beautiful, bottomless blue eyes. I could barely believe he was real. I was still trying to wrap my head around this world. But at its core, there was him. The aura I'd always known, the shadow who had followed me and surrounded me. The protection I'd felt.

And he was there, my shadow and safety, even in the chaos and terror of this new world.

The creature gave a soft grunt, turning toward us. I screamed, turning and leaping back at Arafel, hoping to God he would catch me. A breath later, I was back against his impossibly hard body, the thick, heavy muscles of his chest pressing against my cheek as I curled into a ball. Fear choked me for a moment, and I sucked in the air there, trying to drown as much of the smell of him into my body.

It was a balm, soothing my soul. And I shook there, my body on its last reserves.

"Lucia, don't be afraid." Arafel held me closer, the warmth of his breath on the side of my face. "This mahr is a creature of dreams. One of my most loyal citizens. The creatures you met earlier no longer serve me. They were corrupted, turned against me."

The words flitted across my mind, forced out by more grunts and noises from the sharp-faced creature before us. I curled tighter, forcing my mind to take in his words, to let the thoughts and ideas slip into my consciousness.

"A mahr?"

"Yes, a mahr. Perhaps you would know them as nightmares. But I know them as citizens of my realm, soldiers and workers. He will not harm you."

I raised a hand to press hair from my face. The deep-brown strands were falling out of my braids and sticking to my face where fearful tears had left tracks. I shoved them back, forcing myself to meet Arafel's glowing blue eyes. Looking away, I let my wide eyes find the creature again and forcing my body to remain still and silent. "Hello."

The creature bowed low, its body quivering. It spoke in a long stream of words then, foreign and rough to my ears, so high-pitched that I actually flinched.

Arafel answered it in short, curt terms, and it bowed again, even deeper this time. Its chattering made my ears ache, but I forced myself to wait and watch. It didn't look inherently dangerous, like the snarling ones from before. It didn't speak English, and the noises weren't all that aggressive, now that the fog of fear was clearing from my mind.

Not to mention it wasn't going to do anything to me with a six-and-a-half-foot tall demon holding me. I relaxed in Arafel's hold, and I could tell that relaxed him as well. He seemed to shrink against me, and I jerked my chin up to meet his gaze.

"Did you just…?" I felt too stupid to finish my question. Had he grown and shrunk in a matter of minutes? That couldn't be possible. I broke off with a shake of my head and swallowed hard. "You can put me down. I won't freak out again."

Arafel's dark brows raised in a smooth arch, and I felt the hot blush crawling up my cheeks. "I mean, I'll try not to."

He breathed out hard, a laugh, and turned. With one powerful hand against my side, he ushered me past the mahr, who was continuing to chatter and bow as I walked by.

"What is he saying?"

Arafel remained silent then looked at me slowly. "Mostly repeating himself. He is quite besotted by you."

I jerked my head back around to stare at the mahr. "Really?"

Arafel nodded, his face solemn. "It has been a long time since something new has come into this land, Lucia. A very long time."

I didn't know what to say. I looked around, staring at the manor before us. The immense brick home was as real and lifelike as one I might have seen driving across the countryside.

"Are you talking about the house?"

Arafel's palm was warm on my back. "No. No, I am not."

I hid my face, staring down at the bright-green blades of grass surrounding my shoes. Suddenly it all seemed…too much. I was in the Underworld. It was all real. *He* was real. I reached out, my hand finding Arafel's forearm for a moment, and I clenched on.

"I need to lie down for a minute. May I?"

Stepping forward, my body shaking, I stared down at my footsteps, forcing my brain to take one step after another.

"Lucia." His voice was tight, a warning.

And then I was falling, the grass rushing up to meet my face as I gave up and darkness came rushing for me.

***

When I woke, I was in a dark room, light shining in from under the doorway. I sat up straight, my body tense at the strange surroundings.

And then it came all pounding back through my mind. My mother. The man and the demon dogs. The creatures in the woods.

Arafel.

And I was the other half of his soul, Simeon claimed.

Breathing hard, I pressed my hand against my chest, as if calming my racing heart would calm the thunderous pound of confusion in my mind.

"You're awake, miss," a soft voice said. "I'm so glad. I hated the way we left things earlier."

I pulled my hands back, surprised at the voice in the room. And then I shrieked because standing there, a coy smile on her lips, was Susan. Susan, who had given Mom and me a rainbow knitted soup koozie for Christmas last year.

She was sitting at the foot of my bed.

In Hell.

Oh God, not quite sitting.

She was standing, but her form was misty, nearly transparent as she came even closer.

"Oh, Lucy, I'm so sorry. I didn't mean to scare you. Lord Arafel thought it was too early, but I couldn't resist when I heard you waking up."

"Susan, what are you?"

Susan swatted at the air with one shadowy hand. "Oh, me, I'm dead. I've been dead since the early 90s, darling."

I stared. "What?"

Susan gave me a small smile. "There's so much for you to learn, but you should know that a large number of the citizens in Lord Arafel's realm are like me, displaced souls."

"But..." I swallowed. "Are you all right? You attacked that man."

Susan snorted again, this time walking to the bureau and picking up a glass of water there, her hands surprisingly steady. "He got the better of me, but I slowed him down plenty. It's been a long time since I've seen a full-on possession."

I took the offered water. "He was possessed, then? Like in the movies?"

"Yes, with the Drude's dark magic." Susan shook her head of gray curls, taking the glass back after I'd had a long sip. "I've seen plenty of nasties in my time, my dear, but he was a real piece of work."

My throat ached. "I'm so sorry."

"Don't be. That was my purpose, you know, to watch over you and your mother. She was a human but had always known you would be special. Ever since Arafel came to her and told her what you were. And when the cancer came, she bargained with Nephesh herself for more time."

"Nephesh."

"The Judge, Lord Arafel's eldest brother. We don't talk about him much; they've been in a tiff since the First World War."

I swallowed, suddenly feeling faint once more. "Oh, of course."

"Don't worry, darling, it will all make sense the longer you stay here. The Underworld is another stage of our lives. I'm happy to have served my lord. And he's granted me permission to continue to watch over you as your personal maid." She cut me a quick look. "As long as you're all right with it."

"I really don't need a maid," I started, surprised at the hurt in Susan's eyes. I went on quickly. "Does that mean you'll stay here? Teach me what all of this is..." I gestured around the room.

Susan followed my gaze then smiled, her expression already brightening. "Of course. Lovely choice of home, by the way, dear. Very Julia Quinn of you."

I chuckled because she was still so Susan. I reached out, unsure but still wanting to make contact. Her eyes met mine, and then her hands slowly nestled around mine. Her touch was different, soft and delicate as a rose petal. "Thank you."

"You are pure light, my lady. Now, let's get dressed and I can give you a short tour about these new grounds you dreamed up. Lord Arafel will return shortly with the remaining Brotherhood."

"The Brotherhood? How many of them are there?" Instantly I wondered how angry they were at me. There was no way Arafel wasn't furious at them. And it was all because of me and my stupidity. I swallowed hard, focusing on Susan as I attempted to stem off the tears. I'd cried more in the past seven days than I had in the past year combined. It was exhausting.

Susan considered the question, puckering her lips, which were covered in a dark lipstick. "You've met his three closest companions, but there are dozens of members across the Underworld. The Brotherhood are his ears and eyes within the realm. You've already met Simeon, his most trusted advisor."

nodded, unsure how to ask more. There was one question I forced myself to ask. "They've been following me for a long time, haven't they?" Guilt made my voice waver.

Susan offered a kind smile then handed me a soft knit dress, the stretchy fabric settling against my skin with a sigh. "You are important to Arafel. He would trust your safety to only the best." Before I could ask more, she waved a hand over my hair, her fingers catching the ends of my braids and tugging lightly. "Let me fix your hair before we go out. It is so lovely when it's down."

I pulled the long strands out of her hands, running my hands over the braids protectively. "I like it the way it is."

Susan raised a brow. "Dirty and messy?"

A flush warmed my cheeks. I choked back an embarrassed noise. "Fine. Do your worst."

The older woman ushered me into a chair by the vanity, standing behind me and freeing my long hair from the braids before running a brush through them.

I wasn't used to this kind of treatment and immediately pushed away, feeling awkward. "You don't have to do that."

Her light grip on my shoulders made me stop fast. "It's my pleasure, Lucia. Please, let me."

I stared into the mirror, watching her behind me. "I don't know how to ask this..."

"What's that?"

"What are you?"

Susan chuckled. "Your lady's maid, remember."

"No, I mean—"

"I know what you meant." Susan patted my shoulder. "No sense in letting you off the hook that easy. I am, so to say, a soul made sturdy. If you were to run into a soul moving through the

River Styx or awaiting judgement, they would be far too flimsy to do this." Susan ran her fingers through my hair, and I could feel the gentle rasp of nails there. As if she were as human as I was. "I'm not like the Brotherhood; they are given bodies designed for their stations. But my soul has been given form permanently."

"And you...like that?"

Her smile was soft. "I do. I hoped your entire life I might be given the chance to see you shine."

I gulped a little. "How do you do that, then? Wouldn't every soul want that?"

"Perhaps." Susan's eyes found mine in the mirror. "Arafel and his family are the only demons powerful enough to grant this type of power to a soul. Being the caregivers to souls is no easy task, and I'm grateful that my lord has the ability to keep me here. Now, sit back. We need to get a move on."

The cushion shifted as I settled back into it. Unsure of what to do with my hands, since they weren't doing the brushing, I curled them around my knees to hide the shaking of my still-frazzled nerves. "I feel silly like this."

"You shouldn't..." Susan's words died, and her hands dropped from my head. "My lord." In the mirror, I saw a wide smile on her face, even as she dropped to a curtsey.

My heart leapt in my chest, my skin heating instantly as I saw a tall, horned shadow in the doorway.

Arafel.

6

Lucia

He was even more beautiful now that I truly had a moment to observe him. His deep, silver-toned skin was wrapped tightly over an angular face. His ears were delicate and pointed at the ends. The black horns I remembered so well shone in the light of the room. But it was his smile that made my heart thunder in a surprising rush of delight. It radiated warmth and made me think of curling up against him, the way he'd held me on our journey here.

I blinked quickly, suddenly worried about how that had looked. I had made a huge mistake, forced his hand, and now I was staring at him like he was a tourist attraction. Embarrassment made my face burn as I lurched to a standing position. Susan hissed a warning, capturing the chair I'd upset as I stood.

Cheeks hot, I tried to smile back at him.

"I'm glad to see you awake. May I come in?"

I nodded, my brain unable to put any words together as my eyes took him in once more. Yes, he was real. My formerly invisible protector was standing right in front of me. Susan patted my shoulder, sliding across the room.

Arafel took his cue and stepped in closer. "You look stunning. Especially considering what you've been through." His voice was deep and rumbling. It washed over me like a wave, making my chest heavy and the muscles in my legs and belly clench.

"Thank you." My tongue felt thick and strange in my mouth.

His eyes were so inhumanly blue, they seemed to glow as we stared at each other. "Are you well? Is everything to your liking?"

I swallowed twice before answering. "Yes, everything is great. It's not exactly what I pictured Hell to be like."

Arafel's lips curled in a soft smile. "The Underworld and Hell are two very different things."

I felt the heat of mortification warm my face again. "Oh, I didn't know."

"I know." Arafel's chin dropped, and he took a purposeful step away from me. His knee-high boots appeared custom made, and their soles were silent against the hardwood floor. "That's not your fault. It is mine. I was actually coming by to see if I could show you more of my home."

My heart hammered, the emotion surprising me. I was excited to see more. "I'd love that."

Arafel nodded, his horns catching my attention as his dark hair slipped free from the knot at the back of his head. It was black as ink, and for one rash, incredibly wild moment, I wished I could stand, smooth the strands back for him.

But I didn't. I shouldn't. I had no idea if I was even allowed to touch him. Yesterday was a blur, including the powerful pull I felt toward Arafel. And I was determined to figure out why this was all happening to me. "Actually Arafel, I was hoping we could talk about a few things. This is...quite a lot to take in."

The big male moved as if to sit at the edge of my bed, his thick thighs making the tight leather-like leggings he wore stretch as his muscles moved underneath. "Of course—"

Frustration welled up in my chest as I scrambled for words to explain my feelings. "I want to know what's going on, Arafel. I want to know everything. Why am I here, what do you want from me...and..." My throat closed tight, but I forced it on. "Why did my mother have to die?"

My words ended on a sob, and for a moment, grief overwhelmed everything else, and I couldn't imagine needing to know anything else. I needed to know why I was alone. I needed to know now.

"Sweetling." Warm, heavy arms settled around my body. "I'm so sorry. I should've been there."

"No." I pushed at him, his chest thick and strong under my palms. I could feel the way my body instantly responded to him. My skin tingled and heated as I urged him away from me. "I don't want your pity. I want answers."

"And you will have them, Lucia. I will never keep things from you again," Arafel said, his voice low. With a quick move, he stooped down to cradle me against his chest again. The next instant, we were perched on the edge of my bed.

"I need to understand."

His lips pressed against my temple, and I shuddered against him, the tears flowing easily. "I am one of the Lords of the Underworld. My father, Lucifer, rules the Underworld as King, but we are his leaders, his generals, his overlords. He knew we would be incredibly powerful, so he took our souls, shearing them in half. One half would be ours to have, the other implanted in a mortal for safe keeping. Only when we find our other half do our true powers emerge. Until then, we are driven to serve our purpose in the Underworld, while always hoping and searching for the human whose soul-bound to us."

I stared down at my fingernails, realizing they still had dirt under them from the chaos of yesterday. "Do I not have my own soul?"

Arafel's chest rumbled with a soft chuckle. "Oh, you do, Lucia, and it's as bright and powerful as any I've seen in my time. Think of my soul as a parasite. It's wrapped all around yours, completely embedded."

"How do I give it back to you?" A horrifying thought occurred to me. "Oh my gosh, are you going to kill me? And then I'll be like Susan?"

Arafel stiffened under me. "You are misunderstanding me. I've spent your whole life protecting you, and that's not about to change." His hand was human-like, save the long black claws tipping each finger. Arafel stroked my arm, up and down, over and over as my panic receded once more. "I have been searching for a way to extract the other half of my soul for many years, with only minor success."

I curled further up against him, the scent of him filling my nose as I pressed my cheek against his tunic. "What now?"

"I'm not sure yet. The most important thing was keeping you safe."

I bit my lip. "And keep your soul safe."

He sighed, and I could feel his thighs tighten under my bottom. "Do you truly think that?"

I shook my head. Because I didn't. I was only tired and overwhelmed. "This is a lot to take in." My lips quivered again, and my frustration gave way to raw, overused emotion.

"I know, but consider it this way. You are my other half, Lucia. The soul I am bound to above all others."

His lips quirked, and I was briefly distracted by how full they were and what they might feel like against my skin.

"I saw you all those times, I think. It's all foggy when I try to remember." My head pounded, and I let it fall against his shoulder once more.

Arafel shifted, one large palm stroking up and down my back. "You called for me." There was a soft laughter in his voice, maybe a touch of awe. "I'd never heard a mortal's call before. When I moved through the realm, imagine my surprise when this child looked up at me, scared of the dark and shining with the light of my soul in her chest."

"How old was I?"

He cocked his head. "You must've been six or so. I came to your mother shortly after to explain to her what you were."

I breathed in and out, trying to slow my heartbeat. "And all this time? You've been watching?"

Arafel made a noise in his throat. "In comparison to my lifetime, Lucia, I waited but a breath for you to grow up. I would've waited a hundred more lifetimes to know you."

Something in his words struck a chord in my brain, and I recoiled, pushing away at him. "But I don't know you."

"You do, Lucia. You will remember."

I turned away, my mind a blur as I sorted out this information. "Those creatures, what did you call them?"

"The Others. They are corrupting souls, pulling them from the safety of their realms and using them against us."

"And how do I fix any of that?"

Arafel sighed, the sound loud in the suddenly quiet room. "I don't know exactly. I believe the best course of action is to try to find a way to extract my soul from yours."

"But you don't know how?"

"My father has been less than responsive, and my eldest brother, the only one of my brothers who found the human he was soul bound to, is in too much pain to respond to my missives."

"Pain?"

Arafel's silence was palatable. "His soul bound died only a few weeks after they met. There are dangerous forces at work, Lucia. That's why I had to bring you here."

Dread curled in my belly. "Someone like the possessed dog walker?"

Arafel's brows dropped, but he nodded after a moment. "A lost soul, possessed and desperate to do their master's bidding."

"And they were after me because...?"

"Because if they succeed in killing you before I extract my soul, the cycle will start all over again. My soul would be moved to another."

I stared at him, letting the words sink in as much as they could. I think I was about done with absorbing new and horrifying details today.

"Why can't we stay like this, with me holding both souls? I'm a fast learner. I can help with whatever you need."

But he was already shaking his dark head. "You do not understand how important it is for me to utilize the entirety of my power, Lucia, but you will."

"You're scaring me."

His sigh was soft, the warmth of his breath on my face making me still. Even his scent was addicting to me. "I know, but you need to know. I wanted you to understand why I'm doing the things I'm doing."

I pulled away, suddenly chilled by his words. He felt the change in my mood in an instant, rising and letting me slip off his lap to the bed. "I will give you space to settle in. "

Arafel moved to the door. "And Lucia?"

I looked up at him, my vision blurred by frustrated tears. "What?" My voice was all wrong, thick and choked.

"It was the greatest joy of my life to find you and also my sincere sorrow it meant the end of your mother's life."

I stared at him, a tear slipping down my cheek.

"She cared for my most precious possession for as long as she was capable. I will mourn her for the rest of my days."

And with that, Arafel closed the doors.

With a ragged cry, I moved rigidly and climbed into the bed, pressing my face against the cool pillows and surrendering to it all.

Minutes later, or maybe hours, I heard a voice whisper nearby. "So should we wake her up?"

"No, you idiots, get out of here."

I blinked slowly, the familiar grit of crying myself to sleep in my eyes. But this time I was surprised to find both Simeon and Gatam on my bed with me. Susan stood a few feet away, arms crossed, tongue clucking.

"Hello," I said, my voice rough with sleep. I cleared it and tried again.

"Ahh, see, she's already awake. No need to get all worked up, Susan."

Susan grumbled, walking to the other side of the room and throwing back the gold-threaded curtains on my windows. Sunlight, or whatever it was here that lit up the outdoors, streamed in. I lifted an arm, pressing it over my eyes, unable to meet the eyes of the Brotherhood warriors. "How can you stand me right now?"

Gatam looked at Simeon for a long moment, and then as if agreeing with each other, both warriors shrugged. "We may not understand everything about humans, but we understand you did what you thought you needed."

"I thought Arafel would be mad at you."

Simeon grinned, one brow quivering. "Why do you think we are here?"

Sniffling, I blink furiously. "Wait... What *are* you doing here?"

"We came to take you on your tour."

I swallowed, surprised by the pang of disappointment. "Oh. I thought Arafel was going to take me."

Gatam stood, carefully avoiding my gaze. Simeon, on the other hand, patted the bed. "He's away, checking in with one of his brothers. Besides, it will give us some time to make it up to you."

"His brothers?" The idea there might be more like Arafel both delighted and horrified me. There was so much I didn't know about his world.

"He's hoping one of them might know how to extract his soul from yours."

Gatam moved across the room to stare out the window, and Simeon slowly stood, massaging his back as he straightened to his full height. "Don't look so disappointed, Lucia. He'll be back soon."

Throwing my legs over the edge of the bed, I pushed to a standing position and moved away with a flip of my long hair. It was still down from earlier when Arafel interrupted Susan and me. "Of course. It's no big deal."

Simeon's voice was charged with humor as he got more comfortable on my bed. "Clearly."

"How many brothers does he have, anyway?" I leaned against a wall, my fingers easily parting my hair and dividing it into sections for braiding.

"Arafel has five brothers, the unholy and inimitable sons of Lucifer."

I mentally tucked that away for later. Not only was Lucifer a real living creature, but that he was some kind of Underworld family man. I was not in a state to deal with that yet. Nodding as if this were a completely normal conversation, I finished one plait and moved to the next. "And they are all like Arafel?" I released my hair to gesture over my head, trying to replicate the horns that curled over Arafel's brow.

Gatam made a rough sound, and I raised my eyes to him, my fingers moving quickly back down my head, pulling as the braid formed. The smile on his face made it clear that he was laughing.

"Why is that funny?"

Simeon crossed his arms, thick muscles flexing under his spotless white tunic. "Because Arafel is one of a kind. And comparing him to his brothers is a little like comparing day and night. Each of them rules a separate part of the Underworld, and each is uniquely qualified to rule those kingdoms."

I tied off the second braid. "Makes sense, I guess. And no one else besides his older brother has found their missing soul?"

Simeon's cheerful expression slipped. "No, only Nephesh. Bad business. That was before we understood what the Others were after."

"The others?"

"Those who serve the Drude. A combination of stolen or corrupted souls, demons, half demons." Gatam nodded along with Simeon's list. "Your friend from the park was Other, same with the mahrs who attacked Tim's house."

"And what do they want?"

The big warrior ran a hand through his shaggy blonde hair, the gesture born of habit. "It's only a guess, really."

His avoidance of the subject only made me more interested.

"Simeon, what is it?"

"You will give Arafel the greatest gift of his life—complete power, the other half of himself returned." Simeon's eyes met mine. "Imagine finding that, only to lose it immediately after. Safe to say the Lord of Judgement isn't necessarily excited to chat about it."

I nodded, tying off the second braid.

Gatam moved a step closer, flicking my braid over my shoulder like a brother might do. Then, with a soft, breathy noise, he pointed out the window between us. "He says—"

"I know," I spoke over Simeon, offering a small smile to Gatam. "We should get to the tour."

Simeon grunted, climbing off the bed and going to the door. "After you, my lady."

I rolled my eyes but passed through the door, Simeon and Gatam ominous shadows at my back as we strolled through the elaborate manor halls. Other than my rooms, there were several rooms. I peeked my head into one, finding a small library with a heavy desk and walls lined with books, as well as a warmly lit kitchen, which was empty and silent. I already knew, or at least sensed, the matching set of doors down the hall were off limits to me. I wouldn't go into those, my cheeks heating when I realized those had to be where Arafel had been staying.

"He's a king, right? Arafel?" I couldn't stop myself from whispering.

"Yes, King of Dreams."

Glancing over my shoulder, I saw that Gatam was smiling again, his eyes dancing. "Well, does he have a castle or something?"

Simeon shrugged, a grin on his friendly face. "Or something."

I snorted, and Gatam laughed at my reaction as we passed through a dining room that could sit twenty-five Arafel-sized guests easily. My eyes bulged out of my head as I moved down the room, my fingers brushing against the polished wooden tabletop.

"And I dreamed all of this up?"

"It's more complicated than that, but Arafel's magic gives people the opportunity to build something for themselves, something of comfort or need while they are in his realm. You are the first we've seen to act so independently, but the end results speak for themselves."

I looked at him nervously.

"It is beautiful, Lucia. Remember the soul is most vulnerable while dreaming, and so our mahrs, as well as several warriors from the Brotherhood, are all protecting the souls who are visiting during their dreams."

Simeon leaned on a doorway, observing the décor around us. "Personally, I think you have great taste. It's not hurting Arafel a single bit to stay here."

Gatam pointedly bumped into Simeon, and the bigger man frowned by stopping talking.

"Where now?" I looked out the back door. A wide yard filled my immediate vision, a small greenhouse in one corner. I'd always wanted a greenhouse, and the sight of it there, the panes fogged and warm, made me smile. Every inch of the property was lush, green, covered in flowers and as real and lifelike as anything I'd experienced in…in…

"What do you call, uh, my home? Where all the human souls live?"

The pair of Brotherhood warriors ushered me forward. Simeon waved his arm around the wide, well-stocked kitchen before moving back to the entryway. "You mean the living world? That might be odd for you to hear, but that's what we typically call it."

"You mean I'm the only living soul here who is not dreaming?"

The warriors nodded.

"That's a little eerie," I confessed, peeking into a pantry, surprised to see a variety of food that I ate regularly. "But I guess eerie is relative? Holy shit, is that a twinkie?" I held the plastic-covered pastry out to Gatam, who took it and examined it with interest.

"Hey, it's your dream house, not mine." Simeon took the twinkie from Gatam as the other man began to open the package. "Don't eat that, trust me."

Gatam snatched the treat back and shoved it into his pocket while ignoring Simeon.

"This is so weird," I whispered to myself as I followed them back toward the foyer, turning in a circle underneath the biggest chandelier I'd ever seen. "Amazing, beautiful...but oh so weird."

We continued on, winding around the vast estate, where I had the chance to run my hands along perfectly polished banisters and across the tapestries that covered much of the walls. My favorite space might have been the cozy-looking den in the back of the house, with dim lighting and deep velvet green couches; I immediately pictured myself curled up there, talking to Arafel and—

My feet froze in place. Arafel. I'd always remembered him, or at least bits of him, but now that I was here, it was as if I couldn't stop my mind from calling out for him, wondering what he was doing, where he might be. I imagined that was his soul calling to him, but nevertheless, I couldn't get my mind off of him.

"Do you want to see the hall of dreams?" Simeon rubbed at his chin, tapping a finger into his dimple. "I don't think Arafel would mind us showing you."

"The hall of dreams? Is it dangerous?"

"Not as long as you stay with us."

I offered my guides as much of a smile as I could muster. "Then yes, I would love to see that."

"Right this way, then. It's a short walk or a quick shadow jump."

My stomach clenched a little at doing another shadow jump so quickly after the last one, where Arafel brought us here. "I'd rather walk, if that's okay with you."

They looked at me knowingly and then opened the door wide. Down the stone-paved drive, the bright-green grass slowly lost its color and turned to short, stiff-feeling stems that bit into the edges of my feet around my sandals.

But before I could complain, I realized we were walking toward a stone, wide-columned building. It looked like a library, or maybe a big-city museum. And it was larger than I could ever imagine a building being. From the front, I couldn't see the end of it, the sides of the building so long my vision blurred before I could see where it turned a corner.

Weird. But also so, so interesting. I hurried up the stairs leading to the high glass entryway doors, eager to see what was within. The doors were covered in stained glass, the colors so at odds with the drab grays and creams of the stones around it—beautiful, nonetheless. There were five shapes positioned around the outside of an elaborate tree of life. But in this one, the tree was upside down, branches facing down while the roots curled in on top. I pressed my finger against the first, a gavel, simple and poignant. The second was a moon, silver and iridescent. The third a swooping arch.

"A wave, for the ferryman," Simeon said from behind me.

I nodded, my hand continuing on. The next was a shield, and finally a perfectly balanced measuring scale.

"One for each of his brothers?" I was whispering again, my palm falling to rest on the flames at the center, backing the tree of life. The glass heated under my palm. "And this?"

"Hellfire, Lucifer's magical gift. The center of this world."

I turned to him. "Hellfire?"

"A powerful symbol for a powerful ruler." He leaned in, as if telling a secret. "Remember, fire brings death, but it also creates new life. A poignant symbol for the King of the Underworld, don't you think? The Court of Hell is not something to be feared, especially for you."

"Have you been there?" I swallowed hard. "To see the devil?"

"Many times. This world is not what you think it is, Lucia."

Tears unexpectedly filled my eyes; I choked them back. "I'm so confused. Why is this happening to me?"

Simeon put a hand on my shoulder. "You were chosen for a reason, my lady."

"So far, being chosen sucks."

Gatam's soft, rasping laugh broke me from my pity fest, and I wiped my nose with the back of my hand. "How long have you been here?"

Simeon's shoulders grew stiff. "A little over three hundred years."

My eyes were bugging out, I was sure, but I couldn't stop them. "Three hundred?"

"Give or take a decade."

"Same with Gatam?"

"Nah, he and Paran are younglings."

I waited until finally he shot me a wide grin. "They were born around the beginning of the twentieth century."

"Oh God, that's it." I threw my hands up. "I've gone completely mad."

Simeon stepped around me, opening the door wide. "Perfect timing, then. Please allow me, my lady, to introduce you to the very center of the dream realm."

7

Lucia

"Everything in the dream realm is centered here." Simeon's thick frame blocked a cool breeze as we entered the building, the stained glass closing behind us casting a rainbow effect on the floors. Checkered marble floors and Roman-looking columns decorated the three-story entryway.

I stopped, spinning in place as I looked up above me. "Wow."

"Inside here is what you can call your run-of-the-mill dreamers. The folks who are living their lives. The more complicated dreams are handled by our mahrs and branch out across the realm as needed."

Gatam pressed a hand to my shoulder, ushering me to a wide, half-circle reception desk, where a mahr sat, its dark, unblinking gaze watching me. My memory dragged me back to the clearing at our safe house, to the corrupted mahr, with his red eyes and dripping claws. The memory of the pressure of his power on me as I'd fallen to the ground in front of him welled inside me.

"Lucia?" Simeon's voice was gentle, pulling me free from the memory.

I blinked rapidly, back in the present, back with the Brotherhood.

With suddenly dry lips, I leaned over. "Hello," I whispered to the mahr. This one, something about it seemed feminine, and it cocked its head to stare up at me then back at Simeon.

"Hey, Jackie." Simeon leaned in, a charming grin on his face. "We are going to give Lucia the tour."

Jackie sat back in her raised chair, blinking those huge eyes at me. I really had time to look, and they were a bit comical. I offered her the best smile I could muster. I wasn't sure which one of us was more scared of the other.

Simeon chuckled. "Please."

The mahr offered what looked to be its equivalent of a smile, and I tried not to flinch away from the display of razor-sharp teeth. Behind her, the wide double doors swung open. Gatam patted the top of the desk in thanks, and Simeon placed a hand on my back, guiding me away.

"Thank you." I quickly added, "Jackie." As Simeon ushered me through the doors, I took a moment to look back over my shoulder to see Jackie leaning off her chair to follow our little party with her obsidian stare.

"She likes you."

I jerked around to stare at Simeon. "What?"

Both men laughed, Gatam a bit roughly, and I let myself smile at their enjoyment of my acclimation to the Underworld. As soon as we passed through the archway, all thoughts of Jackie, and even Simeon and Gatam, were swept away. I was standing at the base of what had to be one of the longest and most elaborate staircases ever dreamed up. It rose up seven—no, eight stories into the air, the staircase zigzagging through the air above us.

"What is this?" I stared up at the staircase, my head tilted back so far my neck ached. "Oh my God!"

"Meh," Simeon grunted from beside my shoulder, his tunic swaying slightly as he looked from side to side. "Nah, this one is Arafel's design, although I've heard God's library is impressive as well."

Gatam gave a humored grunt as he passed us, and I swatted at Simeon's shoulder, my body still tingling in shock. "This... This is absolutely incredible." I spun in place, trying to absorb everything I could see. We were standing at the beginning of a library, but the depth and vastness was inconceivable. From here I could see the beginning of row after row of books. The vaulted ceiling was painted a bright white, with skylights scattered above, bringing in the sun-like glow from outside straight into the library. Every corner, every nook was positively stuffed with books and light.

I was instantly infatuated.

"It is," Simeon said after I finally stopped gaping at the room around us. "Like I said, there is so much you don't know yet. But you will."

Gatam gestured forward, his hands sweeping wide at the base of the staircase. He clearly meant for me to start climbing. But my throat closed; clearly I couldn't scamper up there. It was so high.

"Up?" I hoped to God the Brotherhood didn't notice how high my voice sounded.

Simeon shrugged. "Let's start with the second floor. Just don't touch anything unless we are together. And I mean *anything*."

Relief made me sag for a moment. "Done," I said and took off toward the stairs, my legs pumping as I lunged up the staircase to the first landing. I hated heights, but the second floor was completely possible. As I slowed at the top of the first turn of the stairs, I found myself staring down the beginning of even more rows than I would have imagined from the first floor.

The library was endless. Books in every color and shape covered the shelves. And as I got near the shelves, I saw the ink on their spines, elaborate scrolling words and names.

"What does it mean?" I said loudly as Simeon approached. My chest was rising and falling quickly still, a combination of fear, excitement, which made my heart race.

"It is hard to explain. Hmm." The warrior drew closer, looking at a large red volume closest to my eyeline. "This one should be fairly safe."

"Fairly?" I echoed, a bit worried. "What do you mean? It's a book."

Simeon grinned and then pulled the book from the shelf. Jerking his chin, he ushered me closer. "Nothing is quite as it seems. Come here."

I propped my fists on my hips. "Come where? I'm practically on top of you, Simeon."

The big man cleared his throat and then stepped a bit closer. I raised my brows, surprised at his boldness. But before I could say anything, Simeon opened the book wide, nearly splitting the spine as he held it out between us.

"And breathe" was all he said as his hand gripped the back of my neck and tilted me forward. Off-balance, I let out a screech and tipped forward onto my toes and then fell. Straight into the book he held before us. I screamed. The feeling was the same as when Mom and I would go on road trips and she always sped up going up the hills, knowing on the other side my stomach would flip and drop dramatically.

Only this time, the hill went on and on until I wondered for a moment if this feeling would ever end. And then my feet slammed into warm, deep sand. I could feel the harsh little beads of earth making their way around my shoes, sticking wetly to my skin. I grimaced, staring up at Simeon as he quickly stepped away from my side, his hand dropping.

I blinked up at the harsh sun above us. "What happened? Where are we?"

"We," Simeon said, turning me with a quick push on my shoulder, "are inside someone's dream." To my surprised face, he grinned. "More specifically, Leah Albertson's dream."

I stared around us. We were on a beach, wide expanses of sand meeting bright-blue waves right in front of my eyes. I stepped forward, gasping when warm water washed over my feet, soaking my sandals.

I squealed, scuffling out of the water and into the dry sand, where even more grains adhered to my wet skin. "It's real!"

Simeon shook his head, blonde locks blowing in a salty breeze that I could nearly taste. "Not quite. It's a dream. But to her, everything she's experiencing is real. Therefore, everything here is real for us as well."

"This is a dream?" I wiggled my toes, feeling the sun on my shoulders, the distant call of gulls filling my ears. Joy, simple and heady, filled my heart.

"It's her favorite, and I have a feeling the mahrs encourage her to continue coming here for their own benefit too." Simeon tilted his head back, rolling his shoulders as he sucked in the sea breeze. I didn't stop my smile as I watched the warrior.

I was standing inside someone's dream, someone's fantasy. It felt completely inappropriate but, on the other hand, completely normal. Sighing, I nearly plopped down in the sand, but a soft female voice spoke across the beach, and I jerked my head up. "Oh my God, is she here? Leah?"

"Of course she is." Simeon nodded to a lawn chair, where a curvaceous blonde sat perched, a tall, dark-haired man rubbing her shoulders as she sipped a frozen white drink. I couldn't stop the soft chuckle that slipped out of my lips. Her head turned to Simeon and me as if noticing us for the first time, and she raised her drink in silent cheers. Unsure of what to do, I simply waved in her direction.

When I turned back to Simeon, his expression was serious, surprised. "What? I like her style." I looked around us, feeling the warmth and peace of the tropical breeze on my face. "I was expecting it to be a dramatic thing, like you forgot to put on pants at school or something. But this is lovely."

"We have those too, but not as much as you'd think. The mahrs are particularly tired of that nightmare, so most of them get weeded out pretty quickly."

Leaning down, I picked up a perfectly shaped white seashell. Awestruck, I turned it over in my palm. "It's amazing."

"You can ask Arafel to show you some of the more impressive ones sometime. I chose Leah's because she's usually on some kind of vacation and I figured you might need to feel the sun on your back."

Clutching the seashell, I could feel the ridges and points of the edge of the shell in my hand. It was warm in my palm. "It was a good choice." I turned my hand over, letting the shell fall back to the sand. It looked so real, I went to pick it up again to be sure. But then the air around us wavered, and my stomach tugged again, a hint of the feeling I'd withstood to get here.

Simeon's head rose, and he looked out across the beach. Then he stepped close, placing his hand on my shoulder as he did. "We need to go—"

"Already? I want to try a pina colada."

But Simeon wasn't laughing. His lips puckered, and with a quick move, he stepped up beside me, the red book back in his grip and his hands on my shoulders as he jerked me back. With an ungraceful squawk, I tripped, but instead of my body meeting sand, there was nothing. Just more of the gut-swirling movement as I fell back to the Underworld. My feet hit the hardwood floors of the library of dreams, my knees feeling jellylike as Simeon snapped Leah's book closed.

I stumbled forward, leaning against the bookshelf to catch myself. My fingers separated a book, and I cringed away. I wasn't ready to go falling back into another dream yet, even one as nice as Leah's.

Simeon looked no worse for the wear. He cast a worried glance over me and then tilted his head, as if listening to something.

My legs were feeling more secure, and I straightened, tugging at the hem of the dress I'd tossed on before our tour. Looking over the bookshelf around Leah's paradise dream, I let my fingers ghost over the other spines. Most were names, written in neat, scrawling script. Occasionally, there was a second or third line, written in tiny minute writing under the name. I leaned in, squinting. "Each book is a dream? That's why there are so many." I took his silence for agreement. "Do they change?"

"They change constantly," Simeon answered, but his voice was brusque, tense. "We need to go. Where's Gatam?"

When I looked around, the only things I saw were a pair of mahrs who were walking down the aisles several sections ahead of us, running their hands over the spines of books as they went. I only got to observe for a moment before someone grabbed my hand and hauled me back toward the stairs. My feet were wet still, the sand making me cringe.

"Simeon, what's going on?" I grunted as we began to descend the stairs.

I couldn't help but notice his free hand was perched on the hilt of his sword. My belly clenched. Something was wrong, I thought to myself, hurrying to keep up with him.

"We need to get you back to the house."

"All right," I said and then tried to move faster to keep up with his bigger stride. "Okay, I'm hurrying."

For a second, all we heard were the slapping noise of my sandals against the stairs and the deep footsteps of Simeon a stair ahead of me. Then there was something else, someone else in there with us.

Because I'd never heard silence quite that loud.

"What's the hurry, Brother Simeon?" a deep, husky voice said, coming from all around us. It was beautiful, lyrical.

The hair on my arms rose. Simeon stopped at the base of the stairs and pulled me close, practically dragging me into the enormous entry room of the Hall of Dreams.

Jackie was nowhere to be seen. Her desk was abandoned, chair still swiveling ever so slightly.

"You're far from home, aren't you, little soul?"

In a movement borne of habit and practice, Simeon drew his broadsword, pivoting to face a tall male who appeared in the corner of the entryway.

Simeon growled, a dark and threatening sound. I stared at the newcomer, shock making my blood run cold. Because whatever stood before us, whoever stood between us, was even further from human than Arafel was. It had to be one of Arafel's brothers. But which one? This creature was nearly as tall as the King of

Dreams, but instead of horns, he had a marine-like quality to his features. My gaze took in the slightly pointed ears and the dark lines along his throat that looked distinctly like gills, had they not been sealed tight, flush to his pale-blue skin.

Even the way he moved toward us, long, lean lines graceful as he approached us.

A demon, maybe.

But not like Arafel. But then again, Simeon had said Arafel was one of a kind. Which would make this…male…something else entirely.

Simeon growled again, and this time the demon male looked at the warrior, his expression surprisingly mischievous. He was wearing a tunic and pants not unsimilar from what Arafel wore, but his were a deep blue that, coupled with the soft-blue tone of his flesh, made him seem even more other worldly.

"Is there something you wish to say, Brother Simeon? Or may I talk to your guest?" The male drew closer, stopping a few lengths away when Simeon growled another warning. Arafel had made it seem like the Brotherhood served each of the lords, not only Arafel, so the open hostility in Simeon's face made my fear bloom anew. While this new demon didn't appear outright hostile, Simeon was on alert. I should be too. The realization crept over my skin, replacing curiosity with anxiety as it moved through me.

"You shouldn't be here. Your brother—" Simeon dropped into a crouch as the newcomer raised his hand up, a swirl of bright-colored liquid forming against his palm. As soon as the droplets swirled around his fingertips, the male dropped back, his eyes flashing a bright white for just a moment.

I didn't know a lot about combat, but I recognized a threat when I saw it. And both of these males were ready to fight at a moment's notice.

"My brother brought a soul into the Underworld, a living soul, and didn't feel it was necessary to inform any of us? We have processes for a reason." The newcomer tutted at us, one side of his lips pulling back into a sanguine smile. Chills erupted along my arms. Without thinking twice, my mind leapt to Arafel. He may have been a monster, some kind of demon, but he was mine. He was warm and safe and God, er, Lucifer help me, I needed him. Now.

Fear thrummed in my veins, making my head light. And then a breath later, it was gone. Replaced by a shining heat that nearly burned as it flew through my veins. But I recognized it for what it was.

Him.

I stepped back, straight into his chest. Long, powerful arms remained at his sides, his posture relaxed, but as Arafel's chest rose and fell against my spine, I could feel his heartbeat against me.

"Brother." His voice nearly echoed through my body. My knees quivered as I stood against him.

"Arafel." The newcomer smiled again, showing off a pair of white fangs, this time broader. "So glad you could make it. Did your little soul call for you?" He clapped his hands together then tilted his head as he bowed his head to observe me closer. "How convenient. I love that feature of the whole soul bound situation."

"What are you doing here, Kharon?" The question was quiet, controlled, but I felt the tightness in Arafel's form behind mine. My body hummed at his proximity, my muscles relaxing into him.

"Am I not allowed to visit?"

"To visit, yes. But not to harass and scare my mahrs." Arafel's hands slowly moved to rest across my belly and tuck me close. "Or my soul bound."

That term again... It lanced across my brain a mixture of pleasure and pain all in one endearment.

Kharon raised a brow, his features relaxing at his brother's tone. For the first time since I noticed him, I recognized that in many ways, Kharon might be considered handsome. His high cheekbones and sharp, angular features were appealing. What I couldn't get past were the eerie inhuman green color of the eyes that continued to stare at me. There was something there, some kind of strange thirst he emitted when I met his gaze. I broke it just as quickly, uninterested in seeing more.

"Scared mahrs? Well, I'm sorry about that. Please point me in the direction of which ones I've frightened before I leave, and I'm happy to make my apologies. I can hardly tell them apart, so please, be clear."

Arafel released a soft chuckle, and the tension lessened between them. "After all these years, you still can't?"

"Come down to the river realm, and we shall test your knowledge of ancient creatures and services."

I glanced up to see Arafel wrinkling his nose. "Maybe later. First, I want you to tell me what you're doing in my library."

"Ah, yes, of course. Always on task, aren't you, big brother? I came to see the soul you snuck past Father and me. Nephesh has been oddly unhelpful in the matter." Kharon cast a graceful hand in my direction. "She is quite interesting, you know."

The broad hand at my waist pressed again until I was flush against Arafel. Heat blossomed from where his hand lay, making my entire body restless. "She is not your concern, Kharon. She carries the other half of my soul, and she is under my protection."

Kharon snorted. "I'm not blind, Arafel. I can see that. Call off your soldier, will you?" He gestured at Simeon, who still had his sword drawn, his eyes fast on the newcomer.

"Simply doing my job, River Lord," Simeon said softly.

Kharon looked pointedly at Arafel and then at his hand, still holding me tightly against him. "I won't trouble you any longer, then. But if you change your mind, perhaps if you find someone else who strikes your interest, please let me know so I can come and get this wayward soul."

"She is not yours."

"Neither is she yours. Perhaps she would rather spend her time with someone like—"

Arafel moved faster than my eyes could register, disappearing from behind me to emerge in a puff of deep-silver smoke in front of his sibling, his hands wrapped tightly around Kharon's throat. "Never."

113

"So sensitive," Kharon whispered, the words choking. Full lips curled into a devious smile for just a moment before he said, "Until next time, dear brother." Raising one fist, Kharon snapped, his body instantly turning to water and dripping down over Arafel's fist as Simeon and I both recoiled from the splash.

Arafel straightened, his shoulders heaving as we all stared at the puddle where Kharon had been.

The awkward tension became too much for me. "He seems great. Any other family drama I should know about?"

Arafel looked at me, handsome face grim. "You have no idea." He turned to Simeon. "The others will surely be coming. Make sure the gates are all secured, and warn those at Castle Fel. My brothers are as nosy as ever."

Simeon nodded, bowing to his master before turning to run from the room, leaving Arafel and me alone.

I moved to face Arafel, my hands twisted in front of my body. "I'm sorry I caused such a commotion."

Arafel's eyes narrowed, the blue within them flaring with his power. "Why are you apologizing? It was my brother who came here to poke around and challenge us. You did nothing wrong."

"I..." I closed my mouth, considering his words. He was right, but it was odd to have it be stated so frankly. My heart lifted as I glanced up at him. "Thank you."

The ghost of a smile crossed Arafel's lips. He moved to stand before me. "I'm glad you're all right. When I heard your call and felt Kharon's power..." He shook his head, a stray dark hair slipping free from its knot at the back of his head. "The thought of him touching you, talking to you, it... I don't quite understand it."

He reached out a hand, the rough callus of his thumb stroking down my jaw. I barely resisted the urge to shiver at his touch. Swallowing, I lifted my eyes to his, soaking in the fire in his blue depths. "Was what he said serious? Will he try to take me away?"

Arafel's face changed in an instant, his mouth parting enough I could see long, sharp canines descending from his gums, his eyes glowing bright blue, his muscles bulging and making his shirt tight. "You will never belong to Kharon. If I have to pull you from the depths of the Styx myself, I promise you this."

I pressed my hand against his, flattening Arafel's hand against my skin. His was so much larger than mine that he cupped the side of my head while I barely covered his palm. "I believe you." His other hand came to rest against my waist, claws pricking against my skin even through the dress.

Arafel was breathing hard, fangs still showing.

"Arafel, I'm here. I'm safe." My eyes darted around the vast space for a moment, but we were alone. Arafel's eyes glowed bright for another breath, and then just as suddenly, they dimmed back to their normal ice blue, the pupils reappearing as his muscles shrank and his fangs receded.

"Lucia," Arafel whispered, his voice ragged.

I instinctively relaxed into him. "I'm right here."

He sighed, lowering his forehead until it pressed against mine. "I don't... I apologize. I'm not sure what came over me."

I breathed him in, confused but entranced at the feel of his skin against mine. It was lightly textured, almost like a fine leather. My fingers curled around his forearms, my heart hammering in my chest as I soaked up the feeling of him against me. "It's okay. It's nice to have someone looking out for me." But as much as I wanted to stay like this, our bodies so close, the smell of him making my body feel achy and needy, I knew I couldn't. I was in the Underworld; I was supposed to be helping him so I could get his soul out of me and let us both get back to our normal lives. His people needed his power.

And I needed to find out what was next for me.

I stood on my tiptoes to brush my lips against his forehead just in front of his where his curling dark horns began, and then I leaned back, moving away from his embrace. "Your library is extraordinary."

Arafel blinked several times, his hands falling from me to swing by his sides. He glanced behind me at the rows and shelves visible through the still parted door. "Yes, they are quite remarkable." He ran a hand through his hair in a human-like gesture, which made me smile.

"How did you get here so fast?"

"This is my realm, Lucia. I can bend and move it at my will." He ducked his chin, and I could've sworn his cheeks darkened. "That said, I was only down the hall at my desk."

I didn't bother stopping the laughter that slipped from my lips. "You have an office? The Lord of Dreams?"

His smile was quick, fangs flashing. "Of course I do. Every respectable demon does. Would you like to see?"

"Yes, absolutely." I looked back toward the reception desk. "But I have to check something." I walked across the room, wrinkling my nose when I realized my sandals were still wet and sandy from Leah's beach.

"Jackie?" I approached the desk slowly. Shoving down the remaining bit of fear of the mahrs, I leaned over the polished surface. "Jackie, are you down here?"

A soft squawk answered me, and then something moved in the dark shadows of the desk.

I smiled. "You can come out now."

At first, she didn't move. If anything, her dark form seemed to move back faster. "Kharon is gone," I said softly, reaching my hand out to her. "Lord Arafel is here. It's safe to come out."

I didn't think she would. At first there was no movement, not even more of the shuffling sounds I was starting to believe were their language. But then, fingers, or rather claws, filled my palm. They were cold and bony in my grasp, but I ignored the small swell of revulsion as I looked down at those black, skeletal fingers on my own. With a smile, I pulled my hand back, guiding Jackie back out into the light of the room from where she'd hidden beneath her desk. She flinched at first, and I offered her a mumble of kind words.

After she had emerged and I got her settled back in her stool, I backed away, her enormous eyes watching me, unblinking. With a shrug and a twinge of awkwardness, I moved back to Arafel. He was watching me with a strange expression, waiting. When I reached his side, I tried not to think about how natural it felt to have him place his hand on my back and guide me back through the doors to the library of dreams.

8

Arafel

Nothing was as it seemed.

She had embraced my monster. Not just any monster. Not the human-like ones like the incubus or the harpies that roamed my realm. She had reached out to a mahr, the very creatures built to turn a soul's dreams into nightmares with a touch of their skin. Even after she'd been attacked in the woods yesterday.

I glanced at the woman at my side. Her blonde head didn't even reach my shoulders. Another visceral reminder of how fragile she really was. How human. How alive. My hand at the small of her back clenched, and I longed to move it along her spine, to offer her comfort as she tried to find her footing in my world.

She'd let me hold her last night. I'd picked her up, expecting her to resist me or push me away. But instead, she'd turned into me, her body curling against mine as she not only took comfort from my presence but asked for more. I had barely known what to do.

It was the first time anyone, since perhaps my mother, had treated me as if I were even capable of the softness they needed.

It had felt...blissful. The powerful need to keep her close thrummed in my veins even now.

But this morning, feeling her fear and knowing my brother was close... It had awakened another side of me I barely knew what to do with. For not the first time in my existence, I cursed my father's ideas of making me with a human male in mind. I was neither angel nor human. I was a demon.

But still, in these moments, I wished for the knowledge of what to do with emotions I rarely felt. This woman, she drew them from me effortlessly. She always had, but having her here, the depth of these feelings was nearly overwhelming.

We drew even with my office doors. "Here we are," I said.

Lucia took a few steps forward, and I didn't stop myself from taking a deep breath of her scent as she moved past me. She smelled like the sun and, I realized with a start, me. The thought rooted deep in my mind, and my hands felt cool where they had once been touching her. I liked the knowledge that she smelled like me. It was another claim, one I might not have the right to but appreciated nonetheless.

"I can see why you spend so much time here," she said softly, moving to stand by my desk. Smiling, she brushed her hands over the deep cushions of my office chair. We did not function like the humans above, with their endless technology and computers. We had magic of our own. But then, I did quite enjoy the look and feel of the opulent office, much like an executive suite might appear in the human world.

I glanced around the familiar space. There were two plush sofas facing each other, a small fireplace on the end, and wide, illuminating, heavy-paned windows behind my desk. It was comfortable, warm.

Lucia moved to sit in my chair, and a sharp pang of warning filled my chest. "Lucia, I—"

My words died off as her eyes caught on the subject of my shame. Her books were open on my desk, her dreams stacked neatly in a corner.

Her eyes grew wide. "You were watching my dreams." The accusation hung between us, growing heavier by the moment.

I forced myself to meet her intense blue gaze. "I was."

She swallowed hard, the bob of her throat distracting. "Why? Why would you want to do that?"

I moved around the office to stand by her shoulder, letting my finger trace down the spine of one book. I didn't miss the shivering movement of her shoulders as I did. "After last night, I couldn't imagine the pain I had put you through. You had lost your mother, and I brought you here to protect you, but I actually have no idea how to get either of us what we need."

The excuse felt bitter on my tongue.

Her cool eyes watched mine. "And so you watched my dreams?"

"I wanted to be sure they were calm, relaxing." I left out the part about how I'd been wondering who else might have been watching my soul bound. Obviously the Drude knew about her. It wasn't a far reach to imagine they were already invading her dreams. My boundaries, both physically and mentally, needed to be strengthened again. My muscles stiffened and grew under my shirt as I pictured someone getting too close to Lucia because of my weakness. My fangs bit into my lips as I barely resisted a snarl.

"Isn't that kind of the opposite of what your people do here?" She moved a fraction away from me. "They aren't called nightmares for nothing, Arafel. They are meant to be scary."

My temper still lurked beneath my flesh, a living thing. "No, that's not what they are meant to do. They are meant to be a guide."

Lucia's pretty face twisted, suspicion lacing her voice. "How do you explain the boogeyman? The things kids dream up and wake up screaming over? That's not guidance."

I gritted my teeth. "You speak to me as if you understand what my world is, when you have been here mere hours compared to the centuries I have spent building it. There are roughly eight billion people in the world, all dreaming at various parts of the day. Do you think we can manage every dream, every fear and worry? Sometimes things get away from us."

Lucia looked like she was thinking it over, so I pushed onwards. "The reason these dreams are coming through the Underworld is because many times, if they do not make better choices, or if we do not guide them, these souls will end up here, in my brother's realm to the east, serving a lifetime for their sins.

Would you rather have a few nightmares or an eternity of servitude? It may seem an ethical dilemma, Lucia, but trust me, we have looked into all facets of this process, and this is what has to happen." I swallowed, trying to slow my words. "I apologize for invading your privacy and looking at your dreams, but I wanted to be sure."

She was quiet for a long time, the crackling fireplace behind us the only sound in the room. Finally, she raised her gaze to mine. "I'm sorry. I didn't mean anything by it. I'm so confused." Her breath rushed out. "But please, I don't want you to be wandering around in my dreams." Bright-pink spots appeared on her cheeks, and I barely resisted smiling at her response. Before last night, I had stopped peeking into Lucia's dreams some time ago, as it had felt too intimate, especially when I'd had no idea when we would truly be able to meet. "But I want to know how you affect them. How do you guide people? It doesn't make as much sense to me."

I leaned over, picking up a small book on the other corner of my desk. Its bright-yellow cover read *Theo Huggins, Grandpa at Baseball Practice*.

"Simeon showed you how this works, right?" I showed her the spine, holding the book out to her so she could read the script across the cover. Her lips pursed as she read, and something in my chest kicked as the adorable look on her face as she became even more confused. My earlier anger vanished in a moment.

"Yes, kind of. We visited Leah's beach vacation. There were drinks and cabana boys and a lot more sand than I was expecting."

I chuckled. The day that woman stopped dreaming of her tropical vacations, all of us would be sorely disappointed. "Perfect. Now Theo, he's been struggling lately. Life is hard, marriage is complicated, so on and so forth."

Lucia nodded solemnly, taking a few steps closer to me. My lips curled in pleasure. She truly did not fear me. And while that did not bode well for her self-preservation, I couldn't deny that I could get used to having someone close.

Tempting fate and rejection, I held open an arm. Without hesitation, Lucia moved under it, nestling close to my torso as we looked down. "Remember, you can't interact with the dreams but are there to simply experience them with the souls."

She was nodding, dark brows lowered. "Can you interact, though?"

I didn't hesitate to answer. "I can—if I chose to."

"That's scary. How do you know what to do?"

I stared down at her, unsure of how to answer that. "It's sometimes necessary to intervene, Lucia. Take my hand. We are going to step in."

I placed Theo's book on my desk, careful to restack her dreams on the far opposite edge. Opening to the first page, I wrapped an arm around her waist. She emitted the tiniest gasp, and I hid the heat that followed the noise, trying to focus instead on young Theo's dream in front of us. Every breath I took in her presence made it harder though. She smelled so good; I wondered immediately what she would taste like.

Demons were not immune to sexual hunger or desire, just as my cousins in the skies weren't, though the seraphim often liked to pretend they were. Feeling Lucia against me, it reminded me how much of me really was human. Or at least the part of me that craved companionship like a starving man craved sustenance.

She was the darkest, deepest temptation, and I barely understood my body's reaction to her. It had never been like this before she came here. Before she knew me for what I was. And I knew if I admitted it aloud, I could and would ruin everything. She held my soul in the balance, the full reach of my power within my grasp.

I could not let myself be tempted by her. No matter how much my heart ached for her.

Not now.

Not ever.

Forcing my hand to loosen its clenching grip on her hip, I looked down at my soul's keeper, her slender hand already smoothing down the page of Theo's book, as if she knew what I needed.

I pressed a finger to the page. My magic slithering from under my skin to gather there was a mere shadow of what I had once held.

"Hold on." I leaned us forward, and then we were there, standing in Theo's dream. The sun was bright and burning in the sky above us, humidity clogged my chest, and a sluggish southern wind blew sand against my face.

No, not sand. Dirt.

Frowning, I glanced around the baseball diamond Lucia and I had stepped into. All around us, teenage boys were playing catch. The slap of rawhide on leather baseball mitts filled my ears, as well as the chatter of the boys themselves. They looked happy, carefree, as all young boys should be.

I stepped away, freeing Lucia to observe on her own. I was endlessly curious about this woman, and I wanted to see what she thought of this type of dream. Not everyone dreamed of beaches and pina coladas.

Most dreamed like this. Remembering moments, days, even people in their best and worst moments. And it was our job to move them through it, to ease their souls through the darkness or pain. I wanted her to understand what we did. Who I really was.

"Theo." Lucia's voice was gentle, barely a whisper as she spotted the boy at the end of the bench. He was digging through a bag, his movements growing more and more frantic as other boys moved past him to begin playing catch,

I motioned for her to get closer. I was the only one here who could affect the dreams. Her presence wouldn't be a problem. If she got too close, she might find out how uncomfortable it was for a dreaming soul to pass through you, but it did no harm, not really.

Lucia grew closer, and I followed her, already familiar with this child's plight.

Theo's voice was soft, shaking. "I can't believe I forgot it."

"What did you forget?" A tall, skinny redheaded child moved to stand next to Theo.

"My glove; Coach is going to kill me," Theo said. His hands were clenched in fists, the desperate attempt to control his emotion visible to all.

"No, he won't. He'll get it, especially with...you know...everything."

Theo stopped moving. The redhead stilled too, bright cheeks revealing his mistake. "I'm sorry, Theo. I didn't mean it like that."

Theo's narrow chin quivered, and I saw Lucia's arm rise, reaching toward the dreaming boy. Her empathy hit me like a force of a hundred bricks as her fingers brushed across the dreaming soul's shoulders, and to my surprise, Theo seemed to startle, wide brown eyes searching the air where Lucia stood. He couldn't see her. Souls never could, not unless I wished it for them.

But still, those eyes, they searched over Lucia, not seeing, but knowing, feeling her there. His soul's reaction made my skin break out in goosebumps.

"Oh honey, it's going to be okay," Lucia murmured. The boy's shoulders dropped, his face temporarily relaxing.

My brow furrowed, and something dark curled in my gut.

Was she soothing this soul? Was this something each of our soul bound would be able to do? Because from where I stood, it seemed like she was using my power without even realizing she was. Simeon's words about how Lucia had spoken to her mother's soul before Kadmiel took her flashed in my mind.

"Lucia," I said before I could stop myself. "Come here. Watch what happens."

Obediently, she turned to me, her hand falling away from the boy. His shoulders stiffened instantly, and I watched the movement with curiosity. Lucia moved by my side, tucking herself in closely, which immediately made my chest ache once again.

"What are we watching?" she whispered, shifting from one foot to another impatiently.

"There." I leaned into her, pointing up the hill and the parking lot beyond. A large red truck was pulling in, a shadowed figure in the front seat. "Watch."

"But...who?"

I smiled a little, shaking my head. I loved this part. Out of the truck popped a medium-height silver-headed man, his large sunglasses at the edge of his nose as he hurried down the hill toward the dugout.

"Theo!" the older man called. He was in a pair of worn overalls and a flannel button-down shirt. Work clothes. There was a smudge of grease on his chin, and his hands were thick with arthritis.

"Grandpa?" Theo's voice came out shaky. He appeared frozen, standing by the dugout bench.

"There you are." The older man walked right into the dugout, his boots so at odds with the cleats on all the surrounding feet. He reached under his arm, pulling out a glove and handing it to Theo. "There you go, my boy. Can't have you miss out, now, can we?"

Those words... They were the entire reason for this dream. The power in that statement would live in this boy's heart for the rest of his days. It was the reason I had chosen this dream, not only for Theo, but for Lucia too.

Theo's throat was working. I glanced at Lucia to see her eyes glossy with unshed tears. Her hand was curled against her chest.

"Thank you," the boy managed in a hushed whisper. His grandfather moved quickly, his arm jerking around Theo's shoulders to clasp him close for an embrace. It only lasted a moment, but I knew it would last a lifetime. Every time Theo dreamed about this moment of his life, he latched on to the feeling of his grandfather enveloping him.

Fingers, shaking and cool, slid against mine. I opened my hand on instinct, and Lucia wove her tiny palm into mine. Together we stood, watching as Theo's life was temporarily righted. After a moment, I drew her hand up to my lips and pressed my mouth to her knuckles. "Come." Together we shifted, trying to pretend that it didn't feel completely natural to wrap an arm about her as we let my magic pull us back out of Theo's dream.

When my feet hit the floor of my office, Lucia staggered a little, falling against me. I bore her weight easily, shifting so she could sit on one of the sofas. With a flick of my fingers, a fire bloomed in the fireplace. Traveling in this realm obviously still took a toll on her, and worry filled my chest.

"Are you all right? Was that too much?"

Lucia was shaking her head, her shoulders low. "No, I loved it." She met my gaze with those wide, curious blue eyes. "What happened to Theo? Is he okay?"

I sat beside her, my knee brushing hers as I stretched out my much longer legs. "Theo Huggins is a thirty-three-year-old man. He and his wife run a successful car dealership a few miles from where you and your mother were living. He named it for his grandfather."

Lucia pressed her hands to her face. "But you said—"

"I said he was struggling, not that he was still twelve." I stared at the fire. "We dream often about what we need. The gaps in our lives that we are trying to fill. Theo needed comfort, support. This dream, this memory, would serve that purpose."

Her face stilled, turning up to me. "And you knew that?"

"I did."

"How?"

"Probably the same way you knew to reach out to him when he was upset." I gestured around the office. "This is why I exist."

Between us, the fire blazed, warming the room and casting her lovely face into light and shadow.

"It's beautiful, what you do for them," Lucia breathed, and I heard the awe in her voice. But I was consumed with something, someone, else entirely.

"*You* are beautiful," I said solemnly, reaching out to brush a stand of mahogany hair behind her ear once again. My hands shook, longing instead to pull her hair free from the intricate braids. It would be easier then to bury my hands in the heavy locks, turning her head to mine, holding her still so that I could devour her. My chest ached.

"Arafel, are you here? There's trouble at the south gate." Paran's voice sliced through the air between us, and I sat back quickly. But not so fast that I didn't see the flash of something in her eyes moments before I turned to the door.

"Come in, Paran. We are in here."

Lucia cleared her throat, scooting a few inches away as the warrior stepped into the room. Paran's brows lifted when he saw the pair of us, but he didn't hesitate to keep talking. "My lord, your assistance is needed at the south gate."

I stood slowly. "Of course." I reached out a hand to Lucia, pulling her up to stand. "I'll go. Paran, can you deliver Lucia back to her room and then meet me there?"

Lucia's face was tensed as she looked between us. "What's wrong? What's the south gate?"

I shook my head. "An old problem, rearing its head. I will see to it and join you for dinner tonight."

Lucia's mouth opened, and I wondered for a moment if she would ask to join me. But she changed her mind, snapping her mouth shut as she stepped toward Paran.

My trusted soldier bowed his head. "Yes, my lord."

Every footstep was heavy, and my body rebelled against leaving the room. At the door, I turned and looked back. "Keep her safe."

Paran's face grew hard. "I will."

9

Lucia

My manor, as I was calling it in my head, was warm and welcoming as I stepped back through the doors. Paran was gone after a quick bow to me at the front door. I closed it after him, feeling the first pangs of loneliness as I moved down the hall to my rooms.

They looked exactly as they had from this morning, save the neatly remade bed and a large leather-bound book on the edge of my vanity. That was new.

Curious, I edged closer, a bit wary after seeing the power of books in this realm. But this book didn't look like the books of dreams did; its binding looked haphazard, and instead of a cover, it simply had Arafel's moon-shaped seal stamped upon it in gilded paint. I recognized it in an instant from the library's stained glass.

Boredom was a powerful motivator, and after a brief walk around the manor, I found myself looking at the book once more.

"It's just a book. No harm ever came from reading a book," I quoted, laughing a little at myself. The cover opened easily, and the pages inside were not all uniform in size or type. My fingers flipped over them; it was full of letters, each addressed to Arafel.

Taking the book, I curled up on my bed, thumbing through the first few, the lines intricate and scrawling. They must have been in another language. Blinking and rubbing at my eyes, I looked closer.

"Why would he leave me a book I can't read?" Frustrated, I looked again, focusing hard. "It must be important."

Frowning deeply, I picked up the book and ran my fingers down the page, staring at the strange symbols. To my shock, the ink seemed to shift under my touch, moving and reshaping as I watched until lines and lines of text in English filled the page.

"Oh my God." I stared, my heart hammering in my ears. "That is so cool." I barely resisted the urge to squeal at the features I'd somehow unlocked. "This place is amazing."

"Happy you think so, dear," Susan said suddenly, walking through my open door and across to the bed. "But is there something in particular you've found?"

"I made the book—" I clapped my hands over the page "—turn into English."

"Oh good." Susan's voice was filled with relief. "I couldn't understand a word of it, but the mahr I asked insisted it would be helpful to you." The older woman looked up, her nose scrunching. "Jackie. Her name was Jackie."

"Oh." I looked down at the book. "I met her today at the library."

"Well, she sent this over with a messenger." Susan bustled around my room once again. "I'm glad you're happy about it, but I'll stick to my Harlequin romances, thank you very much."

"So scandalous," I teased, and then grief gutted me with a single thought.

Susan paused, noticing the way I physically gripped my middle.

"Lucia?"

"She loved them too, you know."

Susan's hesitation was palpable. Finally, she let the words slip free. "She did."

I looked at her sharply, realization dawning. "Did she know who you were? Who you really were?"

Silvery brows lifted as Susan moved away, busying her hands by folding and refolding a stack of towels on my dresser. Finally, she responded. "After some time, yes, she did. Juliette was a deeply suspicious woman, for good reason, but I'd like to say that I have a good soul, and she saw that in me.

"One night she confessed that she was hiding you from someone, something. And I admitted to her I had known all along." Susan cut me a sharp glance. "She almost packed you up and ran for it that night, but I convinced her to stay a little longer. You were practically done with high school then. It was so important to her that you have as normal a childhood as possible because she knew once the spell was lifted, things would never be normal."

The book was heavy in my hands. I cleared my throat before talking again. "I can't believe she never told me. There is so much I want to know, so many questions I have for her."

Susan puttered by on her way to fluff a pillow on the small settee in the window. "Perhaps in time you will be able to answer these questions for yourself. I imagine that's what Juliette would've wanted."

"Maybe." I didn't bother to keep the disappointment out of my voice. Suddenly disinterested, I placed the book of letters to the side and stared down at my bare feet. There was still sand sticking to my ankles, and I decided there was no time like the present to take care of that.

"I want to get cleaned up, Susan. Is there anything I should know about the bath?"

"No." Susan moved toward the door. "Arafel said he'd be home by dinner, so I'll check in with the cook and make sure everything is up to snuff." Her eyes softened as I picked up a towel and headed toward the bathroom. "You have had more change in the past three days than most mortals have in their entire life. You will find your footing, Lucia. I know it."

I nodded, my throat feeling thick as I moved into the bathroom and closed the door. Turning on the bath and filling the room with thick, delightful steam, I let myself slip into the water.

Everything would look better after I got cleaned up.

And after Arafel returned.

Without him, the dream realm simply seemed less. And as I let myself sink beneath the scented water, I tried not to think about what that meant.

***

I must've dozed off in the bath, because it was over an hour later when I finally opened my eyes. The water was cool against my skin, and I grimaced as I got out of the tub and wrapped myself in one of the enormous towels Susan had left for me. Looking at the mirror, I laughed at the ridiculous length of the towel. It covered me from shoulders to shins and was wrapped around me several times.

Looking at my reflection, recognition bloomed in my belly. The towels were huge because of the male they were designed for. I blinked, looking down at the fabric. Arafel was much larger than me, and I knew that, but seeing the proof of it against my skin made something deep in my chest twist and my body heat.

I forced myself to step away, toweling off my hair as I shrugged into a robe. Fumbling around my closet, I realized I had no idea what to wear for dinner. Susan would know, I thought to myself. I had taken only a few steps out of the vast closet when there was a crash outside of my room.

I stilled, worry flickering on the edges of my mind.

Had someone found me? One of the Corrupted that I still didn't understand? I almost screeched for Arafel in my mind, but held back, waiting. There was another crash, this time from farther away, toward Arafel's room.

"Arafel?" I peeked my head outside into the hall and immediately noticed the hallway table was out of place and had clearly been bumped. I moved past it, drawing my robe firmly around my body.

"Arafel, is that you?"

The door to his room was open, and I moved quietly in that direction. There was a soft grunt and then a lot of swearing in both English and a few other languages I couldn't understand. But the way Arafel was saying them, it was clear something was wrong. As I turned the corner into his rooms, I was expecting to find a furious demon lord.

But I didn't. Instead, there was Arafel, sprawled over a high-backed chair, Gatam and Paran flanking each of his sides as they deposited the demon lord into the chair. Their faces were all tinged red from exertion, and Arafel's usually rich pewter-toned skin was paler than I'd ever seen it. He must've heard me, or God help me, smelled me, because his eyes snapped to me.

A growling sound slipped from his, lips making me freeze in place for a moment. But this was Arafel, my guardian, my oldest protector. I stepped closer, raising my chin. I had never been afraid of him before. I wouldn't begin tonight.

"Arafel, what happened? Paran?"

The big demon male's chest was rising and falling faster than I'd ever seen it. Paran pointedly ignored my question, instead reaching into a bag at his feet to reveal a variety of bandages.

Settling one out, he kneeled before Arafel and motioned at his shoulder. Gatam did the same, echoing his brother's movements exactly.

Arafel shifted with a soft grunt, and for the first time I noticed that Arafel's shirt was stained a deep, crimson red.

I could feel my heartbeat in my fingers as my body filled with panic. "You're hurt."

Arafel sat up a little, jaw ticking with the effort of moving the injured side. "I heal remarkably fast." He flicked his good hand at his injury. "This will all be gone in a matter of minutes."

"Or hours," Paran mumbled from his position, ignoring Arafel's glare by reaching for another bandage. "Shirt off, my lord."

I moved a step closer, and Arafel's face changed again, turning to look at me with a strange expression. Even from here I could see his nostrils flare. "Lucia, you shouldn't be here." His rumbling tone made my skin break out in goosebumps.

"What? Why not? Maybe I can help."

I took a step toward him, and Arafel's form seemed to grow before me.

Both brothers leaned away, casting a wary glance at each other. "Boss?"

Arafel grunted. "I will be fine. You two get out of here, get some rest."

They hesitated, but he nodded at the twins. Gatam turned to me first, offering a ducked chin in greeting as his brother set down an enormous broadsword across the coffee table in front of Arafel. He gave me a quick nod as well then moved to his brother's side.

They gripped each other's shoulders, and with a telling look at Arafel, they both disappeared right in front of us.

I couldn't stop the small gasp of shock, but I pressed a hand to my belly and willed my nerves to settle. "Are you really going to be okay?"

Arafel sighed then reached over his head to pull at the fabric of his shirt. I stared for a long moment, confused. But when I'd rushed forward, I'd said I could help, and then I froze the first moment he needed help. Not a great start.

Scolding myself, I helped pull the last of his body through the sleeves and looked down at the injury. It looked like... "Are those teeth marks?"

"A corrupted mahr," Arafel says casually. "Amongst other things. I was distracted, and Paran nearly lost a hand coming to help me."

"He seemed to be fine," I said, reaching down to pick up a towel from the bag at his feet. I looked around, wondering if I should run to my bathroom for hot water.

"Paran may be a pain in the ass, but he's among the best of the Brotherhood. I'm lucky to have him by my side, even if it makes me look pitifully slow."

I snorted. "I doubt you are ever slow, Arafel,"

"And it is my sincerest desire you never see a battle, little soul."

"So, I can't see how slow you are?"

Arafel chuckled then pressed a hand against his shoulder once more, the reaction making his injury bleed once again. "No, Lucia, so that you are never that close to danger. But I guess it would serve a dual purpose."

"I can hold my own." As if to prove this, I moved to his side and leaned over the injury again.

"That much is clear," Arafel murmured. When he turned his head, we were suddenly so close. Close enough I could feel the warmth of his skin, see the subtle designs in the gray of his flesh. I ran a finger over one of the whorls, far from the injury. Arafel shivered, which sent a curling stab of pleasure straight through my center.

Taking a slow, shuddering breath in, I pulled my eyes back to the bite. The cuts weren't deep, but there were a lot of them. Truthfully, they already looked better, but I needed to do something, to explain why I felt this need to be here against him. Anything. "What can I do?"

Arafel must've read my mind, because a moment later, his fingers moved through the air, leaving a steaming bowl of warm water by my feet.

"Do they... Should I stitch them?" I prayed to God he would say no, because I had no idea how to do that.

His unearthly blue eyes met mine, the slightest crinkle of a smile in the corners. "If I said yes, would you?"

Nausea filled my gut. "Of course." A lie. But at least I would try.

He nodded, his lips curling. "You don't need to. Cuts like this will close on their own in a few hours."

I let out a short, nervous laugh. "Thank God."

Arafel relaxed back into the chair, smiling a little, even as I began to wipe away the blood from the injury. It was dried in some places, and I bit down on my lip as I was forced to scrub harder on those parts, leaning heavily against the male. I propped a knee up on the base of the chair and leaned over him when I worked on a particularly difficult spot. Arafel groaned, his body tensing and one hand wrapping the wrist I was using to brace myself against the arm of his chair.

My heart leapt to my throat. "Oh, I'm so sorry! Did I hurt you?"

Arafel was breathing hard again, his nostrils flaring as I looked down at him, our faces only a few inches apart. "No, it's..." He took a deep breath. "Hard for me to have you here, like this, so close while I can still smell blood."

"What? Why?"

His eyes glowed and drew me even closer. "Because in my realm, amongst my kind, oaths are sealed in blood."

"What kind of oaths?"

His smile was wry. "The kind my body is longing to give yours."

My heart was in my throat as we stared at each other. "Arafel, I'm..."

But before I could finish, Arafel's hand surged upwards, tangling in my long, damp hair and pulling me down against his lips. We froze there, so close I could practically taste him...and I realized how badly I wanted to.

His voice was a rasp against my lips. "Lucia."

My knees bent and I sagged against him, the pressure in my chest growing to the point where I felt like I might explode from the sheer weight of it. This thing between us burned white hot, and he was at the center of it all.

"I shouldn't," he said, the words coasting over my skin like a caress.

"But you will," I responded, my body smoldering with want. His nostrils flared once more, and his eyes flew straight into the bright, glowing blue I'd only seen a few times. And then he wrenched me forward, my knees falling into the other side of his lap as I tumbled into his arms. I squeaked a warning, trying to avoid the pressure of my body against his injury, to protect him from my limbs. But then those thoughts fled my mind, along with every other. Because I was being kissed, and it was completely unlike anything I'd ever felt before.

I'd had a few boyfriends, kissed a couple of times. And I liked it. I enjoyed myself.

Enjoying wasn't enough of a word for this feeling, and as soon as Arafel sank his other hand into my hair, the wide palms cradled my head as his lips swept over mine. They were soft, warm, and absolutely enthralling as they moved gently against mine.

He was savoring me. The delicate sweep of his tongue against my lips made me groan and sink into him. His thighs were big enough that I was spread across his lap, my robe riding up a dangerous amount, high enough that I was afraid to glance down, to see how much of my body was at his mercy.

My thighs shook, holding my body over his. One of his hands left the back of my skull, coming to rest against my thigh. His flesh was hot against mine, and by the way he was touching me, I was quite sure that far more of my skin was revealed to him than even I had planned on. But still, I didn't have it in me to be shy. My body quivered against him, and with a jerk of his hand, his grip tightened.

"Relax, sweetling, let me feel you." His hand softened and tugged me close, urging me to settle on his lap. And for a moment, my body protested. And then he was kissing me again, and I let his hand guide me down, until my bare, naked skin was pressing against his pants.

I gasped, arching against him. His body was so hard. Every line of him was covered in thick plates of muscle. And between my legs, right where I was pressed against him so intimately, he was rock solid, the thick, heavy length of him that made him specifically male.

Unable to stop myself, I traced my hands up his chest, feeling the rough skin of his jaw. My skin burned everywhere we touched, and even with my eyes closed, it felt like my vision was bright and white. Need threaded through my mind, and my hips rose and fell against his; his mouth continued to ravish mine.

My fingers teased at the edge of his hairline, and with a startled gasp, Arafel pulled away. We sat there, nose to nose, belly to belly, hip to hip. My robe was absurdly high on my body, and I knew he had to be able to feel the heat coming off my body. He was a demon lord; I was a mortal, and I could feel the throbbing heat there.

For the first time in our history, we were on the same level, and I found it quite disconcerting to be suddenly so close to him. Not bad; merely deceiving. Because from here, he looked like a man who wanted a woman. I couldn't see the horns or the cusp of his wings hidden behind him.

My eyes traced his features, my fingers slipping forward to press over his mouth. They were still warm and soft, and I smiled a little as they puckered under my touch. But then I noticed my other hand; it was bright crimson.

Shocked, I pushed up so I was sitting up in his lap. "Arafel, you're bleeding!"

His eyes didn't leave mine. "I was bleeding before, and it didn't seem to upset you."

"Not like this." I searched his chest, my hand running across his chest, his belly. "I must've missed a spot."

"Lucia." His voice was deep, rumbling against my belly as I leaned forward, my breasts pressing into his chest as I searched his shoulders. "You must know what you're doing."

His hands rose to capture my hips as they rose over him once again. We groaned together, both from the touch and the possessive way that he slowly brought me back down.

"The corrupted harpy got me on my way out. It's merely a scratch."

I pivoted, pushing up again. "Are you serious? How did you not tell me about it? I need to clean it. Or something."

"Again, you have to know what you're doing. You come in here, smelling like pure sunshine." He gave me a hard look. "And get close enough I can practically taste you." His eyes darted to my lips again. "I would gladly take another slice from that harpy for the chance to have you take care of me."

I snorted, shoving myself off his lap and tugging frantically on my robe belt until I was sure everything was covered again. "Well, you shouldn't have." Tears leapt into my eyes. "I've lost a lot in the past few weeks. You're the last constant thing I've had in my life. Seeing you covered in blood, it's not what I would call ideal. So please, don't tell me it doesn't matter."

The last words came out high-pitched, and I backed away from him, crossing my arms across my body. Then I realized I was smearing blood on my arms. His blood.

Arafel leaned forward in the chair, his face anxious. "Lucia, I'm sorry. I should've thought."

"No, it's okay. I want to go to bed." I walked to the door then balked. "Do you need me to—"

"The wounds are already closing, Lucia. I'll be fine." Arafel stood, his impressive form immediately making the room too small. I backed away again, too tempted by the warmth he offered, the security I wanted, and the kiss. Oh God, the kiss had been more than anything I'd ever imagined.

"Are you all right?"

I nodded brokenly. "I have to go."

He started toward me, and I raised my hands. I wanted him to stay back. If he got closer to me, I was not sure my mind would keep working correctly. And I needed that.

"Goodnight, Arafel," I said, stepping into the hall and willing my feet to keep moving. Little by little they cooperated, until I could no longer see any part of him. And then I ran until I was safe in my rooms, the door closed loudly between us.

10

Arafel

T he mahr who cooked for us tonight was a favorite of mine. He still withheld his own name, as many of them did in my realms. Names held great power, and remaining unnamed, he was granted the ability to not be called to service individually. It would take far more power for me to call this mahr, as I would need to overpower not only his will, but also his sense of self. I did not ask for their names.

I had never needed to and hoped I would live out the remainder of my days as this realm's lord without needing to.

The mahr was a genius in the kitchen, his slender hands moving so quickly, so expertly that after only a few meals, I had requested him to serve me specifically. He'd been in my home in the nearby mountains until yesterday, when I requested he come over to Lucia's manor.

Before Lucia had come here, I'd had little to look forward to but the passing of time and the meals with my most trusted advisors. Chef, as I called him, always made more than enough. Which honestly made tonight even more difficult. As I sat in front of the table, a stack of reports from the east propped up on a butter dish, I hated the empty chairs around me.

I especially hated the one Lucia would've been in, its empty wooden form mocking me for my earlier behavior.

I'd vowed I would let her heal, that I would bring her here to protect her while we found a way to complete my soul.

But in the end, it felt like something else entirely. I leaned back in my chair, the taste of her lips still fresh in my mind. Even better, the perfect weight of her form across my lap. The bite of food on my fork suddenly lacked flavor as my mind was consumed with what had happened an hour ago.

My injuries were healing well. But I couldn't stop the memory of her fingers fluttering across my body, the urgent way she had ridden up against me. I wasn't a youngling. It was common for demons, especially high-ranking ones such as myself and my brothers, to find our way into the living world during full moons. I had known what a woman felt like.

Or I'd thought I had.

This pull between us, what I had so certainly thought was the soul bound ties, seemed to be changing. My craving for Lucia grew by the moment, exacerbated by any distances between us. Even one so minor as from one room to another. It wasn't right for me to be beside myself, but I couldn't help it. Her every move wrecked my self-control. I wanted to be around her, to make her smile. To have the privilege of feeling her skin against mine once more.

"Fuck," I said aloud, throwing my napkin on the table and standing up. I would never force her to be around me, but I wasn't going to be able to find any rest while thinking she might still be upset.

I had caused enough sadness in her life. I couldn't add any more.

"Chef, I'm taking a plate to Lucia. I'll be back." I only raised my voice a bit, knowing the mahr was in the room one over. Picking up a plate, I added a small helping of each dish to the plate and moved down the hall. I was growing accustomed to Lucia's manor. But a huge part of me wished to show her my home, to take her flying from my tower.

But that would wait. I looked down at the food in my hands, a small smile tugging at my lips. It was better this way, for her to know me this way.

Castle Fel lacked this manor's warmth, but perhaps that was my fault. Most of what time I spent in my home was devoted to my work, to building the library up, to easing more souls. There hadn't been time to add warmth, yet Lucia had done that with a breath of her existence. It sank deeper and deeper into my skin with every passing moment.

I stopped outside Lucia's bedroom door, knocking gently. There was a moment of silence, and then I heard the quick padding of footsteps from the other side. She cleared her throat, and I could hear the shuffle of fabric again.

I'd not spent very much time with Lucia as she grew. Not really. And as she grew older, my power waned, and it became easier to send the Brotherhood in my place. I was needed here, in the dream realm, serving my souls and my creatures. That's what I'd told myself.

Really, I was terrified Lucia's pull Lucia. It had always been my most dangerous weakness. But now I knew I had no chance of avoiding it. It didn't compare to knowing her. The woman whose soul was so precariously wrapped around my own. There was so much I needed to tell her, so many things to explain. But I couldn't.

My weakness was laid bare for all to see. And I didn't care one bit.

Especially when she opened the door a crack, one curious blue eye darting out into the dim hallway where I stood. It felt as if my gut was punched, that hesitation in her gaze. Hiding my reaction, I ducked my chin, stepping back until the tray of food was more clearly visible.

"I know you missed dinner. Would you like something?"

The door pushed open wider. Lucia's soft-gray camisole was nearly the same tone as my flesh, and my mind instantly stuck on how sweet it looked against her skin. Reminding me of the way she had writhed against me. My baser instincts told me to toss the tray aside and grab ahold of the woman before me, to make her mine in every way.

Because she was. Deep in my chest, the ache, the one I'd always assumed was the hole where my soul belonged, panged hard.

I shifted back. This could never be. She didn't belong here. Her world was beautiful, perfect, untainted by a life of blood and battle. I would do my part, fulfill my promise to keep her safe, above all else. A strange coolness seeped into my core as I held the tray out to her, determined to play the part of protector.

Even at my own pain.

Slender fingers twitched in the air for a moment before they plucked the tray from my grip. A sunshine-filled smile temporarily drove back the coolness in my chest. I returned it, the muscles of my face stretching to accommodate the expression I'd made so little of late.

"Do you want to come in?"

Yes. Desperately. I wanted to tug her back onto my lap, to tease the ends of her silky hair and let my tongue taste every inch of her. If I stepped one more foot toward her, I would break everything. The laws of my home, the oath I'd just made.

Temptation loomed, and I shoved it down.

"In the Underworld, relationships with humans are forbidden."

Lucia's jaw went slack, and she stepped back, shrinking into herself. "I didn't mean to assume; I was trying to be nice." The curves of her cheeks were tinted pink. I had embarrassed her.

"I have fought battles great and small, seen the rise and demise of entire empires. And I have withstood them all." I let my eyelids shut, hiding her face from my view. Fruitlessly, as I had every bit of her face memorized. "But you, Lucia, you bring something out in me I don't truly understand."

"Arafel?"

"Be ready at dawn, little soul." I turned, forcing step after step as I moved back down the hall. For the first time in decades, I was unsure I had chosen the right path.

***

I had told Lucia to be ready to go at dawn, but that didn't mean it was any less surprising to see her, sitting in the kitchen, wide blue eyes steady on Chef as he mixed some eggs in a bowl between them. I had to duck my chin to hide the smile that curled my lips.

My soul bound wasn't sure about these creatures yet, but she was trying. I could see the flashes of her courage shining through, even as she gave Chef a wry smile.

He was speaking to her, the same chittering language as the rest of his kind. We were born understanding all of the Underworld's creatures. Which meant I knew Chef was merely listing off a variety of food options that they had in store. But as far as Lucia knew, it couldn't be anything.

Maybe her death proclamation. Maybe an ode to her loyalty.

Either way, Lucia was nodding along, her eyes flickering to my form as I entered the room. Something moved across her expression as she took in the sight of me. It wasn't fear. It wasn't even the relief I had seen on her face so many times before when she called me. This was merely...pleasure at seeing me.

My flesh heated, remembering how she'd looked last night when I'd come to her room. It drove a spike of need and frustration straight through my veins. I shook it off, moving through the room until I could stand behind her. Her shoulders were stiff, and I longed to soothe away any lingering fears or worries she may have from yesterday.

Chef moved away, pouring eggs in a buttered skillet.

"Good morning," I murmured, my hands twitching as I stood close enough to her that I could smell her. I longed to reach out, to press my claws through her silken locks. But I held back. "Did you sleep well?'

"I did, thank you." Her words were as tight as her body. Foreboding bloomed in my belly, and I moved to perch on the stool beside her. It groaned at my weight but held.

"Are we going somewhere today?"

I nodded, holding my hand out as a piece of fruit leapt from the bowl to my fingers. I tore into the soft freshness of it. I felt, rather than saw, her interest in my movements and immediately held it out to her. "I thought you didn't like pears?"

"I also thought you were an imaginary friend I made up when I was four." Lucia reached out to take the fruit from my claws, her slender hands careful. "Perhaps I'm more open to broadening my horizons these days."

I chuckled, popping the remainder of the fruit into my mouth. Lucia turned to me, her blunt teeth working the edge of the crisp green flesh of the fruit. Mesmerized, I watched as her lips gripped the fruit, sucking on the sweetness briefly before releasing and then trying again.

"Most people just put it in their mouths," I said with a purr.

Her gaze narrowed, and finally she bit off a large chunk, turning back to Chef as he approached her with a steaming plate of scrambled eggs.

"Thank you," Lucia's voice dragged out. Sensing her worry over how to address manners in the situation, I leaned across the bar a little, my elbows making the marble creak.

"Thanks, Chef. I'll take it from here."

The little creature clicked at me then cast Lucia a long, curious stare.

"He wants you to try it first," I relayed, humor making my throat itch.

Lucia's eyes widened, and she hurriedly picked up her fork, scooping up some of the eggs and blowing on them. The steam filled the air for a moment before Lucia pushed the fork inside, her jaw working slowly.

For a moment, we all held our breath. And then Lucia's expression bloomed into one of pure joy. "Chef, these are amazing. Did you put cheese or something in them?" Then she began to help herself to more from her plate, taking big bites then huffing the morning air into her mouth to cool the food enough to swallow.

Mahrs didn't have the same expressions we did, but I could see by the sharp little jerk of his face that Chef was proud of himself. He chittered at Lucia a moment then offered me a bow, stepping back until his body was enveloped in the shadow of the cabinets. And then he was gone. Likely to check in with his tribe.

Lucia was staring wide-eyed at the shadows he'd disappeared into. "Did he just...?"

"He did."

She turned to me, eggs still in her mouth. With one hand covering her lips, she attempted to ask me a question. "So where are we going.... Do we have to shadow hop?"

"Shadow hop," I murmured. "I like that."

Lucia's cheeks bloomed with a soft blush. "You know what I mean."

"I do. And honestly, I don't have a great answer for you, other than the fact it is much, much more fun to travel the way you and I will than to shadow hop."

"And that is...?"

I rapped my claws against the countertop. "Finish breakfast, and I'll show you. Meet me out front when you're done."

With that, I forced myself to get up, disguising my grin behind my hand as I headed to the back of the house. I couldn't wait to see her face when I disclosed a little more about the realm she was in.

The realm she seemed to belong to as much as I did. Even if I didn't understand what it meant yet.

But I would.

***

Lucia

"You're kidding."

"I don't kid," Arafel said, his sharp features relaxed and patient as I walked a long circle around where he stood on the patio.

"You do too." I propped a hand up on my hip, trying to disguise the shaking in my limbs as I did. He had to know. Everyone knew how I felt about heights. And Arafel knew practically everything about me.

The fact that I'd walked out here, and he'd been grinning, telling me how we were going to fly the distance between the manor and his home in the mountain, had me doubting. Sure, Arafel was pure muscle; his oversize gray body loomed over me, the expansive stretch of his heavy black wings making the eggs in my stomach churn with devastating intent.

Flying. He wanted to take me flying.

His features softened as I drew in a rattling breath.

"I don't think I can do this."

"You can." He moved a step toward me, his claws shining in the brightness of the morning. I flinched away, my stomach heaving desperately in my gut.

"No, no, no," I chanted, curling in on myself as Arafel moved in front of me, his hands on my forearms as he drew me closer. The delicious scent of his skin wafted over me, settling my nerves only a little this time. I focused my eyes on the whirls of darker skin that decorated his shoulders.

"Tell me, Lucia, what's wrong?"

I pressed my face forward, feeling the rigid, cool leather of the lightweight armor he was wearing over a black tunic. Suddenly I was desperate to hide my weakness from him. Stubborn, irritating tears bloomed in my eyes. I pressed my hands to the sockets, willing the tears away. I wished my fear wasn't palpable in the air.

"I'm not sure about this. Last time, we shadow hopped."

His hand came to rest on my hip, his warmth invading in an instant. I sagged closer, swallowing repeatedly.

"Are you scared of the sky? You have to know I would never drop you."

I scoffed, hoping I sounded convincing. "I know you won't drop me."

Silence fell between us as his fingers slowly caressed my hip. "But I can't deny there's something about the quick stop at the end if you were to accidentally let something slip."

Arafel's laugh was deep and rich. "After all of this, mahrs and demon lords and possessed neighbors….you're afraid to go for a short ride with me." I didn't answer, and he pushed on. "I have protected you your whole life, from every danger imaginable. You can trust me, Lucia."

My stomach quivered, and I dragged a breath through anxious lungs.

He was right. He'd been my shadow at night, my angel in the day, and the Brotherhood had spent my entire life making sure I would survive. Making sure I could survive this life. He wasn't going to stop now.

I stepped back, letting my gaze sink into the patient, sky blue eyes of the demon lord. "I'm ready."

His lips curled. "Okay, but only if you're sur—"

"Do it, before I change my mind." My words were hissed and a bit desperate. I don't know what I expected, but without another word, Arafel slipped his arm around me, whisking me off my feet and against the leather armor once more.

Then we are airborne, the powerful beat of enormous wings sending us into the swirling silver sky with so much power that my eyes watered.

Which was probably good, because by the time I blinked the tears from my vision, Arafel had leveled out, his arms cradling me like an excited bride even as wind whistled past my ears. My stomach dropped away, and I muffled a small shriek as I accidentally looked downward. The manor was falling away from us, looking more and more like a miniature dollhouse from this vantage point. Or at least it did for the half second I spent looking.

After that, I slammed my eyes shut and curled closer to Arafel's wide chest as his wings flexed, striking out at the air with another long beat. Maybe I hadn't gotten a good look at the ground, thank God, but I had seen his wings plenty. They were easily the length of Arafel himself, and while they seemed to be tucked away by his magic while he walked the manor, he seemed most comfortable with them out, peeking over his shoulders.

I could feel the brush of them, the silk of those feathers against my clenched hands. I cracked one eye, watching as Arafel drew us up and back, wings pumping through the air. They looked like a crow's wings, or perhaps an eagle, with long, glossy black features. They shone in the light of the Underworld with an iridescence that reminded me of an opal or a swirl of ink. Together with the rest of the male against me, they completed the image of him. The demon lord, the powerful King of Dreams, and my beautiful guardian.

Not an angel.

But so much more.

11

Lucia

We glided through the air effortlessly, his grip on me both constant and comforting. Only the breeze on my cheeks and the occasional pulse of the muscles of his shoulder told me that he was still urging us forward with those big, beautiful wings.

"Do you want to open your eyes? The mountains will be within sight soon, and our—my home only a small distance later."

I peeked out, staring at the powerful gray throat working in front of me. A gust of wind ushered us upwards, and I clamped my eyes shut once more.

"Maybe in a minute," I said softly, suddenly worried he wouldn't be able to hear me. I tightened my arms and brought my mouth up as close to his ear as I could. Then I repeated myself.

His fingers tightened against my flesh, and I gasped in the icy cold air at the spike of heat that washed through me.

For the next few minutes I lay against him, my body warmed by him, even as the cool air we flew through surrounded me. I was glad he'd told me to dress warmly. Even as it seemed to drop in altitude, making me clutch onto Arafel anew, I felt his warmth on my face, my throat as he leaned in.

"We are nearly there. In front of us are the Sleeping Mountains, the border of my land."

"Did you say Sleeping Mountains?" I couldn't stop the bit of humor that slipped into my voice. At last, something simple to remember.

I felt his chuckle in my belly. "Yes, Sleeping Mountains. In English, it sounds quite simple. When I first acquired this role, this place, the word for Sleeping Mountains was far more majestic."

"I like it. It makes them sound sweet, something out of a fairy tale."

Again, that laugh. "Open your eyes, Lucia." His lips were warm against my ear. "I would never let you fall."

Clenching my body tightly, I turned my chin to the direction I believed him to be looking and slowly opened one eye then the other. I was expecting a few peaks, perhaps some snow on the top.

But what was before me was nothing like that.

In fact, I actually recoiled from the vision in front of me. Not out of fear but of awe. In front of us, taking up the entirety of my vision, was a range of mountains, green and heavily wooded. They rose from the smooth belly of the Underworld, stabbing far into the sky above us, and consumed my entire vision.

"Oh my." The words slipped from my mouth as I stared at them, my eyes unable to take it all in. The thick silver of a stream running down one of the closest mountains, craggy peaks illuminating the vastness of the range before us.

Arafel banked to the left, but I barely noticed, my eyes glued to the lush green of the mountains. Guilt made my chest tight for a moment. I'd pictured a lonely peak or maybe some desert-like rock features. But this... These were mountains teaming with life and virality and...and towers?

Watch towers, I realized as we flew over one of the carefully laid out grid of stone structures, a group of small mahrs perched across the top floor. They shrieked at us, high-pitched voices cutting through the atmosphere as Arafel turned us to the side, following the landscape up the second highest peak, right to where an enormous castle emerged from the center of a deep green flock of trees.

As I stared at it, something slipped over my heart, something sweet and painful all at the same time. It was beautiful, and it felt... It felt like I was supposed to be here. I tightened my fingers against Arafel's broad shoulders as we approached the castle, his body shifting as he slowed. Out of fear, I drew my knees up, unsure of how the landing worked.

But it wasn't anything like I expected. There was a short thrust from his wings, and then we dropped, rather unceremoniously, to the stone floor atop a flat watchtower at the peak of the closest corner of Castle Fel.

Arafel held me tightly with his arms, bringing me closer to his face. His expression was unreadable as he spoke the words slowly. "Welcome to my home, Lucia."

He let my legs fall and steadied me on my feet as I looked around. We were up high, the drop off over the wall enough to make me want to be sick, but the railing was high, sitting at Arafel's waist, and I knew there was no way I would be getting close enough to check it anyway.

Instead, I looked over the wall to the interior of the castle. Down three levels were a courtyard, empty save a few cloaked figures. They moved more gracefully than the mahr, and they were much larger.

Immediately I wondered if they were the Brotherhood. But instead of the bright-white robes they typically donned, these figures were wearing black, their long cloaks dragging over the stone-covered ground. I was still staring down at them when Arafel spoke again.

"Come," he said. "Let's find you a room with a view." He waved to the mind-numbing drop over the edge of our tower.

"Uh, Arafel," I started, letting my hand fall to his forearm, stopping him. I'd had enough height for my lifetime. I wanted a room in the cellar at this point. The demon lord looked back at me, and to my surprise there was a teasing grin on his face, his fangs winking out and making my belly clench for a whole other reason.

"Had enough for today?"

I shoved at his shoulder. "Get us down from here, you asshole."

He cocked his brow at me. "Perhaps I do have a sense of humor after all."

"God help us all." I rolled my eyes but stopped when a quick, firm hand suddenly gripped my chin.

"There is no God here, Lucia." Arafel gestured behind me, his eyes glowing with a strange bright-blue power as he looked out over the mountains. "Welcome to the heart of the dream realm."

I shivered at his words, turning slowly as his hands fell to my shoulders, holding on to me securely as I looked out over his home.

My heart was in my throat as I looked down the side of the mountain. It was beautiful, there was no denying it. But I could see the differences there, between my home in the living world and his here. The way the trees were completely still, every leaf and dewdrop in perfect stasis. And the waterfall, the one that seemed to split the mountain range in half... I could only see a portion of it, but I saw enough to know that the water was flowing wrong. It was moving up the mountainside, the boulders and small outcroppings splitting the water also facing the wrong way.

But even as the sense of wrongness surprised me, it immediately was swept away. Not wrong. Just different.

I smiled up at Arafel. "Thank you for bringing me here. I would've never understood, I don't think. Not if I hadn't seen it myself."

"I'm glad you like it. Let's get you a new interior chamber where you can reacquaint your feet with the ground." Arafel offered me his elbow, and I took it without question, letting the Lord of Dreams usher me toward a hidden staircase at one end.

People—or rather creatures—of the realm scattered before us. And I knew in an instant it was because of the look Arafel was sending at everyone who drew too close. From those who were able to see me, I could hear the scratches, the noise as they slipped back into the safety of the shadows.

I blushed, not used to this kind of attention at all. I was so distracted, I didn't even notice we had stopped in front of an intricately carved doorway, the iron and wood swinging wide as we approached. Arafel led me straight through, his body forcing mine to press against him to fit.

"This door is hidden to all of those who wish you harm. To them this is nothing but another section of wall."

I stopped, staring wide eyed around the room before me. It was more medieval than the manor house, but I wasn't about to complain. A canopy bed sat against one wall; from the posts hung heavy black velvet. The walls were covered in bright, vividly painted landscape paintings, and a fireplace big enough for both of us to set foot inside of it easily took up the only other wall. Before it was two wingback chairs, again more of the trademark black, but this time with fine silver threads running through it.

There were no windows, yet every wall was lit by the flickering lights of sconces. In a breath, it felt safe and warm. The last reserves of my doubts about this place slipped away as I breathed it in. The entire room, it smelled and felt of Arafel.

I blushed a little, as I realized the demon lord was still standing beside me, eyes on my face. Waiting.

"It's beautiful, Arafel."

His sigh made butterflies take off in my chest.

"Thank you." Arafel looked pleased, and I knew in an instant this room was his making, not from some recess of my mind this time. I dropped his hand, stepping toward the fire. "I've lost track of time; how much longer do we have before the council is meeting?"

Arafel's sharp features grew serious. "You don't have to come, Lucia. Some of my finest warriors will be present. And in this land, that doesn't exactly mean they are palatable."

I noticed my bag was at his feet, and I moved to pick it up, needing something in my hands so that I could fiddle away the rush of excitement. New creatures. More things to learn and understand. Maybe we would learn something about why I had Arafel's soul.

"I want to. Really." I shot him a wicked grin. "How bad can they be? Can you tell me which one to watch out for? The really scary one?"

Arafel's brow raised. "It is not the scary-looking ones you should be concerned about," he said, voice low. "Some of my most lethal weapons don't fit into your human idea of what we should fear."

I nodded, but I didn't quite understand. "You're saying…"

"Don't touch anyone. Or let anyone touch you. I will introduce you to the council, and they will know you are under my protection, but they are still creatures of the Underworld. Don't tempt them." Arafel's size seemed even more exaggerated in the windowless room. I didn't stop myself from running my eyes over the curve of his lips as he frowned down at me.

"Okay, no touching strangers." I grinned, wanting to soothe his fears and bring by the lighthearted male I'd just traveled here with.

"Lucia," he warned me, eyes dark. "I mean it."

I moved closer, raising my hand to run my fingers over his lips. "I won't, Arafel. I promise."

His eyes fluttered shut for an instant, sending a bolt of boldness through me. I pushed up on my toes, my free hand resting on his armor once more, where he'd held me so closely a few minutes before, and then brushed my mouth along his jaw.

A kiss.

A caress.

His contented sigh warmed my shoulders as I stepped away, feeling a rush of warmth as my thighs clenched and heated. As our faces realigned, I couldn't help but notice his nostrils flared again.

Embarrassment lurked in the back of my mind, but also relief. I didn't know how to explain this pull between us, the power that seemed to call for me to get closer to him.

"Arafel..." I whispered, confused when he stepped back abruptly.

"The others are arriving. I need to see them."

I instinctively wrapped my arms around myself at the chill that appeared every time he left. "You need to warn them."

Arafel turned at the door, his eyes glimmering. "I'll be back in an hour to walk you there."

"I don't need you to do that. Tell me where to be."

"I will walk you."

"I don't need you to protect me from everything."

Arafel turned without looking back, closing the door halfway before adding, "Yes, you do." And then he shut it firmly.

I picked up a small throw pillow and launched it at the door. I wasn't mad, not really. Only frustrated that every day since my mother had died, there had been more and more that I didn't know, didn't understand.

And now this. A male I couldn't stay away from. A power that I didn't understand. And a soul that wasn't mine.

I flopped down in the chair, running my hands over my braids as I watched the fire leap and dance under the mantle.

Absolutely nothing in my life had prepared me for these moments, for what I was about to do. Why did I think I wanted to sit on a council of demons and angels and undying warriors? A few weeks ago, the only thing I'd been worrying about was passing my microbiology final. I looked around the room. I was in the Underworld, surrounded by creatures I didn't think existed and catching an unhealthy number of feelings for a gray-skinned, black-winged demon lord who peeled pears for me and looked at me like I was the center of his entire world.

I pressed a hand to the center of my chest, where I believed my soul resided…happily, I hoped, alongside the half of his soul his father had hidden away for him.

After tonight, I would know more.

I pushed myself from the chair. It was time to get ready.

12

Arafel

I, King of Dreams, Lord of the Underworld, was hesitating for the first time in my life. Lucia was by my side, a soft red dress on her body, sandals on her delicate feet. Her hair was down today, and every step she took sent more of her sweet fragrance straight to my nose. At first, I thought it was soap, shampoo, or even perfume. But after living with her these past days, I knew it was simply Lucia.

Which meant we were royally fucked. Because there was no way I could take this sweet, sunshine-smelling woman into the council room and expect my advisors not to make a move.

Land above, I could barely stand to be beside her without touching her. My fingers were trailing over the cloth that covered her spine. And I was begging for more.

Maybe if I stopped her, maybe she would touch me or slide those pretty lips against my jaw again.

I'd never been kissed like that, with such ease and pleasure.

I wanted her to do it again.

A growl lodged itself in my throat when I realized we had to do something. The advisory chambers were only a few strides away.

"Lucia."

She turned to me, her eyes so wide and blue I could practically fall into them. "What is it?" Lucia licked her lips. Waiting for me to explain to her what was going on.

But there was no way to explain that now. I wanted to whisk her back to her rooms. To curl around her and snarl at anyone who got too close.

Because she was mine.

Fuck. What was I talking about?

The growl escaped then, but it was strangled, lacking any real venom.

Lucia cocked her head. "Are you all right?"

"Stay by my side. They know the rules, but you will be a temptation the likes many of them have never seen."

She nodded, bright-blue eyes serious as she glanced warily at the door.

"Right then, let's go." I couldn't decide if I was talking to her or myself when I uttered the words and then rushed the final steps to the tall arched doorways and shoved my way inside. Lucia stumbled at my side, her smaller strides struggling to keep up.

I looped an arm about her slender waist, steadying her. Even as everyone in the room's interior stopped in an instant, followed by a brief, respectful nod of heads in my direction. Each of them were valued members of the realm, and I didn't require them to bow when we entered here.

Here we were as close to equals as I was comfortable allowing. My father loathed that I allowed such familiarity, but in the dream realm, there was a need for more creatures than anywhere else. It was important they were all represented.

They were my true power, these creatures and powers who resided in the dream realm alongside me. In the decades since my strength began to diminish, they had stepped in, providing aid to not just myself, but to my brothers as well.

"Welcome," I said loudly. All eyes were on Lucia; even the harpy chief had frozen in place, his red gaze fixed on her.

I shepherded Lucia into the room, the round center table taking up only a portion of the vast chamber. As I expected, several demons and monsters raised their heads, nostrils flaring as my human drew closer.

More than a few huffed out a breath. Others growled softly. I stiffened, my muscles and body longing to erupt into battle form and settle this in the ways of the old world. But that wouldn't get my soul back. It wouldn't help Lucia.

For her, I would be...diplomatic.

"Kuddelmuddel," I said softly, tilting my head to the male in charge of his kind. A king in his own right, bright-blue feathers rising from his forehead, brightening to shades of green and yellow as they trailed over his angular skull to broad shoulders. He wore typical harpy garb, a low-slung belted loincloth, the rest of his body dusted in lighter-toned feathers. He greeted us with a short bow of the waist, and his expressionless face seemed to observe Lucia closely, the sharp gold of his eyes flickering over her.

He was powerful, a force unto himself. And deeply, deeply loyal. My advisor on bad days and perhaps even a friend on the good days. Harpies were once common in the living world, and Kudd spent many days and nights patrolling the boundaries between our world and that of the living. His kin were not inclined to aggression, but curious, exploratory creatures that had simply mastered the passing between the worlds a few centuries before and used it to venture out into the living world.

"My lady," Kudd murmured, dropping low on his long slender legs, his claws scraping the floor. He was as tall as me, and that was before the feathering. I could see Lucia's head tilt back as she attempted to take in every inch of him. Her breathing was fast, heartbeat racing, but instead of running, her pale, slim hand broke the space between them.

"Hello. I'm Lucia," she said, her voice shaking. But she stood solid, steady in front of my body as Kudd loomed over her.

I could see from the tilt of his head, Kudd was giving the harpy equivalent of a smile.

"Kuddelmuddel," he murmured, slipping his three-fingered hand over hers and drawing it his face, pressing it to his forehead. "Chieftain of the dream realm's flock, at your service."

"Kuddel...muh..." Lucia tripped over the name, her cheeks pinking.

A deep chuckle ushered from within harpy's feathered chest. "Call me Kuddel, my lady."

"Then you must call me Lucia."

I could see the glowing eyes in the sockets rise to my face for approval. I gave a short, brief nod. Kudd dropped his chin again, giving another brief bow of the body to Lucia. "Then Lucia, it is. Please, come and sit with me."

The growl rumbled free before I could stop it, but Kudd ignored me easily, guiding Lucia toward the table with the barest touch of his claws on her hand. Standing behind the chair, Lucia seemed to look around her, shoulders tense as the harpy reached down to pull her chair back for her.

"Please, allow me," Kudd murmured.

"Kudd, my dearest skull-faced friend, do not steal away our queen so quickly." A smooth, heat-laced voice filled the room.

I moved forward, knowing that nothing I could do at this point could prepare Lucia for what was coming her way.

"I wouldn't dream of it, Albtraum," Kudd said, easily stepping back.

"Be careful, succubus," I said, stepping up to take the empty chair beside Lucia.

"A succubus?" Lucia's wide eyes fell on Albtraum. I could see her take him in; he was the furthest you can get from Kudd in appearance. Albtraum was everything a woman might dream about in her fantasy of a monster. He had human-shaped features, much like the other high demons, soft purple-toned skin, with dark brows and darker eyes. The thick hair on his head was pulled back in a heavy braid, and he was wearing only a loincloth over a lean, muscular form. The tongue that swept over his teeth was thick and so inhumanly long that I knew it would catch her attention. I wouldn't blame her. It was the same with any woman.

"It's a pleasure," Albtraum said softly, leaning forward in a bow to Lucia. "You will have to excuse me from the customary kiss of the hand." His brows waggled at my soul bound, making me prickle with jealousy. "Who knows what fantasies we might strike up."

"That's enough Albtraum," I warned from the side. "Where's your mate?" Cydia was much more enjoyable company. At least in my opinion.

Albtraum straightened, shooting a perfectly white smile in my direction. "Home, growing our first youngling."

"What?"

Albtraum straightened, his hands twining together as he gushed on. "Yes, I know. We found out a few days ago. The first in our tribe in nearly a hundred years."

I stared, shock making me slow to respond. Luckily Lucia stepped up to Albtraum. "How exciting! How's she feeling?"

"Nothing exciting so far. Tired and especially wild at night."

Lucia laughed, the sound a bit manic at the blatant sexuality of the creature, but she didn't stop asking. "Can I ask something else? Is that normal? To go so long between babies?"

Albtraum's gaze was on my face, reading my expression carefully before he answered her. "We haven't had a new youngling in many, many years. The magic that allows the

Underworld to function also affects us, its creatures. It will not usher in creation for creatures it cannot support."

Lucia was nodding, her face serious. I could feel her absorbing his words as she did everything else, cataloging the information. "You will have to offer your mate our congratulations, from Arafel and me." I could see her face flip to me and back again, bright spots of pink appearing on her face. "Right, Arafel?"

I reached out, letting my magic cloak my hands as I embraced his forearm. "Congratulations, my friend. This is great news for everyone."

I didn't need to explain what this might mean to the others. To the harpies and the mahrs and the higher demons. The chance to have families again, to find mates and live real lives.

"We are just as shocked as old Arafel here. We gave up on hoping for younglings years ago, and then a few days ago, it hit Cydia like a ton of bricks. She's thrilled of course, but we don't know what changed."

My gaze snapped down. The succubus wasn't lying. He didn't know what he was saying, but I did. My chest ached at the realization. Nothing had changed for hundreds of years, until something happened a few days ago.

The only soul to come into the Underworld, to create life and change with the whisk of her hands.

Lucia.

Albtraum prattled on for another minute or two as a variety of mahrs scuttled in, followed by Simeon, who immediately enveloped Lucia in a bone-crushing hug. When he held on a little too long, a soft rattle in my chest was enough to set them all back to their chairs and Lucia to my side.

Feeling even more sure of myself, I drew back the chair to the person at my right, as each of us did, effectively opening the circle to each other. Kudd pulled back Lucia's and offered a friendly tilt of the head as she settled in and gave him a wide smile.

"We are gathered here to discuss a very important matter." The chambers were so silent you could hear the creak of my chair when I leaned forward in it. "My soul has returned to the dream realm."

Wordlessly, everyone again looked to Lucia, who, while flushing red, didn't duck her chin or hide. Her dark curls drifted over her shoulders as her sun-kissed scent permeated the room.

"Each of you were already in existence when my mother was taken, forcing the spell that split my soul and my brothers' from our bodies. Lucia is only twenty-one, her life barely begun. Yet she carries the missing half of my soul within her, residing alongside her own."

Whispers broke out.

"What I've come here to ask you tonight is if you have ever heard of a magic to reunite the souls, to remove my soul from Lucia's without damaging her future."

Lucia's fingers crept across the tabletop and folded over my claws.

"I will open the table for discussion."

13

Lucia

A yawning quiet stole over the airy chamber and made goosebumps rise along my forearms. Or maybe that was the part of my brain that was slowly registering that I was in a room full of predators. Lethal. Brutal. Creatures that might have crept directly from the screen of a horror movie or out of the pages of a fantasy novel.

Arafel's warmth was my grounding force, his steady presence enough to wear away at the part of my brain that screamed for me to retreat to my rooms and stay there.

Kudd, the claw-tipped monster to my left, cleared his throat. The idea of that alone sent a hysterical chuckle to my throat, which I smothered as the demon slowly stood.

"Our chief told tales of your mother's kindness and magic for centuries, Arafel, her prowess a legend in both the Underworld and the living one. Is there a chance the humans may know the answer? Since she was dragged to the living world, there's very little record of her here. It was her magic that tore your souls, wasn't it?"

Arafel shifted a little, nodding as Kudd sat again. "I have sent dozens of members of the Brotherhood to the living world over the course of Lucia's life, and even before that, in an attempt to locate any of these details. But there is nothing."

"What about your father? What does he have to say in this?" A willowy figure whose entire being seemed composed of shadows spoke up from a corner. The tiny mahr beside them jerked its chin in agreement.

"My father doesn't want to be bothered with this. At least not right now. He's busy maintaining the watchtowers."

"He likely won't, not until the Drude comes marching right up to the gates of Hell," Albtraum said sweetly.

"Meanwhile, our demons are slaughtered by the dozen holding back the corrupt at the edges of the living world," snarled a short red demon with blunt horns and black lips. "Why you prattle on about how to extract souls, our people die at the Drude's hand, Lord Arafel."

He turned beady eyes to me, and I flinched before I could stop myself.

"Kill the human, take the soul."

Arafel's rumbling growl slid down my spine, leaving a heavy dose of calm as the others in the room shifted in their chairs. Obviously his growl didn't have the same effect on them as it did me. I reached over to put my hand on his.

"It's my belief," I started, the buzzing conversation around me slowing, "that when Nephesh lost his soul bound human, he wasn't able to gain the soul."

"But he wasn't there. Her soul would've come here, to be reborn if she wished," spoke a feminine-sounding mahr, yellow eyes sharp. "You, my lady, are already here. Here the brothers are the masters of souls. They could control the transition."

"And if it doesn't work? And we have to wait for his soul to show back up? What then?" Kudd spoke slowly.

While I was briefly offended my neighbor was even joining the conversation about murdering me for Arafel's soul, I tried to stay quiet.

I could sense the change in Arafel, the way his body seemed to fill, grow at every word. Briefly I wondered if he noticed his body preparing to defend me. When he spoke again, his words were calm, placid. "It doesn't matter what you think. Lucia will not come to any harm while she is here. Anyone who moves against her will have me to contend with."

Silence. "Even to save your realm?" This time it was Albtraum, black gaze on his king.

Arafel bared his teeth, fangs shining. "We will find another way."

His response hit me right in the gut. The shadowy figure from before grew, the edges of their form flickering with bright light, as several other demons growled and rumbled their disapproval. Distantly I felt someone come to stand behind my chair. Risking a glance back, I see Simeon, in full white armor, standing at my shoulder. His sword was still sheathed at his hip.

"Good," Kudd said, turning his harsh face to us. "Because the Drude is coming, my lord, and it doesn't care how or what you feel for the soul carrier. It only knows we are what stands between it and the freedom of the living world."

The room erupted once more, this time in cries for help for their homes, at the need for more of the Brotherhood to be sent to assist. I even thought I heard someone beg Arafel to ask his brother to send some of the imprisoned souls to fight. But it was all too much. My stomach roiled in my gut as I tucked my hands between my legs. I didn't want Arafel to see how badly they were shaking as I was faced with the reality of the situation. This was no bedtime fairy tale; this was a real-life war that had been going on longer than I could imagine.

And it all stemmed from me doing something I had no idea how to do.

As if from a great distance, I heard Arafel meeting their answers and cries with his calm, rolling voice. And after some time, I could tell he was wrapping up the meeting.

"There is only one more thing, Arafel," Albtraum spoke up as the others began to stand, his black gaze landing on me once again. There was no denying the demon's good looks, however unhuman he was, and the room grew silent once more. "I'd like to address the open and flagrant breaking of one of our oldest laws."

Arafel stood slowly, expression tight. "Albtraum..."

"For generations, you haven't allowed the creatures of the Underworld to seek out their human mates, requiring them to stay below, to stay hidden and quiet." Albtraum looked right through me, and my heart raced in my chest. "Yet you bring her here, your soul bound, and expect us to believe you aren't already breaking our laws."

Something deep in my chest twisted.

"The laws exist to keep the living safe from demons who cannot control their bonds," Arafel began.

"You mock us and go behind our backs, my lord, and people will notice." The incubus's jaw flexed. "What happens after you retrieve your soul and decide to keep the pretty package it came in?"

Arafel's snarl silenced Albtraum. "I can assure you, Albtraum, this is not the case with the human at my side or any other. They do not belong in our world, and that will not change. The old law stays."

Cool, sharp pain raced along my spine, aching and permanent as the demon lord beside me twisted and marched from the room. The wide doors swung shut again after his broad form disappeared. As if a trigger, several demons moved off, disappearing into the shadows. A few others moved through the door after their king.

Kudd offered a solemn-feeling bow of the head and disappeared as well.

Woodenly, I stood and moved around the huge table, my watery gaze intent on my feet.

"My lady." Albtraum was suddenly in front of me, his booted feet only a step from me. I slowly moved my gaze up his form to meet his stare, surprised to find deep pain in his eyes. "My lady, I apologize for…"

"For forcing your king to admit he feels nothing for me publicly. Yeah, no problem." I moved to walk around him. But he held an arm out, careful to not touch me.

"No, Lucia, it's clear he's lying to himself and to us." Albtraum let out a soft sigh. "Many, many things changed after Lucifer's mate was taken by the humans. But before that? There were living souls here, the fated mates of creatures who reside here. But now, my people, they live their entire lives, knowing their soul mate will never know them. We have long memories; our heartache will be eternal compared to the lifespan of our humans."

I blinked at him. "I am only a carrier. We just cleared that up."

"You and I both know that isn't true. But Arafel fears what he doesn't know, and I have a distinct feeling that the emotions he has now are quite foreign to him."

Looking away, I bit my lip. "I don't understand any of this. Is it the soul tie that makes me care about him so much? Or is it something more?"

"Only you two can decide that." Albtraum nodded, his braid dancing down his back. "I believe his feelings for you will help us change the laws, to bring more life into the Underworld and hope back to my people."

I thought then of what he'd said about his youngling, about the creatures of this world and the pain they must feel knowing how close they were to their soul mates but completely unable to reach them.

"I understand," I said with a quick nod. "At least partially."

"Will you talk to him?"

"I will."

"He cares for you; I can feel it."

"I carry his soul, nothing else." The denial was strange on my tongue.

Albtraum gave a slow smile, white fangs shining. "You carry much more, I believe."

My cheeks flushed hot, and I ducked my chin. "Goodbye, Albtraum. It was good to meet you."

"Goodbye," he said softly as I moved past him. "My queen."

I stumbled, twisting to face him. I'd heard the whispers, but never so obviously spoken. With a gasp, I stumbled forward, catching myself on Albtraum's forearm. Immediately heat raced across my skin, making my breath come short in my aching lungs as I slowly met Albtraum's gaze.

"Oh no," I practically whimpered as my entire body curled toward the incubus.

"Get out of here, Lucia, now," Albtraum hissed, pulling his hand back. "Go! I'll tell Arafel."

"No," I said, backing away. "I'm fine. You don't need to tell him anything."

Albtraum's eyes narrowed as I backed away, each footstep nearly painful to take. When I got to the door again, I tucked my hands to my chest and forced myself to turn away. To run. Far away from the incubus who had touched me and the fantasies of a demon king who wanted to keep me for himself.

No matter how big of a lie it might be, the magic of the incubus overruled it all. And it was Arafel's bright-blue eyes that filled my mind as I raced down the hall toward my rooms.

***

I hurried down the hallway, my bare feet slapping against the polished marble tiles. Every inch of my skin felt like it was on fire, and I couldn't get to my room fast enough. I needed to get out of this dress, out of these clothes. I wanted to throw my overheated body straight into the tub and stay there until I stopped aching.

I came up onto the door, still only visible for Arafel and myself, and hurtled through it. The cool darkness of my room was a comfort, but only for a minute. This dress, which I'd loved so much a few hours ago, needed to go. And I needed to be able to see all those pretty little buttons down the back.

"How do you turn the lights on in the freaking Underworld?" I grumbled, twisting around until I could see the beginnings of the buttons. To my surprise and relief, a set of sconces by my bed brightened in an instant. It wasn't much, but it was enough that it made tearing this dress off slightly less stressful.

Even as I stood there, my back to the mirror, my flesh crawled and burned, begging me to turn around, to go back to Arafel.

I needed to see him again. Maybe he would hold me once again, bring me up against the powerful lines of his chest until this dreadful heat dissipated. My thighs shook and my heart was pounding through my mind. I needed him. I needed him badly.

Damn that incubus.

Pressing a warm hand to my neck, I moved to the bath, kicking off my slip and underwear as I switched on the cold water. The tub began to fill, and I bounced from one foot to the other, desperate to distract myself from the endless images of Arafel bombarding my mind. I forced my arms across my chest, gasping at the unexpected pleasure my own touch brought.

"Oh my gosh, this is getting out of control." Unable to wait another moment, I stepped into the huge clawfoot tub and forced myself to sit. The moment the cold water hit my skin, I let out a little cry, equally loving and hating the splash of the water across my needy, desperate flesh. As soon as the water was deep enough, I slid in deeper, submerging myself completely.

Even there, in the darkness behind my eyelids, my body screamed for Arafel to come closer. I prayed he wasn't listening or that it was not the same type of call my body instinctively used to get his attention.

"Lucia?"

My eyes popped open, and I jerked to a sitting position. Surely not. The voice I'd just heard, it had been muffled from a door. "There's no way. I must've imagined that."

"Lucia, I'm coming in."

"No!" I cried out as Arafel and his mass of muscle and bulk came straight through my bathroom door. As if in slow motion, his face swept the room and immediately came to rest where I was still half submerged in the freezing cold water.

My body screamed in delight, and I groaned out loud, arousal coming over me in waves as I watched Arafel's chest rise and fall as he stared at me. I knew the water must be translucent. But I couldn't make myself cover my bare skin; I couldn't even move.

"Lucia...I—" His voice was a dark rasp I could feel on the raw nerves of my body. I tilted my head back, and I couldn't stop the moan that slipped out.

Arafel took another step into the room, and it was as if every part of my body lit up for him, my hips rising, my knees dropping open. I couldn't stop my hands as they slowly reached up to grab the edge of the tub and pull my skin toward the air, baring more of myself to his eyes.

Arafel let out a gentle rattle that made my eyes slide shut, fantasies of us together filling my mind once more.

"Arafel, what's happening?"

"Albtraum told me what happened." Arafel's voice was a growl. "He said he accidentally touched your bare skin before you left." I could see his powerful throat work as he swallowed. "It can cause a rather...visceral reaction."

"Visceral," I repeated dumbly, my eyes glued to the way his thighs filled out his pants. His wings were glamoured away, and a voice in my head was disappointed they were missing. I wanted to see him, all of him.

"Yes, that's how they work. They inspire desire and need and tend to leave their victims aroused and wanting after they are touched."

I groaned, leaning back in the tub again. "Like a sex dream?" My breasts broke the surface of the water, and I saw his hands turn to fists. I knew I should've been embarrassed. I should've been screeching at him to go away, yelling for all of the Underworld to hear that he had to get out of my rooms. But instead, all I felt was an overwhelming sense of relief, because I knew he would protect me from this too.

"How do I fix it?"

Arafel's eyes flashed bright blue before they dulled to the more human-like irises once more. "You need...to complete the spell, Lucia."

"Complete the spell? How do I..." My words died as realization washed over me, relief and embarrassment warring as I squirmed against the porcelain tub.

"I should go," Arafel said, seemingly to himself, but his position never changed. "But I cannot seem to make myself go."

Instead of shock, his words filled my body with ever growing need for more. One of my hands slipped off the tub edge and moved between my legs. I couldn't stop myself when I ran my fingers along my most intimate part, feeling the slick heat as I slowly looked back at him.

"How do I complete the spell? Like this?"

Arafel growled, his booted feet moving him a step closer to me.

My finger teased deeper, and I moaned softly at the relief and pleasure that little touch brought. But I knew in a breath that it wasn't enough. Probably because the male I was picturing between my thighs was standing a few feet away.

But he was only watching.

I licked my lips. "Like this, Arafel?"

"No." His voice was a deep rumble ricocheting through my body, from the tips of my toes, straight to my chilled skin of breasts. "Not like that."

"Then how?"

With a snarl, Arafel ripped his tunic off over his shoulders, revealing a gray chest smattered with scars and layered with thick muscle. I didn't stop myself from licking my lips. And then he was there, by the tub, his knees hitting the tile floor as he loomed over me, so large and powerful that I should've leaned back, flinched away.

But instead, I leaned in, my entire body pulsing with his proximity.

Arafel leaned in, his mouth so close to my ear. "Let me ease you, Lucia, and the spell will be broken."

I knew I could do it on my own. But why would I ever want that when the male from my fantasies was kneeling before me, his thick body preparing to give me the pleasure I was so desperate to have?

"Yes, yes, yes," I chanted, my hand leaving my core in order to grip the tub again. Arafel's nostrils flared, and with his claws retracted, he reached out and picked up that hand, bringing it slowly up to his face.

For a moment, he stared at me, his eyes heavy lidded, and I thought he was going to smell me again. But instead, he brought my hand to his mouth. With a wistful noise, his tongue slipped from his mouth, longer and thicker than any tongue I'd seen before. It wrapped around the fingers I'd had inside my body and tasted them.

I cried out, and my other hand gave out, sending me sinking back into the water. But for a moment, because the next, Arafel was there, his arm curling around her and holding me up in the water. His other hand rested on my knee, his grip tight.

"Arafel." I chanted his name as he moved against me.

"You know what kind of torture it has been to smell you every day? I thought the only way to make it better would be to have the chance to taste you. But now, I know I was all wrong. Because you taste like the sweetest fruit I've ever tasted. And I don't think it'll ever be enough."

I was panting, watching as his hand slowly traced down from my knee to my thigh. "Never?"

He kept moving, those thick, strong fingers reaching the place I needed him most. I moaned softly, arching my hips against his touch. But still, Arafel held back, his fingers grazing my clit before digging a soft touch down my lips.

His answer was a growl turned to a soft rattle at the end. "Never." Arafel rolled a finger around my clit, his touch making me squirm in desperate need. I reached out, gripping his arm and digging in my nails, deep enough I imagined I might have made him bleed.

"I need you. Arafel, I need you so much," I gasped up at the demon lord.

His mouth ducked down to press against my hairline, even as his finger curled and slipped deep inside me.

14

Arafel

I'd been so wrong.
There would never be enough. Enough time to touch her, enough time to taste her, enough time to savor her.
Never.
Never.
Enough.
Her aching, clenching flesh was hot against my palm, my finger buried in the sweet perfection of her body. And as I stared down into that dear, beautiful face, I felt something deep inside me tear wide open. Something more terrifying than pain. But I couldn't look away. Not from her. Not ever.

The reason for my obsession, my drive to save her, to keep her close, was becoming more and more clear. I wasn't sure if I was ready to allow this theory room in my mind. But it was there, nonetheless.

"Arafel." Her voice, rasping my name, set fire to my blood, making my heart pound loudly in my ears, making my control weak and tremulous.

"I'm here, Lucia." My finger curled gently inside her, making her neck and back arch up in a wanton display of need. "I'll always be here."

"More," she whispered, her hips working against my hand, the bathwater soaking my arm and splashing onto the tiled floor under my knees. Not that I cared. I was so far invested in her pleasure that I couldn't think of anything else.

I growled, and she quieted, her body trembling against mine. I knew what she needed. It was as ingrained in me as my powers, as my need to seek her out, as my loyalty to my brothers and the forces we served.

She was mine. I was an idiot to try to believe anything else. Whatever had brought us together, the end result would always be the same. She was destined to be mine.

I would make her forget anyone else.

And after we freed my soul and sent the Drude back to the nothing from which they came, maybe I could convince her to stay with me. I retracted my arm from behind her back, urging her to sit up as my fingers danced up her arms, feeling the silken skin there prickle with goose bumps and need. I found my way to that sharp little chin, finding it and holding it tight until I could lean over closer, trying not to scare her with my size.

But needing to kiss her.

The human male in me demanded her touch on my skin. I was desperate for it. And so, before I could think twice of it, I leaned in, capturing those sweet, soft, pink lips with my own. Her body was flush against the side of the tub, her hand eager on my chest.

Even my hand felt the flutter of her inner muscles against my finger.

Every part of her was craving me.

Fuck the incubus for putting us in this situation. But also, I couldn't get enough.

I began to move my wrist, slowly pumping my finger into her. I swallowed her moan the first time, but she pulled away as I guided a second finger into her. Her body rolled up against me, her hips desperate as she adjusted to the pressure once again.

"Yes," Lucia cried. "Arafel, please." Her eyes snapped open. "I want you. I need all of you, not just your fingers." Her hands were on my shoulders, her short, blunt nails digging into my skin, leaving water running down my body.

I couldn't stop myself from looking down, seeing the sharp contrast of her smooth, pale skin against the gray leathery texture of mine. Light and dark. Entirely different, yet somehow coexisting so beautifully, as if we were always meant to be this way.

My cock was hard as iron in my trousers, my mind pounding with the need to see all her beautiful skin against my own. On top of me, under me, against me.

"Fuck, light walker, don't ask me for that."

"Why not?" Her face turned serious, a pout on her lips. I wanted to kiss them again, to kiss away her questions and forget all of our responsibilities.

"Because you are going to break me, Lucia, right here. I'm on my knees, begging." I took a ragged breath in. "Do not ask me this. For you know I cannot deny you anything."

Lucia sank back into the water for a moment, her lust-dark eyes wild on mine. "Then why are you waiting?"

I leaned in, my face right against hers, feeling the quick little pants of her breath against my face. "I'm waiting because when I finally have you, Lucia Walker, the carrier of my soul, I want no other influence upon you. So that I know when you are screaming my name, there will be no doubt in your mind how badly you want me."

Her eyelids fluttered shut, and slowly, she ran her hand down my arm to where my hand rested, still and gentle against her most intimate space. Her fingers tightened around my wrist, and she pulled me back inside her.

I moved my fingers, picking up speed as her hips rose to meet my thrusts. "Good girl," I murmured, my thumb circling that part of her that made her jerk against the water's pull.

Her lips quivered, and her other hand reached up to play with her own breast. She was close, her muscles jerking and trembling in the tub.

Lucia's lips parted, the pink of her tongue slipping out to wet them as her eyes rolled back. The hand at her breast left it to clutch the edge of the tub.

"Arafel." Her voice sounded different, fearful. Nervous perhaps.

I leaned in, pressing my lips against hers again, my tongue sweeping in to taste hers. The slick sound of her flesh was muffled by the splashing of water.

"Let me feel you, Lucia. Let me feel on my hand what I'm so desperate to feel on my cock."

Her chin jerked up, and a ragged cry filled my mouth as her body clamped down on my fingers, clenching and pulling at them as the pleasure consumed her completely. I wanted to pull away, to watch her expression as she fell apart in my arms.

But I couldn't.

Because if I did, I knew I wouldn't be able to get up, to stand up and walk away from this room tonight. Not tonight. Not ever. I would stay here, on my knees, at my soul bound's side. Leaving the dreams and lives of the souls who relied upon me to damnation.

I wouldn't care.

I kept my eyes shut fast, instead letting my ears soak up every little noise, all the muffled cries she made until I finally pulled away. My fingers slipped from her, and I forced myself to rock back on numb legs to stare at her.

Wide, shocked blue eyes stared back. They swept over my face, my chest, landing on the marks on my shoulders and chest where she'd tried to dig her nails in. I breathed in, forcing myself to stay still under her eyes.

The spell would be wearing off, sated by her pleasure.

"Lucia," I finally said. "Are you…" I didn't know the correct word. "Better?"

She gave a soft laugh, her arms crossing over her chest as she settled a little deeper in the water again. "I'm not sure better begins to cover it. But sure, we can say better."

"And you're not having any regrets?"

Lucia swallowed but still had a smile on her mouth. "No regrets, Arafel. I...um... You did exactly what I asked you to do. And I understand why you did it."

The silence between us felt tight, strained, and my fists clenched. If I had ruined this thing between us tonight, first by lying about the feelings that I held for her and then by aiding her through the incubus's spell, I would hate myself for a century.

The human before me cleared her throat. "If you don't mind, I was hoping you could hand me a towel and maybe we can start fresh in the morning." She flinched, curling up a little in the tub. "Without any incubuses?"

Worry flooded my mind, but I nodded, standing up and grabbing one of the huge bath sheets from the vanity. I turned back to the tub, surprised when Lucia turned her back on me and then slowly rose from the tub. I bit back a groan as water sluiced over her back and lowered down to her feet.

"Arafel?"

Fuck, she was holding an arm out, trusting that I wasn't staring at her like a letch.

But I was. I hurried a step forward, blinking rapidly as I forced my eyes to stay on her hairline while I wrapped the towel around her slender shoulders.

As soon as the fabric was secure, I stepped away, ignoring the throbbing in my groin as I moved to the door. "I'll leave you to get dressed. One of the mahrs will bring a plate for you later since you didn't get to eat dinner."

I was sure she was nodding, but I didn't look back. I couldn't. I yanked my shirt on as I walked through her rooms, forcing my nostrils to not inhale the scent of her, even as it seemed to have seeped into every part of this room and of me.

I needed to get out of here before one of us did something we shouldn't.

But suddenly I was having a much harder time making my body follow directions than before. The feelings I was having about my soul mate were going much further than simple protection.

As soon as I hit the corridor, I stepped into a shadow and back out in my personal chambers. After all, they were quite close, a floor above Lucia's. But I didn't want to risk any of the creatures seeing me walk from her room, dripping wet, a little manic, and with my cock heavy and thick.

I was supposed to be better than a man, but here I was, pining after the woman I was protecting. I slammed my way through my chambers, finding new clothes and stepping into them. I was only alone for a few moments before Paran knocked twice then came in at my beckoning.

"News from the mountain?"

"Kharon met us by the river delta, and he agreed to take a message to Nephesh." Paran sat in the chair by the window, casting a wary glance out at the gray sky then back to me. "It's looking brighter out there today, my lord."

Pressing a hand against my chest, I sighed. I knew it was. I didn't need to look through my windows. "My magic has been growing stronger every day since bringing Lucia here. I think it must have something to do with having the other half of my soul close." I turned to gauge his reaction. Of all the Brothers who served me, Paran was the least capable of hiding his true feelings. It was a gift and a curse.

"Do you agree, Paran?"

Paran was rarely silent, so his pensive, thoughtful face made me still, straightening the collar on my new, dry tunic. "I believe you should be careful, Arafel."

"Of what?" I asked, knowing exactly what he was saying but uninterested in the conversation. I began to pace, unable to keep still, all thoughts of Lucia making me itchy, unsettled.

"There are many eyes here, more than ever before."

Spies. I wasn't surprised. Whether they were my brothers' spies, my father's, or even the Drude's, I didn't know. "And what are they seeing?"

"You and Lucia." Paran flicked at an indivisible speck of dust on his pant leg. "They are wondering if you are truly trying to get your soul from her or whether you are simply besotted by her."

"Besotted? I believe I cleared that at the meeting yesterday."

Paran's laugh was humorless. "They are wondering if you will be able to do what is needed when the time comes."

"I don't know what you're saying."

"There is a way to collect a soul, Arafel. The oldest and most simple way of all."

"You mean to kill her? I can't believe you."

"Arafel, please."

"Get out!"

"Arafel, listen to me. My old friend."

"You are no friend to me. You have protected Lucia her whole life. You have seen her grow up, seen her come into this world. Just as I did. How could you say these things to me?"

"I can say them to you because while you are in here playing house, I'm at the wall, watching soul after soul be torn apart and lost to us. Those are who we are trained to serve. Those are who we are supposed to be saving. Lucia may be the carrier of your soul, but she cannot wield it like you can. Take it back, Arafel. Before more innocent lives are ruined."

"I will not take anything from her."

"Then you should be prepared for those who would do it for you."

"Are you looking to be killed tonight, old friend?" My growl was so loud, I could barely hear when he spoke again.

"I am not. I am your friend, Arafel, but in times such as these, friends must speak the truth. Even if it hurts." Paran's shoulders slumped in submission as my wings slipped from my glamor and spread, darkening the room in an instant. My magic leapt to the surface of my skin, eager to defend my soul bound.

I bared my teeth at him, my jaw aching with the need to gnash my teeth. "Get out, before I slice you from the body I gave you."

Paran nodded, rising slowly to his feet.

"If you hear of any others looking to discuss this soul removal, then tell them they will need to go through me first. Do I make myself clear?"

Paran shut the door behind him, and it was only closed a moment before I hurled a chair at it, the splintering of wood and furniture giving me momentary satisfaction. Then my temper returned at full force.

I stalked to the window, staring out at the light-gray sky, the blue and silvery streams of light threading across. I moved my shoulders, stretching my wing joints. The wingtips brushing each side of my balcony as fury at what Paran said flooded my system. And then I leaped from my balcony, letting the air rush over me as I plummeted off the side of Castle Fel and the side of the Sleeping Mountain.

Maybe a long, thorough flight would clear my mind and remove my rage at one of my most trusted advisors. As I pumped my wings, headed for where my army was camped at the east wall, I forced temper from my veins. In its place was a very real fear that what Paran said was correct.

I was a Lord of the Underworld, the keeper of dreams, a son of Lucifer. Would I sacrifice everything to keep Lucia safe?

I tucked my wings in tight, letting another nosedive force the answer from my mind. I wasn't ready to face that truth yet.

15

Lucia

I was eternally glad the room Arafel had chosen for me suited my every need, because I didn't think I was ever going to be able to leave it again. There was no way I was going to risk bumping into Albtraum again. Because there was no way he didn't know what happened last night.

People would be coming to conclusions about what had happened, despite what Arafel had said, denying any feelings beyond a strange sort of ownership that he felt for me.

My hands covered my burning cheeks. I still couldn't believe the things I'd done and said in my desperation for him. But the moment the spell broke and my brain was able to catch up with my body, all I felt was the same bone-deep connection with Arafel that I didn't know what to make of. I'd believed it was the soul binding us together, but now…now I didn't know.

I scrubbed at my face, staring at the book in front of me. Since I wasn't ready to go traipsing around the castle's myriad of halls yet, I had gone back to reading through Lucifer's letters to Arafel and his brothers. I hadn't learned much yet, other than the obvious fact that before the lords ruled hell, they had been Lucifer's most trusted advisors and warriors as they'd worked to carve this world into something all its own.

I glanced down at a page I'd fallen asleep reading last night. A letter from Lucifer to Nephesh, Arafel's eldest brother.

Nephesh,
My son, I've heard good news. When you are able, bring your soul bound to the Underworld. Only here can we reunite your soul together. The exchange is as powerful as it is dangerous. Tread lightly. They will not want your power unleashed.
Lucifer

On the same page, scribbled in quick stabs of ink, was Nephesh's response.

We will be there soon.

My heart in my throat, I turned the page, noting the return of Arafel's name and handwriting.

Father,
I have caged Nephesh for the time being. Kharon will perform his duties until we can sort out what will happen next. For what it's worth, her death appeared accidental. I'm sure he will want to investigate when he is clearer of mind. If he were to find out it was not an accident, then I pray that their soul be

routed to the Elysian Fields and not hell, because there is no other place that will keep Nephesh from destroying them.
Arafel

I rose up on an elbow, flinching as the blood flow was renewed to my wrist, and I gawked down at the book. This had to be when Nephesh lost his soul bound. For some reason, tears were blurring my vision, my eyes watering as I reread the letters again.

Had someone wanted her dead, I wondered to myself. Maybe one of these corrupted creatures working for the Drude? The letters weren't clear, even as Lucifer responded back with directions on how to manage the Judge's territory of the Underworld while Arafel kept his brother under control.

Crossing my legs, I dragged the heavy book back onto my lap. I fluttering back and forth over the next few letters, needing somehow to know what had happened to this other woman. I felt an immediate kinship to this woman, the only other human to be in the situation I was currently in.

My stomach was growling, begging for a midday meal before I finally got my answer.

Father,

Nephesh and I were able to locate the man who hurt Anna. He broke at the end, crying for his master to save him, but he didn't lie. He never meant anyone harm. It was his reckless intoxication that took Nephesh's soul mate from her world and

into our own. He belongs to the Punisher now; Elon has already claimed him.

I paused, my finger pressing against the page. Soul mate here, not soul bound. Something inside me squeezed.

Something that concerns us both greatly is that the other half of Nephesh's soul seems to have disappeared with the woman who carried it. Why is this? Shouldn't the passing of her body free his soul from her body?

Kharon

My throat ached as a combination of horror and fear swept over me. Here it was, written in ink, that my death would not reunite Arafel's soul. I secretly wanted to brandish this at the members of Arafel's council.

Sniffling back tears of confusion and frustration, I picked up a small piece of paper that had been placed between the pages.

My son,
Nephesh's soul is safe. When he is ready, it will reveal itself to him. The process begins anew.

I guessed that officially closed the whole "kill her and that will solve everything" debate. It wouldn't. My heart ached suddenly. This information was both deadly and a salvation. It would keep the creatures of the Underworld from wanting to kill me and the others who kept souls, but it would damn us to a life of being hunted by the Corrupted. By the Drude itself.

Each time they killed a soul bound, it meant more time without the lords in full power. It was exactly what the Drude wanted.

I opened my door, stepping into the hallway, where a sharply dressed pair of harpies stared back at me with their eerie golden eyes.

"Good day," I mumbled, flushing a little as they both bowed to me. "I'm going to go see Arafel. Don't worry, I can walk myself..." I stepped back from them, my shoulders and body slipping into the shallow shadow of my doorway. My words died on my tongue as I stumbled back another step and found myself standing against the wall in another large suite of rooms.

My eyes bulged as I looked around, wondering how I'd gotten here. I passed across the wide room, my feet quiet against the rug-covered living space.

I drew in a long breath, clearing my throat. It smelled wonderful here. My gaze caught on a set of chairs, so large I doubted my toes would touch when I sat in it. A half-smile curled my lips. Arafel's chair. I looked around me. These had to be his rooms.

A shiver moved through my body, leaving a trail of heat and need in its wake. I shook it off. The incubus's spell may have been gone, but all that was left was raw desire.

I badly needed to talk to him. To know what this was between us. "Hello?"

Nothing.

I moved deeper into the rooms, noting a heavy, wide desk in one corner with a variety of bookshelves on one wall, half-empty but bearing a remarkable similarity to the dream library. I ran a finger down the empty shelves before retreating back out to the living room.

He clearly wasn't here. But that didn't matter. I would wait. Grabbing a blanket from the basket by the fireplace, I moved back to the chairs. With a grin on my face, I curled up in the seat of his chair, easy even with my long legs, and yanked the blanket over me. Warmth and comfort and the smell so uniquely Arafel washed over me.

I'd close my eyes for a moment, and when he returned, I would be able to ask him about what happened after they'd lost Anna.

***

My belly jumped as I woke, staring around at the sitting area I was in. I wasn't in my rooms. I was… I swallowed hard, soaking in the room around me. I was in Arafel's chambers. I glanced at the sky. It had grown dark again, and not for the first time, I appreciated the fact that Lucifer kept the Underworld mirroring the days and nights of the world above.

My neck had a crick, and I sat up slowly, rubbing at the site as I looked around the room. The sconces were lit low, ushering in only a small fraction of light in the rooms. Right as I was about to throw my legs over and stand up, Arafel came in from the other room.

I swallowed hard.

He'd been flying. His enormous wings were still out, folded neatly behind his shoulder blades as he strode into the room, a tattered-looking shirt in his hands. My mouth went dry as his torso moved and twisted as he stalked into the room, showcasing all those thick lines of muscle across his dove-gray body.

He was beautiful. Unearthly and forbidden, but beautiful all the same. My eyes rose slowly, watching the way his chest filled with breath, knowing I would be caught in a few moments.

I put my bare feet on the floor, feeling the softness of the rug beneath me.

Glowing and endless, his blue eyes settled on me. I rose out of the chair, crossing the room to him.

Something had shifted between us. Something dark and heavy and throbbing behind my eyes and between my legs. I felt as if I'd run up a dozen flights of stairs, but my legs didn't stop until I was standing directly in front of him.

"Lucia." His voice was concerned.

I raised a hand, pressing my fingers against his lips. "Before you ask, I'm fine. I wanted to talk to you, and your room let me in."

Arafel's heavy brows dropped, and for a moment, I thought he was going to scold me. I pressed on.

"What you did for me last night? Thank you. Maybe I don't understand this world or the creatures within it. But I know you could've taken things down a different road. But you did not."

Arafel stood silent, and my arm ached as I held my hand over his mouth still. His lips were soft, warm.

"But now..." My voice broke. "Now I'm here of my own accord with my own desires and my own needs."

His mouth opened, but I shook my head. He let out a rattling deep breath that I felt in every part of my body. I stepped even closer. I couldn't stop staring at the scars on his chest, across his belly and shoulder. And there, above his collarbones, my nails had left neat, bright-red little marks on him.

"I know you think we should keep our distance. I know that you are focused on getting your soul out of me. But I couldn't let you think that I didn't care about last night. Even if it was nothing to you, it was everything to me."

I stepped back, hurriedly dropping my hand and tucking it behind my back. Panic washed over me, and suddenly I was embarrassed to have snuck in here and needed to leave before he said something to crush my stupidly human heart.

I turned, my feet hurrying as I made a dash for the door. My fingers had just grazed the handle of it when rough hands turned me, pushing me back up against the door. Gasping, I found myself staring up at hundreds of pounds of angry, emotional demon.

"Arafel!"

"I lied to the council. I thought I was protecting you."

"Oh, I—"

"I cannot let you believe last night meant nothing to me." His words were a growl, arching through me with the force behind them.

"Well, I..." Apparently, I'd lost the ability to speak.

"Last night was one of the singular most important moments of my entire existence. And I have lived a very, very long time, Lucia." Arafel's eyes were glowing brighter blue as they stared down at me. "And you are correct. I am desperate to stay away from you because when I told you that I'd protect you from the creatures of my world, I included myself in those creatures."

"You're not like that."

"Oh, I am." Arafel laughed, low and dark. "I'm the most dangerous thing in my realm, sweet Lucia, and you can't seem to get that into your head."

"You wouldn't hurt me."

His claws dragged down my arms, making my nipples pebble under my shirt and my breath come short in my lungs. I rubbed my knees together, trying to ease the ache in my body. His smell, his words... They made me clench with the need to get closer. I leaned in, but his hands were holding me flat in place.

"I would never intentionally hurt you," Arafel said finally, his tongue slipping out to wet deep-charcoal lips. "But I don't know if I can be gentle for you, not like this."

"Why not?"

"Because." He leaned in, running his nose up my neck to behind my ear. "You smell like pure sin, and I'm dying for another taste. And then another. Because once will never be enough for me. Twice is a mockery. I will always want you, soul mate."

"Oh God."

His hands left my arms, and I slipped forward, my knees weak. He stepped back from me, his entire body quaking with the effort it took.

"Leave, Lucia, before I do something that cannot be undone."

I shook my head.

"Leave," he repeated calmly.

"No."

"Leave my quarters at once!"

"I'm done letting you make all my choices for me, Arafel. I'm making this one for myself." I threw myself at him, letting my arms tangle around his neck and my hands sink into the short-cropped, thick dark hair. My fingers brushed his horns a little as I jostled from my jump, and I could hear the groan that slipped from his mouth.

"Lucia..."

"I'm done hiding from this."

He was breathing hard, his face turned into me. I could feel his muscles shake as he battled with himself. "I am barely half man; I would hurt you."

"You won't." I brushed my lips over his jaw. "I trust you."

"You shouldn't."

I pulled back, watching his expression change from the angry, stern look to one of complete reverence. His arms slowly came up under me, one under my butt, while the other ran over my braids, the pads of his fingers gentle against my scalp.

"You want to be with a monster?"

"I want to be with you."

"I can deny you nothing." His forehead was against mine, and for a long moment, neither of us moved, simply soaking in the pleasure of touching each other.

And then his hands moved, one tugging the bands in my hair free and the other moving so it was no longer merely supporting my butt, but rather cradling it. The change was immediate, and my body clenched hard as I was pressed intimately against his lower belly.

As his hand slowly untangled my braid, setting my dark hair free, his other hand flexed and moved, slowly grinding me forward against the heavy plane of his body. My body lit up; every part of my body was consumed with getting closer to him.

When my hair was finally freed, he leaned in, pressing his face to the side of my hair and hiking me higher up on his body. Arafel released a deep, rumbling sigh that made my muscles quiver.

"Beloved, why do you set my soul on fire as you do?"

I couldn't answer. I could only feel, only want. I pulled back to look into his eyes, so full of magic and the unknown. But I could see the creature behind the magic, the male who saved me from car accidents, who peeled my pears for me. The male who knew me inside and out and still wanted me. The one who had given me complete control over this.

I was done waiting.

"I think we both know the answer." I brushed my lips over his, feeling the soft rush of his breath. "I was made for you, Arafel."

16

Lucia

His growl was half pleasure, half anger, and then we were walking across the room toward his chambers. But we only made it a few steps before I was able to run my tongue up the edge of his ear, my hand finding purchase on his horns to hold on as he moved us both.

The noise he made was so startled, I almost laughed. But everything changed when the hand supporting me moved, letting me slide down the front of his body.

"You should mind the horns," he said, stalking forward. For some reason, adrenaline filled my veins, and I took a step back.

"Because they are sharp?"

His lips curled and his wings rose over his shoulders, the gloss of his feathers drawing my attention. "Because they are a demon's greatest asset. To have them touched is"—he continued stalking toward me—"more than I think you are ready for."

My stomach twisted in delight. A weakness or a pleasure. I looked up at him through my lashes. "I'll be sure to remember for next time."

His growl filled the air, and after a moment, he pounced on me, driving both of us to the rug. His hand cradled my head for a moment then deposited it along with the rest of me against the softness of the rug.

From this perspective, I could look up and see all of him from the thigh up. His powerful muscles, the vast size of him, the ebony-colored feathers at the peak of his wings. Even the sharp, angular lines of his face. When his lips parted, I saw the flash of fangs in his mouth.

The Arafel of my youth was gone. In his place was the male I wanted more than anything else in the world.

And he was here. His heat seeped into me as we stared at each other, a bit awestruck. I moved first, my hands trailing from his shoulders to his chest. I brushed my fingers over his torso. His skin was textured yet soft. The spiraling designs across his shoulders and torso made me think of tattoos.

"Soft," I murmured. "But also hard." Blushing madly, I looked up at him to see if he'd heard me, but he was too busy staring at my hands on his body. With a rattling sigh, he bent his elbows, gifting me with even more of his weight and warmth.

Need throbbed at my core, where my thighs shook against his sides. I knew he could feel me, knew he could probably smell me. But I didn't care anymore. No more hiding.

I let my fingers slip around his back and dig in, my sharp nails biting into his skin. His blue eyes moved, meeting mine. "So impatient, little soul," he murmured then leaned in to press soft, open-mouthed kisses along my collarbone and neck, each time letting the scrape of his fangs tease for a moment. By the time I could kiss him, my hips were jerking up against his.

"I want to feel more."

"You will, Lucia. I'm not like any man you've seen," he rumbled in my ear, his tongue running around the cusp of my ear. It was long and hot on my skin. "I want to be sure that you're completely ready."

I rolled my hips. "I don't think that'll be a problem."

Arafel chuckled, the sound echoing through my core as he moved slower. He pressed a hand against my top, and a breath later it was gone. With a satisfied little noise, Arafel continued his kissing until he reached my waistband, shuffling back on the rug.

"Can I touch your wings?" I mumbled, the feathers only inches from my hands.

"Be gentle," Arafel warned, and I briefly wondered if they were similar to his horns and could cause great pleasure. I vowed to ask him later when I could think straight. But now, Arafel was sitting between my thighs, his broad shoulders opening my hips with a deep, rattling sigh. My hands sank into his hair, his wings temporarily forgotten.

His hand smoothed up my thigh, and my pants were gone, probably with my shirt, wherever that was. Arafel leaned in, pressing his nose against the top of my slit, still covered by my panties, and took another deep breath in.

"Soul mate, I need to taste you. Tell me I can feast on you like this. Let my tongue fuck your body until every drop coats me."

My hips arched up. "Yes! Yes, Arafel. Please, I want to feel…" I let the words hang in the air because they said exactly what I wanted. I wanted to feel him. In any way. In *every* way. My heart pounded in my ears as a thick finger tugged my panties to one side.

The first touch of his tongue on my skin was gentle, inquisitive. The second, bold and determined. I cried out, unable to stop myself as Arafel leisurely tasted me, slipping his long, flexible tongue up and down the part of my body I'd never shared with anyone else.

Which made sense now.

Because I was made for him.

Only him.

He paused, humming quietly. "Better than I ever could've imagined." And then was immediately back on me, licking, sucking, his mouth a hot caress as touch after touch of his tongue on my body made me nearly unable to speak. I could only mutter out short words, tugging at his hair as he took me to the edge of pleasure, only to hesitate and draw it out again.

"Arafel, please. I want to feel you inside me."

His only response was to hum against my slick, needy flesh and then harden his thick tongue and slip it deep inside me before curling it back.

My hips jerked off the rug, my hands in his hair loosening until I could only barely feel the rough texture of his horns against my fingertips. "Yes," he growled then thrust his tongue in again before retreating. "Let me have it all, Lucia. Let me feel you come on my tongue so I can taste your pleasure."

His words were a command and a prayer, and my body exploded around him. Every stroke of his tongue drew it out, making my eyes slam shut. My knees snapped shut around Arafel, desperate to hold him against me as rolling wave after wave of pleasure pounded through my body.

Until finally, when I was able to gather my thoughts, I found myself lying spread eagle, his weight still against my lower half as he leisurely licked at my still-shaking core. It was excruciating, this intense need that still curled low in my belly.

"Arafel." I pushed up on an elbow and was rewarded with his face turning to mine. His tongue slowly dragged back into his mouth with a pop that made my core clench. "Let me see you."

He pushed back, rocking to his heels long enough to undo the ties at his waist. Somehow during all of this, he'd already ditched the boots he'd worn flying. I noticed for the first time his feet were surprisingly human-looking, except enormous and tipped with shiny black nails that matched his clawed fingers.

Arafel reached inside his pants, and hitching his trousers down his thighs, he brought out his cock. I stared. I'd had no idea what to expect. I hadn't been sure if it would be oddly shaped, or insanely large, or perhaps completely incompatible with me.

But his cock was none of those things. It was thick and long, a darker gray than his skin, and with a heavy, wide head, it looked close enough to a human man. At least until his big hand ran a stroke down it, making it throb and thicken right before my eyes.

I opened my mouth, a sliver of doubt in my mind. "Arafel, I'm not sure..."

That big cock throbbed again, pulsing and growing as those clawed nails pumped down the length.

"Don't worry. I will fit, Lucia."

He settled back, his wings spreading a little so he would sit on the floor, sliding his trousers the rest of the way down his legs. I sat up, watching, fascinated by this part of him that I wanted so badly.

"Can I touch you?"

Arafel's wings shifted, his cock bobbing in his lap. "As much as you want, little soul."

I moved forward, straddling his lap for a moment so I could lean up and kiss him. His tongue swept into my mouth, battling with mine in a slick, heated twist of need.

"Lucia." His voice was rough.

"I was..." I brushed my tongue over one dark-gray nipple, and he jerked beneath me. I drew back, pointedly letting my gaze wander his body straight down to the heavy cock that bobbed between us. "I want to make you feel good." And then I scooted back, preparing to kiss my way down his belly, when a strong, warm hand grabbed me and pulled me back to his lap. Both of us cried out as the slick, heated flesh of my core brushed over his hardness.

"Not today."

I blinked at him, surprised. "What? Why not?"

Arafel growled and kissed me, his hands on my ass, moving me against him, letting my flesh part against him. I gasped into the kiss, arousal seeping back through my mind.

"Because, Lucia, when I come, I want to be so deep inside you, neither of us can tell where the other ends. And where I can lock you against me and make you scream my name until you are hoarse." He cocked his head. "Am I clear?"

I swallowed, my body shivering as I nodded.

With a satisfied smirk, Arafel shifted and rose from the floor, guiding me to my back before him. My knees fell wide as rough fingertips traced the insides of my thighs.

"This is the last time I will ask, Lucia, if you truly want this."

My toes curled at the sweetness. Everything else twisted with need. "Yes, Arafel, I want this."

Arafel crawled forward, his skin a velvet caress against my own. His long, black tongue slipped out to taste the skin over my hip, then my ribs, my collarbone. I shivered under him, hands clenching on his sides in a pitiful attempt to pull him in closer. At my neck, he stopped, breathing me in.

"You truly want a monster?"

"If you are a monster as you claim, then I claim you as mine." My legs wound around his as his hands turned into fists by my head. "My monster."

"Your monster," he said, as if trying out the words. A part of his lips lifted, and he bore down on me, his hips slipping against mine until the heavy weight of his cock was against me. "And you, little soul, are my salvation."

And then he was inside me, pressing, pressing, pressing that thick pulsing part of him so deep inside me that I could barely take a breath. There was pressure, of course, but no pain. And when he slowed, his breath was hot against my neck. I couldn't help but turn my face into his chest, to bring in great, ragged lungsful of his scent as I offered him everything I was. Even when he was still against me, his cock seemed to move inside, growing and filling until there no more room. Every inch of me was completely conquered by him.

"Lucia." He breathed me in again. "You are beyond words."

I moved my hips a little, trying to relax against the onslaught of Arafel inside me. He groaned, and it was a snarl that fell from his mouth as his hips powered forward, thrusting deep inside me and stilling there.

Together. Completely together.

I knitted my fingers into his hair; my mouth opened wide as Arafel's hips retreated before moving forward again. Pleasure burned through my veins, making it hard to say anything, making it hard to do anything. I simply held on to him, letting my legs fall open for his cock. Each thrust into my body made me pulse, and I knew that I was rapidly approaching orgasm again. I could feel my muscles and body coiling up, drawing tight as I looked up into Arafel's handsome face and watched him come undone as well.

"That's it," Arafel groaned. "Let me feel you. Let me feel everything."

"Arafel," I cried out, my legs suddenly snapping shut around him like a vise. Pleasure like I'd never known swept over me, consuming me until I could do nothing but cling to his body and trust he would deliver us through this.

As my pleasure ebbed, I forced my eyes open, desperate to see the male I was sharing this with as he experienced it. As his hips lurched forward against mine in one last mighty thrust, his head flew back, every muscle in his chest and neck tense and visible as his wings flew to the sides, burying the silvery claws at the tips into the floor in a spray of wood and stone. Anchoring us, I realized, as deep inside something tugged and throbbed.

"Lucia," Arafel moaned, his head slowly falling forward as the throbs inside me slowed. I let my head fall back to the rug, bliss and contentment filling my body as his wings drew tight, cocooning us in a blanket of inky darkness.

17

Arafel

M*ine.* Finally, I had picked us up, holding her body against my own as I moved through the chambers to my bedroom. The vast bed frame within took up half the room, set up so that I could lie in any which direction and still not bang my horns.

I'd never shared it with another.

Which perhaps made it all the sweeter when I carefully sat down on the mattress and pressed us back into the bedding. Lucia was silent, her breath warm on my chest as she simply allowed me to care for her. Every instinct in my body was going crazy, the need to take her again, to keep her against me, to stay inside her was driving me to near madness. Which is why, perhaps, my inner demon was bellowing in the glory of having her locked against me.

I smoothed a hand down her cheek, the satin of her skin so at odds with my heavy black claws.

I needed to explain it all, to tell her why this was happening. But I couldn't, not at the risk she might jerk away or even leave me all together.

I would wait.

Just a few minutes more.

I leaned back into the bed, my muscles delightfully relaxed as her legs slipped over my body to rest against the mattress, her silken head between my collarbones. This was bliss, I realized.

I tugged a blanket over us, raising my leg and making her body shudder a little as she shifted against my still-firm cock. I clenched my jaw, wondering if I had ruined this bubble of contentment around us. But Lucia only snuggled closer and pressed a sleepy kiss against my neck.

Under the covers, I stroked her back, the smooth mounds of her ass. And with a smile, I let myself relax and doze beneath her.

My soul mate.

And one true mate.

My mind was already made up. We would find a way to separate my soul from hers, and then I would convince her to stay here with me. I fell asleep with a smile on my lips.

Pleasure bloomed in my belly, a gentle tugging that had me emerging from an empty, dreamless sleep some hours later.

"Lucia," I said, smoothing my hand over her body once more. She was awake, I could tell by the rapid movement of her chest against mine, her heart pounding under her breast. "Are you all right?"

She rose up on her elbows, bracing herself on me. "Arafel, I'm sorry, I didn't mean to wake you, but..." Her eyes clouded with more than confusion. I saw the fear there, and I sat up against the pillows, reaching out a hand to cup her jaw.

"What is it?"

"Are we stuck together?"

Something about the way she said it, the whispered, scandalized way the words fell from her lips set off a laugh from deep in my chest. I shifted again, and her fear disappeared in an instant, covered instead by a wave of arousal I could practically taste. "Don't you like it?"

She pushed against my shoulder, but it was halfhearted. "Well...I-I... You should've warned me."

I relaxed back onto the pillows, my longer limbs winding down her body to where her legs were curled on the bed beside my torso. I tugged them forward, changing the angle at which we were so intimately connected.

"I should've. I'm sorry, little light, I should've warned you." Her eyes were sliding shut, her hips rotating a little against my touch as my cock began to thicken even more. "I didn't expect it to last so long."

"It doesn't usually last this long?" Her words were clear, but her head was tilting back, long hair falling over her back as her inner muscles clenched along my length.

"I wouldn't know," I answered truthfully. "I've never had it happen before."

Her chin lowered once more. "Then why now?"

"Sometimes," I said, leaning forward to press a kiss against the pulse in her neck and then letting my long, slick tongue taste the salt of her skin below. "Our bodies recognize what we need far before our minds ever do. And my body, my mind, they want you for our own."

"What does that mean?'

"Stay, Lucia."

All her glorious dark hair swirled over her shoulders. "I don't understand."

"Come with me to ask my father for help, and then stay here with me."

"In Hell?"

"Is it all that hellish? This is the Underworld. And you will live by my side. A queen."

My thumbs found her breasts and circled the sharp peaks of them eagerly. I could imagine her, that beautiful smile looking up at me, light shining from her eyes as we ruled the dream realm. The thought made my back arch a little, pressing my cock deeper inside her, and she gasped and slid a hand into my hair to steady herself.

"I don't know how to be queen."

"Which will inevitably make you the best that there has ever been." My hands were at her hips, my movements becoming more frantic as my need began to outweigh the need to explain this to her. "Promise me you'll think about it. Of staying with me."

My lock loosened, my body satiated by the fact I was clearly preparing to fuck my mate again. I was able to pick her up, steady her over the thick head, before guiding her back down again. Lucia gasped and moved against me, her movements as frantic as mine. We were starving for each other.

"Tell me."

"I'll think about it. But first, Arafel, please, more."

I didn't bother to ask twice or waste my breath on an answer. Because I would show her. My claws teased her back as I showed her how to ride me, how to pull and move her hips against my body as my thrusts slowed, and I watched the pleasure of our bodies united take over her expression. Every slick slide of our flesh together made my muscles quake in awe.

This was bliss.

My one true mate.

And when she faltered, her body growing weak with pleasure, I held her ribs in my hands and ground us together, my eyes glued to the part of myself that was splitting into her body, driving deep and making us one.

I didn't hold back. I didn't wait. And when the pleasure became more than even I could stand, I swept a careful claw across the sweet little nub of her need and sent my cock deep into her womb. There I locked us together again, filling her with all of me.

The feeling of her body clasping mine was enough to make me resolute.

She was mine.

Now and forever.

18

Lucia

"Oh, thank the lords," a cheerful voice sounded from the corner of my chambers. "You two finally got over whatever was keeping you apart."

I started, my jaw slack as Susan sauntered through my not-there door. Arafel must've granted her access to help me pack. "You're here! And what? What are you talking about?"

"Lord Arafel." Susan hummed as she pulled me into a quick hug. "You've always smelled like him, his protection a ward to all others. But today, Lucia Walker, you smell like you've been thoroughly claimed."

"Oh my God, Susan!"

She batted away my embarrassment and moved over to my bag. "Stop your stuttering, sweet girl. We all knew it was bound to happen. That male has been devoted to you for your entire life. It's not a far leap to assume there was something at work far deeper than a carefully placed soul bound."

I pressed the heels of my hands into my eyes, a hysterical chuckle slipping free. "Everyone knows?"

"Not everyone. But honestly, everyone will know soon. The lords do not take kindly to other males being close to their mates. Half the castle will be sent out on assignment soon, I'd bet."

I groaned. "I'm his soul mate, which means something different here than it does at home."

Susan cocked her head. "Did he tell you that?" She gave me a pointed look. "Seems to me like perhaps Lord Arafel was trying to give you space to decide on your own."

"Decide? What, that I was his mate?"

"His true mate, that's what we call them down here. There are chosen mates, of course—those are similar to marriages up top. But here, there is a connection which spans times and worlds. That is the bond of a soul mate."

"And it's different from being his soul bound?"

Susan narrowed her eyes then picked up a sweater and folded it, stuffing it into my bag. "It is. Your body was chosen to carry his soul. That bond is as powerful as anything I've ever seen, save the bond of a soul mate. One that transcends lifetimes."

I trid to pretend like I wasn't gaping at her. Arafel, our connection, it did seem more powerful than anything I'd ever felt before. It explained why I was so drawn to him, why I craved his company, his touch more than anything else.

But was it our shared soul or something else tying us together?

"How do you find your soul mate?"

Susan cocked her head, translucent skin darkening. "They say the fates have a hand in it, but I think those three have got too much on their plates to do anything about true mates."

"It's pure luck, then." It was making more sense. Why the creatures from the Underworld wanted to be able to follow their soul mates, even if they were in the living world. I understood more of their frustration now, what they had seen when Arafel and I arrived together. A king who had found his soul mate and his soul yet wouldn't allow them the leniency to find their own.

If I truly was Arafel's soul mate but hadn't been carrying his soul, we would've lived our entire lives without being able to be together. I rubbed a hand across my chest, above the heart that ached for all those lifetimes of emptiness.

Susan considered my words. "In a way, but there is typically divine intervention in the case of a soul mate."

"That's why they are more powerful?"

"Soul mates are sealed with a vow that cannot be broken. To me, soul bounds seem to be directly related to the old witch's power. Tricky works, both of them. Soul mates may be bound to each other should they both accept the other, but when the queen bound her sons' souls to humans, she must've had a grander plan. Nephesh didn't love his Anna like a mate. He respected her, loved her in his own way. But they weren't together, not like you and Arafel are."

My head was pounding. "I still don't quite understand. Can we talk about this later? My brain is such a mess."

"Anytime, love. As soon as you get back from the Court of Hell. I'm sure we will have plenty of time."

I rubbed my face with my palms, unsure of how I felt about any of this. I had barely come to accept my life had been more about preserving a dream king's power than my own needs and desires.

Yet that was the tip of the iceberg. Arafel believed he was my soul mate. And if I wasn't feeling so cowardly, I would admit the alternative, living a life without him, sent ice straight down my veins.

For the first time, I thanked whatever spell or magic had brought Arafel's soul to me. Whatever happened, I would be eternally grateful for the chance to know him.

"What are you packing, anyway?" I watched as she neatly wrapped up a long, black velvet gown as well. "I don't think I'll be needing a fancy dress for Hell, Susan."

She waggled gray eyebrows at me. "Trust me, you will need it. And probably ten more like it if you end up staying here."

"How did you know about that?"

"I didn't. You told me yourself." Susan approached me, her gray curls wild. "I am only a soul here, and I hold no power over your decisions. But I want to tell you that I've never had someone take to life here so well."

I pretended to pick at the lint on my sweatshirt. "Have there been others?"

"Only a few. Guests of Lucifer or Nephesh who wanted to see the dream realm. It is not uncommon." Her eyes were serious.

Her hands reached for mine, and I gave them to her. "Your mother would be proud of you, Lucia, for doing all of this to help Arafel, for taking a chance on love."

My lips curled in a smile. "You think she would?"

"I know she would."

I cleared my throat, tears threatening at the backs of my eyes. "Thank you, Susan."

"All right, let's get you out of here before that lord of yours comes looking for you. I don't want to be anywhere near here when he does."

I giggled and then began to load everything into my backpack. I was ready to go a few minutes later, and after a quick goodbye to Susan, I found myself out in the hall with my harpy guards.

"Lord Arafel offers his apologies. He had to attend to an issue on the wall and believed you might be happier meeting him in the entryway."

My stomach dropped at the memory of standing on the wall when we'd arrived. Arafel was a smart male. I nodded.

"Could you tell me how to get there?"

Both bowed deeply to me, making my eyebrows lift in surprise, then ushered me forward through the wide hallway. We passed door after door until finally, the hall opened up into a grand entryway. The chandelier above cast a bright, steady light around the room, and I smiled as my feet stepped onto thick, woven black rugs and we passed down the center of the arched room toward double doors twice as tall as Arafel.

Arafel.

He was there, standing by the door, his arms crossed, a bemused expression on his handsome face as I moved closer and closer. The harpies moved away as I passed the center of the room, bowing low to their leader as they did.

"They are bowing for you," Arafel murmured as I got close.

I couldn't stop my arms from sliding around his torso So I could press my face against the leather of his flying armor.

"Not to me, idiot; you're their king, their lord."

"Not anymore," he said with a solemn voice then used his hand to tilt my face up to his. "They bow to the one who will save us."

My heart leapt into my throat. "No pressure."

Arafel's smile was wide, shining. "Never." He captured my hand, bringing it to my lips, eyes dark and lust. "We will conquer this together, Lucia."

My body relaxed into his hold, my hands curling around his as soft, dark lips pressed a kiss against my knuckles.

"All right then, Wings, let's get this show on the road. Before I lose my confidence entirely."

Arafel chuckled at the false bravado in my voice. "After everything that has happened to us, to you, how is it you still fear flying with me so much?" He moved down to a knee, turning his shoulder to gesture that I should climb onto his back.

I crossed my arms. "You want me to ride you?"

The coy look he gave me over his shoulder made my belly curl in delight. "You've already proven yourself quite capable, Lucia. I thought you might be more comfortable starting out this way. If you are not, I will carry you in my arms."

"I feel bad you have to carry me either way. Can't we take a car—er...whatever your equivalent to a car is? Or shadow jump?"

"Because I want to carry you." Arafel turned away from me again, his wings lowering until they swept across the ground at my feet. There was a place along his spine where a long plane of leather ran down his back, between where his wings sprouted from his shoulder blades. I could easily settle there. Biting my lip, I stepped closer. And as soon as my fingers grazed his shoulders, I heard him speak again. "And because I love to have you against me."

I huffed out a small laugh. "You say that now."

"I will say that forever, little soul," he responded. "Hop on."

I didn't hop, but I tried. Leaning forward, I slipped my arms across his shoulders, my nails finding purchase along the seam of his armor even as my legs gripped the back of him. I blushed hot.

"I'm not sure this will work, Arafel."

His laughter was deep and rolling as he straightened. "As soon as I level out, it'll be much smoother."

Arafel nodded to the pair of harpies from my doorway who had reappeared and opened the door wide. I knew in an instant why we hadn't used the front door. It was because there was no path there. At least none a human pair of legs could've traversed. Instead, it was a drop-off into the side of the mountain, a small stream of water trickling down the silver-threaded stone in front us.

"Oh God, oh God, oh God," I chanted, clamping my eyes closed and my legs tight around Arafel.

"As flattered as I am, sweetling," Arafel murmured, his hand sliding up my thigh to providing me extra stability as he moved closer to the edge, "I am no God."

"Arafel, I'm not sure this is—" And then my words died in my throat because as simply as if he might have stepped down a stair in his castle, he stepped right off the side of the cliff.

I didn't scream. Maybe it was because the wind that rushed past us was moving too fast for me to capture it long enough to yell. But it didn't matter. After only a moment, Arafel's massive wings spread wide, slowing our descent.

Under my belly, I felt the pull and flex of the muscles of his back as his wings pumped, taking us up and across the tops of the lush green forest around Castle Fel. I held on tight, keeping my eyes narrowed to slits as Arafel took us away from his castle on the cliff.

"You may open them, Lucia," Arafel said loudly as he leveled out, his wings wide to buffet wind that swept up across the mountain and kept us buoyant as we crossed the area in a blur of deep green and gray.

"It's—" I surprised myself, realizing I'd been staring down. Feeling bold, I pushed my hand against Arafel's shoulders, sitting up ever so slightly and letting myself stare down even more. It was beautiful.

How had I been afraid of this place? This mountain, the lands around it... I glanced behind me at the towering dark towers of

Fel. The Sleeping Mountains were ethereal in their beauty. I turned, staring up into the gray sky above us and felt something bubbling up in my chest, rising inside of me until I couldn't stop it again.

I turned my face to the sky, laughter slipping from my mouth as I slowly released Arafel's shoulders and let my hands drift into the cool air. My fingers trembled, but I held fast to that feeling. And the powerful male under me.

Freedom, sweet and powerful, slipped over my tongue as I watched the sky pass us in a blur. That's what he was giving me. A small taste of freedom. I reset my hands on his shoulders and curled my chin close to my chest.

"Thank you," I whispered to the big male, not sure if he could hear me or not. But it didn't matter. Not really. He knew what he was doing for me, what he'd always been doing for me. Giving me the chance to make my own choices, fight my own fears.

I knew at that moment I would never be able to explain to him what this meant to me. That no matter what happened when we reached the center of Hell, in this moment, I was free.

And loved.

And I would remember that until my last breath. No matter when that was.

19

Lucia

After several hours of flying, my legs grew tired, and my fingertips were numb against Arafel's leathers. He must've sensed my unsteady movements, because even as the sky grew dark silver, he slowed, approaching a barely visible clearing in the Sleeping Mountain's thick tree cover.

His hand slipped back, clutching my thigh as he drew up sharply, landing on the pine needle–covered ground. I slipped down his back, and the moment my soles hit the ground, my knees buckled, and I went down in a heap.

"Lucia!"

I held up a hand as frantic hands ghosted over me in the growing darkness. "I'm fine. I think my legs were asleep."

Arafel's hands slowed but did not leave my body. Instead, they grew in warmth, heating my cool skin until he finally squatted for a moment to scoop me up into his arms. "Allow me, then."

My hands scrabbled for his shoulders. "You're ridiculous," I huffed out finally.

His dark brows rose. "I assure you, no one has ever dared to call me that."

"What if it's true?"

"Even when it's true." Arafel began to walk into the growing darkness. "You seem to have lost a little bit of the inherent fear that most mortal humans feel for me."

"Does that bother you?"

"No," Arafel said calmly. "In my eyes, you have always been my equal. What good is it having an equal if they don't insult you at any given moment?"

"Well, when you say it that way..."

Silence fell, but it was companionable and settled over us like the warmth of a blanket.

"We will be in my father's Court in the morning. I thought perhaps you might like to spend one more evening...just as we are."

I sighed, relieved, making my limbs loose. "Yes, please. Let's do that."

Arafel carried me forward, one powerful arm under my body even as his other twisted in the air. I gasped sharply as a small cabin came into view.

"Did you create a cabin? Just now?"

Arafel looked down at me, handsome face confused. "What?"

"Like whip it into existence?" I felt my cheeks flush a little at how insane I sounded.

Arafel chuckled, his chest vibrating against me. "No, I simply removed the glamor hiding it from view. Do you think you can stand now?"

"Yes, thanks."

Arafel slowly released me, letting me slide down every inch of his chest and body until I was staring up at him, my body tingling, aching, and tight from the presence of his skin against mine.

"Arafel..."

"Come in, Lucia. Let's get you settled."

I bit down on my lip, letting the demon usher me in through the door. Arafel spoke a single strange word into the dark interior, and fire bloomed in the fireplace. Light filled the small cabin, displaying a closed door that I assumed led to the bathroom on one end of the main room, which included an Arafel-sized bed, a dresser, a series of small cabinets, and a fireplace that took up one entire wall.

Everything was perfectly clean, the velvet coverlet on the bed and the shining kitchen counters so at odds with the rustic exterior.

"So, this is glamping," I commented dryly.

Arafel laughed, moving across the room to stand before the fire, his fingers skimming quickly across his leather armor. "Is it?"

"Not that I would know, but it seems like the right word. What is this place anyway?" Without further preamble, I made my way across the wooden floor to Arafel, gently brushed his hands away, and continued to unknot the leather ties and buckles keeping his armor across his broad chest. The task warmed my fingers as I went, and as much as I wasn't ready to admit it, being far from Arafel unsettled me.

His scent calmed me, his presence driving a power in me that I had never felt before.

"We are quite close to the borders of several of the Underworld realms. When I first took on the role as the dream king, I wanted nothing to do with Fel. It was busy, chaotic. The Brotherhood used to use this area for training, so it made sense to have a cabin here to use while I was here to oversee the Brotherhood."

"What lands are we close to, then?"

"Kharon rules the land on the other side of the mountain. You've probably seen parts of his river meeting the waterfall."

I nodded.

"Don't be deceived... His river is as vast and wide as a sea in some places. Quite beautiful too." Arafel kneeled down to help me lift the shoulder coverings off of his body with a soft grunt. "Nephesh's realm is nearby, on the other side of the Court of Hell."

"He is the punisher?"

Arafel hesitated by the chair, his armor hanging from his fingertips. "No, that would be Elon. Nephesh is the judge who decides where souls reside once they come here."

"That sounds stressful."

Arafel turned, shrugging. "We each have our purpose. I am the reformer. I speak to their dreams, show them what could happen should they not change their future. Nephesh sorts the souls into those who are ready to be reincarnated, or who might be better fit to spend time here in the Underworld, and then there are those who are sent to Elon for punishment."

I nodded, fascinated by his descriptions.

"Those are the most difficult souls, and the most stressful, as you said, task between us all. Elon was the most powerful of all of us. And I think Father did that because it would take the most from him." Arafel looked back to me with his expressive blue eyes and said, "In many ways, I think my youngest brother deserves to find happiness more than any of us."

"Will I meet them at the Court? Elon? Nephesh?"

Arafel nodded. "I believe they will be there. As for Kadmiel, he's farther away and therefore not a problem that I'm ready to introduce you to. Yet."

I laughed, walking to stand before him. "After we figure out how to extract your soul, you are formally required to introduce me to everyone."

Something dark passed his features, but it was gone before I could register. "Of course."

"Arafel," I said as he showed me his back, tugging his shirt over his head as he turned. "Did I say something?"

"No, not at all. Why don't you tell me more about what you found in Lucifer's letters?"

"Oh, of course." I moved quickly to the backpack I had dropped when I had moved over to help him with his armor. I opened the pack with a jerk of my fingers and dug in, my finger moving over clothing, clothing, and even more clothing.

I gritted my teeth, turning my pack upside down until it spilled out onto the floor. Where I thought I had packed the heavy book, there was only clothing item after clothing item of silken nightgowns and that blasted velvet gown.

"Susan," I muttered under my breath. "I can't believe you."

"Is everything all right?"

I sighed, glancing back at the fireplace to where Arafel had moved and was momentarily struck dumb by the way his body was carved, beautiful and impossible against the flickering flames. My mouth went dry as my gaze coasted over his naked upper body, following the lines of his body all the way to where the cut of muscles of his hips directed me straight down to the laces holding his trousers on.

"Lucia," he growled. "Unless you want to be thoroughly ravished, you need to stop staring at me like that this instant."

"I…" I cleared my throat. "I-I must've forgotten the book." Even though I knew I hadn't. I'd been duped by Susan and her conspiratorial ways.

Arafel cocked his head, horns casting wicked shadows over the wall behind him. My thighs clenched, and I felt my body tighten deep inside.

Deep where I wanted him.

He took a shuddering breath in and then released it, his entire body growing as if engorged on my presence alone. "Lucia, you smell like sin."

"I'm trying to tell you that Susan switched out the book and potentially the solution to all our problems within it."

Arafel prowled closer. "But what if I'm more focused on the current problem?"

"And that is?"

"How far away you are from me?" Arafel stepped into my space, his arm wrapping around my lower back to raise me up until I was pressed against him, hip to hip. I could feel the thick, heavy aroused part of him against me.

"Problem solved," I whispered, my mouth tilting up for his kiss. Begging for his kiss. There was so much relief in his acceptance of our mutual needs and desires.

I wanted him.

He wanted me.

Whether it was because we shared his soul was still to be determined. Maybe that was something the Court of Hell could elaborate on. My cheeks flushed as I briefly wondered how I would bring that up. But then Arafel was grinding against me, and all traces of thought slipped from my mind.

Replaced with only him.

In a delightful blur of pleasure, I felt him pick me up entirely. I still hadn't gotten used to how he handled me. I was nothing compared to him in mass or size, but the way he held me sent shivers down my body. It was a blatant reminder of our differences and how much I liked them.

He was a demon, Lord of the Underworld, created for one purpose and only that. And yet, he was so much more. And every moment I spent in his company only solidified my belief that

Arafel was the most amazing creature I'd ever had the pleasure to know.

And no matter how long I was able to stay in the Underworld with him, it would never seem like enough.

"Lucia," Arafel whispered against my skin, the tone in his voice rough and grating.

Desire pounded through me, responding to tangible need in his expression. "Arafel, I need you."

He growled, his fingers pinching into my thighs as I wrapped my legs around his waist and tightened my arms around his head. His short, heavy locks were silky in my hands. His claws rose to my back, freeing me of my shirt in a snarl and rip of clothing. The next moment, his mouth was on my breasts, lips hot and eager as they tasted and suckled on me.

I cried out, arching and grabbing frantically for something to ground me as my core clenched, begging to be filled.

"I'd never let anything hurt you," he murmured to me.

I needed him to prove it. On the eve before I faced what every human on Earth feared, I needed it. I grabbed his horns, the rough texture exactly what I wanted as my fingers wrapped around the curling ram's horns tight. I needed to hold him to me, to make sure that he'd never stop.

I didn't expect the bellowed response from the male against me. "Fuck, Lucia, you can't—" He was practically choking on the words. "You can't grab my horns."

"Why not? You seem to like it..." I couldn't help the teasing tone that snuck into my voice.

He growled again. "You have no idea what might happen." He swallowed, and for a moment, I felt a twinge of guilt. He was worried. I loosened my grip on his horns but didn't let go.

"I could hurt you."

"You would never."

Fangs flashed. "I might *want* to hurt you."

My heartbeat thrummed in the fingers I had pressed against his horns; heat bloomed in my body everywhere we touched. I took a moment, wondering. I felt no fear, not even at his confession. In fact, I was inflamed by it.

"I was made for you, Arafel, and I want to be owned by you. In every way." I tightened my hold. "Do not hide yourself from me."

Our eyes met, his piercing blue burning into mine. One of his hands rose to stroke down my cheek. "The things I could do to you, Lucia. The things I could make you believe and make you feel."

"I'm not afraid.

Arafel's fingers tightened on my chin, forcing me to look him straight in the eye. "How many times have I told you? You should be."

And then my back slammed into the wall, the smooth wood cool against my burning skin. I had only a second to determine that Arafel had magicked away my clothes before his mouth was back on my breast.

I tightened my hold, making his hips jerk under my ass. He was grinding against me, and I could feel the tip of his cock brushing against my center.

"I want you inside me." Using my grip on his horns, I writhed against him, making my clit surge with pleasure.

He snarled, his claws tracing over the curve of my waist as he pushed my hips wider. "And you will have me." One hand slipped between us, pressing over my lower belly as he growled again, the sound growing more feral by the second. "Made for me," he murmured, and heat from his hand sank into my body.

I didn't know what he had done, but I knew instinctively that he'd done something. Before I could ask, or even wonder, his cock was pressing into me, bold and strong and so large that It stole both my breath and thought.

The thick head of him slipped inside me, and without hesitation, Arafel thrust deep inside me, retreating only partially before fucking me deep again. My back arched and bumped against the wall as far as he powered into me. Unlike the first times I'd been with him, there was no restraint here. Only raw want and pleasure sweeping me away.

The length of him ground up against my clit every time he filled me, making me cry out. My body was clenching around him, desperate to keep him deep inside me yet thrilled each time he thrusts back in. My mind was already leaping ahead to the way he'd flooded me, the way his face and body contorted with pleasure right before he locked us together.

My eyes slammed shut, my orgasm barreling in on me. "Yes, Arafel, please. I want it all."

His snarl was that of an animal, his claws on my hips and thighs sharp. I reveled in it and the way his desperate body moved against mine. Bliss was nearly pain this time as I dug my nails into his shoulders, letting my convulsing body choke down on his cock. I wanted him to feel this with me, experience this with me.

Because there was no way it would ever be like this with another.

He claimed I was made for him. But as he bellowed out his completion, his hips thrusting deep and holding, I knew that was a lie.

He was made for *me*.

20

Arafel

I should've heard them coming. I knew every inch of this land, every soul visiting it and each creature who called it home. But I had been distracted, holding Lucia in the warm water of a nearby spring. We had only just returned when the bitter smell of anger and jealousy filled my nose.

Snarling, I stepped in front of Lucia, letting my body block her from the hungry gaze of the demons who moved into the cabin with us. My heart pounded in my veins, making my temper short.

"You go too far this time, commander."

The demon in front, his rank and status denoted by the layers of gold chains draped across his armored chest. Commander Alecto, my father's favorite killing machine. Merely having him within sight of Lucia made my mouth dry and my body tighten with worry.

"I go as far as your father sends me, my King of Dreams."

Commander Alecto and two other lesser demons stepped into the cabin. I growled, and I could feel Lucia's hand on my back.

"Arafel, who is this?"

I wanted to tell her to get back in bed, that I was going to dispose of these creatures and then I wanted to go straight back into what we were doing before. But I knew I couldn't. Because these were my father's demons. Unlike my brothers and me, if I attacked them, they would reappear in my father's Court alive and ready to come back here to bother us again.

"They," I said through gritted teeth, "are my father's personal guard."

"They don't look much like the Brotherhood," she whispered back.

"The Brotherhood serves the lords, my lady," Commander Alecto said with a sanguine smile. "We serve a god."

"Oh, well, excuse me," Lucia said, and for a moment I could see the indecision on Commander Alecto's face as he considered my soul mate.

Then he finally nodded. "You're excused, but you need to come with us."

I didn't move. "We aren't going anywhere. It's late, and Lucia needs her rest."

Alecto's eyes narrowed. The look he cast Lucia's way was growing more curious by the moment. Dread curled in my chest as he flared his nostrils, taking in both of our scents. Ruby red eyes snapped back to me, wicked glee in his expression. I met it boldly, unafraid of my father's favorite soldier or my feelings for the human at my side.

"How interesting, Lord Arafel." Alecto straightened his shoulders. "But nevertheless, she can sleep on the way."

"She can sleep where she is." I could feel Lucia step behind me, her hands flat along my back as if she could sense the danger in my words. My wings were glamoured away. They would be a hindrance in this small of a space.

The two demons still standing outside the cabin slowly drew long, dark blades from their scabbards. I bristled, my muscles twisting and growing under my clothing. They were threatening my mate, threatening her life.

"Leave us."

Alecto sighed, turning to his soldiers. "Stand down. It's not worth us getting sliced to bits. Let the girl sleep here, then, Arafel. I assumed you'd have better sense about this."

I growled.

"After all, you are coming to the Court to ask for your father's help, correct? It doesn't make as much sense for your first interaction in a dozen years to be born of all this misguided anger."

"Misguided?"

Alecto grinned slyly. "You always were the quiet one, Arafel. I assumed you would fall in line more easily than this."

My claws raked through the air where he'd stood only a few moments ago. But he and the two demons beside him were rapidly backing out of the cabin, all with matching smirks on their dark lips.

"Out," I ordered, my magic rushing down my arms and forming glowing blue flames in my palms. I was done with their visit and the carefully hidden threat they presented. If they didn't understand what kind of male I was, they would soon.

"As you wish, Lord Arafel," Alecto said. "We will see you soon." And with a heavy-lidded wink, the demon general closed the door with a flick of his burgundy tail.

Lucia let out a long breath, her form wilting. "Well, he's a real peach."

"Yes." I moved across the room to watch their retreat from the small window. "He has always been a delight."

"He's a high demon, though, right?"

"He is. Crafted by my father to serve one purpose and one purpose only." I sighed as the last of their scents finally disappeared. "Anything Lucifer desires."

"Great. Can't wait to see them again." Her arms slipped around my middle, and I sighed, feeling the light and warmth seep into me once more. I was still mad, angry they'd torn even more time from us. But having them come here, it meant my father was paying attention, that he was interested in what Lucia and I had to say.

That could be a gift or a curse. But I hoped it was the former.

"How much time do we have?" Her forehead pressed into my back, and I longed to pull her back into my arms. To bury myself inside her until I no longer had to worry about my father, his guard, or even the seemingly impossible task of extracting my soul from within her.

"Not enough. It'll never be enough."

Warm breath ghosted against my back. "But we have tonight?"

"We do."

"Then let's not spend it wishing for something else."

I turned then, letting her arms go slack until she was loosely holding on to my hips. Her eyes burned into mine, and I looked her over, letting my magic find her soul, its glow vibrant and beautiful as ever. When we were like this, it was so easy to see, my soul so easily beckoned by the brightness of her own.

It was in these moments that it was easy to forget that my soul was slowly killing her and that regardless of what we did, there was a chance we would be unsuccessful. And I would be forced to rule my land with half my power and a very broken heart.

***

As the King of Dreams, I didn't require sleep. We were uniquely equipped to survive and thrive in our own realms. But that didn't mean that we didn't enjoy them.

I'd found sleeping with Lucia was one of my existence's rare joys that I was getting more and more attached to. In sleep, she was soft, sweet, and even a little bit dependent. I smiled down at her, stroking the hair from her face. While awake, the woman rarely let me do much of anything for her, but in sleep, I could caress her, hold her, and in her sleepy state, she would sink into me.

Last night I had been tempted to look in on her dreams or perhaps to see if she dreamed at all. But I held back. Even after all we'd shared, it still seemed too intimate an act.

"Is it time to wake up?" Her voice was drowsy, rough with sleep.

"It is."

She moved against me, one lean leg slipping up and around mine. The near constant needs to have her with me roared back to life. Our desire for each other was endless. I'd taken her so many times last night that I'd thought for now my desperation might be temporarily sated.

But I was wrong. Just like the smile she gave or the sweet way she bit her lips while she was thinking about something, I was addicted to this woman. Her hand stole across my torso, and I bit back a smile. It seemed I was not the only one affected by this pull between us.

"But do we have to leave yet?" Lucia's voice was filled with desire as she moved a little closer, the heat of her core warm against my side. My cock was hard in an instant as her fingers ran across my torso. I shivered.

Still, I knew our time was short, and I couldn't risk one of my father's soldiers stumbling in on me while we were immersed inside each other.

I growled thinking of it.

Lucia's arm relaxed, her body going limp. "I'm taking that as a yes."

I rolled us, pushing her beneath my body. "As much as I'd love to stay here for the foreseeable future, we should get going before my father sends more of his minions."

Lucia flashed me a quick smile and then rolled to the side of the bed, rising and letting my eyes wander over every inch of her skin. She was stunning, every line, every freckle. My eyes caught on the redness of skin around her hips and thighs.

I was out of bed a moment later. My hands shook as I reached for her, only to stop short of touching her. "Are these from me?"

"Oh." She looked down, shrugging. "I mean, they must be; I don't think I've hooked up with any other clawed demon lords in the past few...never."

My blood pounded in my head. "I hurt you."

Lucia bit her lip, eyes hot as they looked between us, settling on something around my collarbones. "Come here."

"No." I couldn't stop the anger in my words. For all my warnings, she hadn't listened. And I'd hurt her. I forced myself to take one step back then another.

"Arafel, come here." This time she didn't take no for an answer and towed me over to the bathroom. A mirror mounted on the wall reflected back at me as I looked at her.

"What is it?"

"Turn." Her hands were on my biceps, moving me to stand to the side. "And look!"

I glanced in the mirror, following her pointed finger, and noticed for the first time the red lines marking my shoulders and upper back.

"Oh my gosh, it's so much worse in the light." Lucia bit her lip again, cheeks bright red.

I leaned in, one hand going to trace the lines. "You did this?"

She nodded slowly.

"And you're embarrassed?"

"Maybe not as much as you are over my scratches, but Arafel, it's okay. We didn't hurt each other. We got carried away."

"Carried away," I repeated, eyes fast on the long marks on my neck and shoulders. From her nails, I realized.

"Deeply," Lucia muttered, her cheeks still quite pink.

I was surprised to find that my chest was filling with pride and something akin to joy as I stared at those little red lines. "You claimed me, little soul."

She snorted, ducking her chin.

"I like them."

That got me another sharp look as I settled my hands on her waist. Her fingers traced my jaw, brushing over my lips as she spoke. "Then you have to understand why I like your marks too."

I brushed my thumb over one small scratch across her ribs. "They don't hurt?"

"They don't, and if you're still worried about it, then you can heal me if you'd like."

I stared down. "I'm not sure I dislike them that much anymore."

Lucia laughed. "Good. Perhaps maybe I like seeing them on me too. Reminders of what we shared here."

I gathered her close, tugging her against me. "My father's Court is the most dangerous place in either world, and you are the first living soul to visit it in a very, very long time. Please, promise me you'll let me keep you safe."

"I will try." I narrowed my eyes, and she grinned up at me. "I will try harder," she amended.

"Good." I swatted her on the ass and smiled as she squealed. "Now get some clothes on. We have a devil to impress."

"A devil I wouldn't worry about. But my boyfriend's father? That's a whole other story."

I wrinkled my nose. "I'm not your boyfriend."

"Excuse me?" Her voice carried through to the bathroom, a little high-pitched.

I moved to lean against the bathroom door and stared out at her as she swept her hair into its trademark braid. "You carry half of my soul; I've spent your entire life protecting you and the last two weeks worshiping you. I don't think the title of boyfriend covers it."

Warm blue eyes found mine in the mirror. "What do you want to be called, then?"

I shrugged, my attempt at nonchalance. "I've told you before, I believe you are my soul mate. I prefer that."

"You did, did you?" Lucia strolled toward me, black silk against creamy skin distracting me.

"I did." My cock throbbed against my thigh as she drew close.

Stopping before me, she held a long piece of black velvet in her hands. "How will we know?" Lucia's voice was soft, her vulnerability shining through. "If I'm your soul mate, I mean."

I dropped my head so I could press my lips against her shoulder. "When you are ready, when you know, the bond will fall into place."

"And if you are only feeling this way because of the soul bond?"

I smiled against her skin. "Then the moment my soul is returned, you will have your assurance of my devotion and the promise that our connection goes far deeper than a soul bound."

Lucia's face was a little pale, but she nodded.

"We have time, little soul. And in the meantime." I wrapped her around her waist, palming the soft skin of her belly and hip. "I will continue to give you a preview of what life as my mate would be."

Her breath hitched, but her face was brighter as she slipped her fingers between mine. We stood there for a long breath, grasping at the soothing connection between us.

"Thank you, Arafel." She swatted at my hand. "Get out of my way, demon lord. I've got a whole lot of buttons and zippers to fasten."

Her hands shoved at me, and I moved willingly, watching as she smiled at me widely and closed the door.

I moved to the bags we'd left on the floor, finding my usual white garb folded neatly at the bottom. With a flick, I freed it from our packing and onto my body. I wasn't changing much to do with my wardrobe for today. My father could see me anytime he liked. And while I knew that Lucia wanted to make a good impression, I was past the point of trying to impress my father. That motivation died a few hundred years ago.

"I'm ready. What do you think?"

I turned, staring. Lucia stood in the doorframe, her features bisected by shadows. Beautiful and bright, the sensuous curve of her lips enough to drive any male to his knees. She stepped toward me, the long, body-fitting burgundy gown showcasing the graceful ease at which she moved, the delicious curve of hip and breast that made every part of me stiffen. She took my breath away. "You look incredible."

She flushed a little again, dark hair swinging forward as she ducked her chin, and I found myself liking it even more than before. "Thank you."

I moved to stand before her, unable to stop myself from tracing the neckline of her dress, the sloping lines illuminating her collarbones. "You will be the envy of everyone in Court."

She paled then, and I raised my brows. "What did I say?"

"Envy? As in they will want me too?"

"Is that so odd, Lucia?"

"Because I assumed you were an anomaly. I didn't realize that would be the norm."

"The Underworld has always been fascinated with humans. And you, my dear, are the picture of everything they want to know about a human. You're beautiful, powerful, kind, and smart."

She gave me a funny look. "They aren't going to want to eat me or something?"

I swallowed back the laugh that rose in my chest. "You've clearly seen too many bad horror movies. They are well fed by my father. The only thing they will hunger for is more of your time and attention."

Lucia blinked up at me through those sooty dark lashes. "Which they can't have."

I growled. "Correct."

She smiled in agreement, moving to the door, where she slipped into a pair of knee-high boots Susan must've packed, and then she smoothed the dress back down. "What did you mean about powerful? Compared to you and your family, I'm only special because of your soul."

I rubbed at the back of my neck. "I did want to talk to you about this."

She looked deeply suspicious. "Which part?"

"You've been showing some interesting capabilities."

"What do you mean?"

"This showed up last night, after we—"

Lucia moved toward me, taking the heavy book I held out. "Lucifer's book of letters. How did this get here?"

"Like I said, you've been showing some interesting capabilities since you came to the Underworld. You said you left this book back at the manor, and yet, only minutes after you wished it was here, it showed up here."

"Showed up?" Lucia glanced down at the pages. "You mean, like you do, pull things from the air."

"That's not quite how I do it, but yes. My realm is mine to form and use, and until you arrived, not even my brothers have been capable of changing that."

"I don't know how I did that, though. The book or whatever else you're thinking of."

"And yet you did."

Her mouth snapped open and closed a few times before she finally cleared her throat. "What does that mean? Is there more?"

"I'm not sure what it means. But I probably should've told you that the manor you dreamt into life with you arrived here, it was the first time in decades any mortal soul has been able to build something that size without my permission and assistance."

"But I didn't do anything. I just showed up, and it was here."

"Exactly my point. You are doing things lower-level demons would never be able to do. And that it took me years to finesse into existence." I stroked a hand over one of her arms, watching as goose bumps covered her skin. "I don't know what it means. Perhaps it's the half of my soul inside you, enabling you to do things in my realm. But either way, we need to be careful. My father is incredibly curious. He will find these new…skills…very interesting."

She nodded solemnly. "Mum's the word."

21

Lucia

When Arafel set us down in the entryway of the Court of Hell, I didn't bother to hide my shock. This place was gothic architecture at its finest, a blend of Dracula's castle and Disney World, with its hundreds of windows, balconies, and seemingly endless turrets and buildings. All surrounded by an obsidian wall that I knew was more than size. There was power in it too. I could feel it on my skin, humming against my mind as Arafel walked us under the arched gate.

A demon met us there, his handsome features marred by a variety of scars. I tried not to stare, but he caught me anyway and sent me a fanged smile that made shivers race down my spine.

These were not like Arafel; however much he might call himself a demon, he was not like these creatures who scratched and clawed the earth with uncovered talon-tipped feet. The wings on their backs were webbed like a bat, and I could see the shimmer of claws at every joint.

They were weapons, powerful ones. And they were waiting for us.

"I thought your father would be more welcoming."

Arafel's jaw was set. "They are not for us."

"Who are they here for?"

He didn't answer. Tucking my arm against his side, he guided me closer to the second set of doors. Were they here because of this Drude they all worried about? Or the Drude's legion of Corrupted?

"Later," Arafel murmured, brushing his lips over my wind-tossed hair.

I nodded, letting him guide me up the slab stone steps. These must lead inside, and as we approached, the flock of demons bristled and moved away.

Arafel's glare kept them silent, but only a blind woman wouldn't notice the way their eyes rolled over me.

"Such a pretty soul," one dared to whisper from the back.

Arafel's fingers flew, a dark shadow leaping from his palm to wrap around the creature's throat, the smoke solidifying until it was clasping the demon high off the ground. His fellow soldiers were silent, eyes on Arafel as he tilted his head.

"You will never speak of her again," Arafel said quietly, his words whipping across the courtyard. "Nor shall you see her."

And then the demon's eyes were gone, the deep-red flesh there smooth and fresh, and it was as if he'd never had them to begin with. Horror and shock rolled over my chest as the demon screamed. The other demons around us backed away hurriedly, casting a more interested glance at Arafel.

Reeling at what Arafel had done, I stepped toward the inner castle. "Arafel." My voice was too small.

But he heard me anyway, his powerful shoulders relaxing as he came to join me. A powerful gray hand slipped around my waist, holding me tightly to him.

"Don't look back," he said in a deep voice.

I could hear the crunch of a body against stone as the demon fell back to the ground in a heap. The others crowed in delight as they shuffled toward their downed fellow.

"You took his eyes."

Arafel leaned in, his breath warm against my neck. "I would do much more to keep their words and wickedness away from you."

I swallowed, my hand falling to the powerful muscles of his torso; under my palm, Arafel's heart raced. "They did not know who I belonged to, but now they do."

His claws swept over my face, brushing my hair away from my eyes. His gentleness was so at odds with the screeching creature beyond those doors.

"What would you do to protect me?'

He slowed, turning to stop us in the front hallway. All around us, commotion raged, and behind us, the eyeless demons still screeched. "You want to know what I would do to protect you?" His lips curled in a deadly smirk. "I will burn worlds, sweetling."

"Worlds? Why?"

"Because I'd rather drown in flames than let you go through another thing that causes you pain."

"You can't protect me from everything."

His smirk turned victorious. "Yes, I can."

With an exaggerated roll of my eyes, I pushed back and stared down the wide hall. Ahead of us, the door to Lucifer's Court loomed, the black iron fixtures dark even in the Underworld's strange brightness. Even as I looked at it, I felt as if it pulled at me, curious.

Arafel's face was turned too, watching the doors carefully. His hand dropped to curl around my waist, pulling me closer to him.

The words were unspoken, but I could feel them as surely as the screams from the demon behind us. There was one thing Arafel couldn't protect me from. And we were about to meet him face to face.

I dropped my hand to press against his arm and before us the massive doors began to swing open.

The Court of Hell was opening to us.

Mom and I hadn't been churchgoers, but that didn't mean I had any less of a stereotypical impression of what I thought Lucifer might be like. He was a fallen angel, a powerful entity all on his own, the ruler of the Underworld. And Arafel's father.

The ruler of these lands.

And my last chance at finding out how to separate Arafel's soul from my own.

The door swung wide, and I walked in side by side with Arafel. He had shortened his step to be on pace with mine, and I wasn't sure if he was doing it to make me feel better, or whether he was truly concerned for our safety. Either way, I reveled in his closeness as we neared his father's throne.

The throne itself was shining, glimmering in the room, brightly lit by a variety of black iron chandeliers swinging from the vaulted ceiling above. The candles that flickered there glowed as bright as any from my world, but they were cast in a strange black glow.

And seated on that throne was the most surprising version of the devil I'd ever imagined.

Lucifer was dressed in a three-piece black suit, his smooth black hair combed back from a roguishly handsome face. He looked more like a mafia kingpin than the biblical King of the Dead.

And the smile he was sending us... It wasn't the wicked pull of sharp teeth or red lips. It was warm, full of what appeared to be an authentic welcome.

"My son," he boomed, a deep voice echoing off the walls of the chamber.

Arafel's grip on me tightened before it released, and he fell to a knee before the throne. "Father. I hope you are well?"

Lucifer stood, his eyes darker than any human I'd ever met.

I flinched the first time they searched over me, not bothering with my gaze or my permission. He was a king, and I was a citizen regardless.

"I am better now, Arafel. It has been decades since we have spoken face to face. Why is that?"

Lucifer descended the stairs before his throne, his fair fingers swirling in the air to one side. Arafel didn't answer, and I didn't think Lucifer was actually looking for an answer. "I think it is because of this soul here, the one you brought to me."

He strolled right up to me, and it took every ounce of willpower in my body to keep my feet where they were and wait for Lucifer to stand before me. His hands, cold and smooth, tipped my chin up to look at him. "After all these years, you found her." He tutted softly. "I am impressed. You've done a far better job than Nephesh did."

There was a noise from one side, but I didn't dare to look. My mouth went dry at the mention, and I was reminded vividly of the letters between Nephesh and Lucifer and then the early days after the woman who had Arafel's brother's soul inside her. She had died, leaving a legacy of unknowns and a demon without his soul once more.

"Father..."

"No matter. She is here now. What do you plan to do with her?"

Arafel blinked up at his father.

"And for Hell's sake, boy, stand up." Lucifer strolled back to his throne and sat down, crossing his legs at the knee and looking at us both.

"Lucia and I—" Arafel began, his hands spread wide and relaxed.

"Lucia," Lucifer interrupted. "What a lovely name. You know it means light, correct? Light Walker. That was your name."

"It still is."

Lucifer's short breath wasn't a laugh, but his face relaxed. "Perhaps. But you are so much more, aren't you?"

My veins pulsed then, filled with ice as I stared down the King of the Underworld. Arafel remained at my side, his immense body tight with anxiety. Lucifer finally broke his stare with me and looked to one side. A jerk of his smooth chin brought a servant forward—a soul, much like Susan, who moved to his side hurriedly.

"Prepare rooms for Lord Arafel and his...soul."

A rolling growl slipped from Arafel, but his father pretended not to notice, watching the soul as it hurried from the room.

"We are having dinner tonight, all of us together. Be sure to be there." Lucifer's eyes snapped to Arafel's. "Her too. Do you understand?"

"Yes."

"Good." The smooth smile reappeared on Lucifer's face. "You may go, Arafel. We will talk soon." Looking past his son, the king gestured for whomever had entered behind us to come in. Arafel's arm was around my waist and pulling me quickly against him as we moved through a throng of faces and creatures. I could barely see in the dark corners. But perhaps that was best.

If Arafel was this worried, that meant I should be infinitely more scared than I was. We slipped through a tall black door, a miniature of the grand entrance we'd entered through. I could feel the atmosphere around us change the moment we made it to the hallway.

The corridor was empty, lit by flickering sconces along the smooth black walls.

Arafel turned to me, his face grave and tense. "Are you all right?"

Was I? I could've happily gone my entire life without meeting the devil, but since I couldn't go back and undo the experience, there wasn't much else to do. I nodded. "A little shaky."

"He was in a good mood."

"That's a good mood?"

Arafel chuckled, his head dropping to press against my forehead. "Yes, Lucia, that was a good mood. The man is the definition of vengeance and sin. The fact that I didn't have to make a deal to get through his doors is a miracle all on its own."

I was nodding again, my hands sliding up his chest. "Dinner tonight?"

I felt his chest rumble with a growl. "Yes, dinner. My brothers will surely be in attendance."

"Maybe that's good. We can all think of a way to extract your soul."

"Nothing good ever came from having a family dinner with my brothers."

"Maybe this will be the first," I said, trying to think of another positive but coming up empty. I flopped my hands to the side. "I'm trying."

"I know," Arafel said, his claws winding down my arms in a soothing motion. "You don't know how he can be."

"I'm about to find out though, aren't I?"

The big demon breathed out, and I took that as a yes.

I watched goose bumps rise along the skin where his claws traced patterns. "Can we go home?" There was a wistfulness in my voice I didn't recognize.

"Yours or mine?" he responded, his voice even softer.

"Anywhere you go, I go."

"Deal."

Something sparked across my lips, and for a moment, I drew away from Arafel to press a hand to my lips. I looked around, but there was nothing around us or on us that would've shocked me like that. After a moment and an odd look from Arafel, I shoved it out of my mind.

The servant from earlier had come back and, with a low bow, offered in short vocalizations to show us to our rooms. Arafel situated himself between me and the Court of Hell at my back then nodded.

And so began my first, and hopefully last, stay in the house of Lucifer.

22

Lucia

I wasn't sure what I expected from the home of the devil. But from the few hours that I'd been here, I knew one thing for sure. The Bible and cinematic universe had gotten it all wrong. This wasn't a world of chaos and sin, but rather a fully functioning world, an empire perhaps. And while there was a devil on the throne here, it didn't take away from the fact that today he'd acted like any other parent or perhaps authority figure when Arafel and I had been presented.

It had been awkward.

Not scary. Not worrisome. *Awkward.*

Even more so afterward when the soul servant had shown us down the winding corridors to two identical doors. When the door swung open to reveal a plush interior, reminiscent of a high-end hotel suite, I had stepped in. Not realizing that when Arafel tried to follow me in, the soul slipped between us, holding his hands up in a defensive manner.

"What is this?"

"His Majesty specifically requested you take the room next door."

I snorted back a laugh as Arafel's jaw flexed. "The devil is shaming us about sharing a room?"

The soul's patient face grew more translucent, as if he were longing to disappear from right in front of us.

"Don't you dare," Arafel growled again, his fist landing on the soul's nearly invisible shoulder and holding tight. Around his claws, the soul bloomed fresher, in a more vivid color. My eyes flashed to that strange, beautiful reaction to his magic.

"Tell me why my father is keeping us separated."

The soul smiled patiently. "It is for her own good."

"Why?"

"Can you imagine, Your Highness, what would happen should your brothers stumble upon the fact you've found the other half of your soul?" The soul's eyes jumped to me and back to Arafel again. "And that she's here, right under their noses?"

Fear kicked in my gut. Did Lucifer think so lowly of his own children that he wanted to hide me? I wet my suddenly dry lips. "You're not separating us... You're hiding me."

The soul nodded, and Arafel released him with a short, angry curse.

"Fine. Be gone."

The soul skittered away, or as much as a footless, legless ghost could, moving to hover in the air by the second door a few strides away.

Arafel's body was shifting, his muscles flexing and rolling under the gray skin. I could feel the indecision, the concern over my safety. "I don't like this," he said finally.

Something in his voice made me laugh. Stepping up so that I could feel the warmth of his body settling over me, I looked up into his face. "It's a little space. Besides, there's only a wall between us. I'm sure if something goes sideways, a little stone won't keep you from me."

Arafel snorted. "It would take much more than these walls to stop me. But..." Arafel ran a claw over the stone of the walls. "These are no ordinary walls."

I put my hand over his. "I highly doubt anything in this place is ordinary."

"Even more reason to keep you close."

I raised a brow; my earlier fear lessened as his breath wafted over my face. I turned my face up for a kiss. "I'll be okay, Arafel."

Arafel's only answer was to lean in, brushing my lips in a light, brief kiss. "Try to relax, I'll have your dress for tonight brought over later."

I cocked my head sideways but then nodded. "I'll see you soon."

I stepped into the room, closing the door between us before I lost all confidence. And then, staring at the dark, obsidian door there, I instantly regretted my actions.

But there was no turning back. I fell into my room, lounging on the bed for a long minute before finding my bags stacked by the corner. On a whim, I moved to take out the book of letters again, my fingers searching out the markers I'd had in earlier.

I still felt like I was missing something obvious.

But what?

I flopped back on my bed, groaning. This was all too much right now. A thousand thoughts swirled in my head as I lay there. Lucifer, the Court of Hell, the Brotherhood, corrupted creatures, even the swirling need the incubus had ignited in me.

I wasn't the same person Susan had run to a few weeks ago. That girl, she would've crumbled at this point. As much as I'd grown, I was still tempted to run as well.

As soon as the thought broke over my mind, Arafel's face appeared in my mind, as clear as if he was in front of me. He was tense, like usual, I thought with a smile, but there was something so dear, so beloved in his face that I couldn't stop thinking about him.

About what he'd made me feel in such a short time.

He had protected me my entire life. The part of his soul that swirled around in my body demanded it. But every moment we spent together, I knew there was more. Had I perhaps hit the destiny jackpot, being both a carrier for a demon lord's soul and his perfectly designed mate?

The way he looked at me made me hope it was possible. That *we* were possible. Because in my heart, human or monster or demon, he was still as much mine as I was his.

A knock sounded from my door, and I rolled off the bed to see who it might be.

"These people think of everything, except for peep holes," I muttered, pushing my ear against the door for a moment. I laughed at myself then, because what would my normal, pitiful human ears do for me at this situation?

Absolutely nothing.

"Well, here goes," I responded to myself, slinging the door open wide. There was nothing in this castle that should want to hurt me.

Emphasis on *should*. I held tightly to this belief as my eyes met the stare of my visitor, and every instinct inside of me clamored to slam the door once again.

Standing there, his body gnarled, skin red and pulled tightly over a too bony frame, was a demon. Not one from the legion standing guard, as he didn't wear the uniform that Lucifer's soldiers had worn. He was dressed in an expensive-looking robe, the black fabric highlighting the deep-ruby tone of his skin.

"Ma'am," he growled, the word barely understandable.

"Uh." I looked down the corridor but saw no signs of anyone. I glanced at Arafel's sealed door for a moment. "Hello there."

The demon bobbed his head, the slick black braid that ran down the back of his head visible as he took a step toward me. He was small for a demon, maybe only my height, but there was no mistaking the ropes of tight muscle that covered every visible inch of him.

"My name is Hiram." The demon held up a garment bag. "I beg your pardon, my lady, but I was asked to bring you a dress for tonight."

I stared at him; this creature, he was a servant.

"Thank you." I steadied my nerves and then reached out to grasp the garment from his claws.

"He did not want you to feel underdressed or underprepared."

"For dinner?"

Hiram's eyes had no iris, just pure black. But instead of the madness or darkness I'd expected, there was shrewd intelligence shining back at me. I got the feeling this servant was more than he seemed. "His Majesty prefers to keep a formal dining table."

I stared at him. "Do I need hells? I mean, heels?"

The quickest flash of a smile curled one side of his lips before it was gone again. "They are already in your room."

I was too afraid to take my eyes off Hiram to look over my shoulder, so I settled for a nod.

"Thank you," I echoed again, unsure.

"It was my pleasure." Hiram bowed, sending a huff of tangy, metallic air over me. Blood, I realized. He smelled like blood. The realization cooled my appreciation toward him, and I was even more scared to turn my back to go into my room.

But the demon wasn't leaving. He simply remained in that half-bent position, his face to the smooth dark floors.

Gritting my teeth, I took a step back, then another, until I was in my doorway. I felt the subtle magic there, washing over my skin as I stepped in. Arafel had been correct. There was magic in these walls. Its pulsing touch lingered on my flesh as I crossed the threshold once more.

"Goodbye," I whispered and then turned to swirl around the door and slam it shut. Hiram's shining eyes met mine the moment before the door closed, and I got the distinctive feeling he was laughing at me, right before I covered my face with my hands and sank into a hysterical heap against the door.

Several deep breaths later, I realized that I was still clutching the dress and probably wrinkling it. With a grunt, I pushed myself up and off the floor then moved to lay the dress out over the rumpled bedding.

My jaw dropped. There was no way this was the dress Arafel wanted me to wear. This male who had wanted me to remain quiet and out of the way that ensured his brothers wouldn't be interested in me.

But then again, he promised he would send something for me to wear.

I reached out, my finger slipping over the glossy red satin. The dress was gorgeous, at least what was left of it after the designer had carved out chunk after chunk of fabric. It would no doubt leave little to the imagination.

I never would've worn this a few weeks ago.

Which was why, when I found a pair of strappy black heels sitting against the window, I took a deep breath and threw all my clothes in a pile by the door.

Whoever I was before Arafel brought me here, that girl was weak, unsure, and content to wait for life to pass her by.

I wasn't that girl anymore. I carried a demon's soul. I was beloved by a powerful mate. It was time to act like it. The dress slipped over my body like it had been made for me. Which perhaps it had been.

I tied up the straps of the shoes, feeling the bite against the skin of my calves. And when I stood in front of the mirror of my room, I looked every part a demon's mate.

I put a small bit of makeup on, smudging the lines around my eyes and darkening my lips. Leaning back, I was pretty pleased with my appearance.

When there was a knock at the door, I answered it, finding Paran standing there. He blinked several times, staring at me up and down as I stepped into the corridor. I reached for the Brotherhood soldier to enfold him in a hug, but something in his gaze stopped me.

"Paran?"

"You look—" his throat bobbed "—smoldering."

I laughed. "It is dinner with the devil. Isn't that fitting?" My confidence coursed through my veins.

"It is." Paran offered his elbow carefully, and I took it. "I'll walk you down there."

"Thanks. You really don't have to do that," As much as I appreciated the steadiness of the warrior at my side, I always felt like perhaps I was a burden to Paran more than the others.

"No, trust me, I do."

We turned yet another corner, confirming that I was completely and maddingly confused by this Court's layout. "Is Arafel already there?"

"Yes. His father wanted to speak to them before dinner began."

"Them?"

"The King of Dreams, the Punisher, and the Judge. They arrived shortly before you did."

That meant Nephesh was here, the only other brother who had found his soul before. As for the Punisher, I knew very little about him. "Nicknames?"

Paran sent me a savage smile. "When you've been around as long as they have been, you receive a wide variety of names. These are simply some of the ones who have stuck over time."

I swallowed instead of responding. And after another short passageway, we were standing in front of yet another arched doorway. This door was nearly translucent, and I could see figures moving behind it.

"This is the dining room." Paran hesitated. "I wasn't supposed to come in with you. But…" He cast a wary glance over me once more, and my cheeks heated. "I might need to."

"Why?" I smoothed a hand down the front of my dress, feeling the satin and my skin under my palm. "What's wrong?"

The brother sighed. "I pity the first person who happens to look at you, light walker."

"Excuse me?"

"Because I have a feeling the King of Dreams might kill them for it. Brother or not." Paran hesitated, bouncing on the balls of his feet. "I'm guessing no one mentioned that possessiveness between soul mates can get a little heated? Especially in the first few years."

I blinked at him, finally understanding. Arafel may have the best manners of any male I'd met, and he might peel pears and hold hands. But tonight was the first time that I would be in the presence of males he might consider competition. And I was wearing…well…not much.

"Fuck."

"My sentiments exactly."

And then he pushed the doors open wide.

23

Arafel

My father was the very foundation of devilry and strategy. But he was also a smug bastard. And as I sat in a high-back leather chair and watched his servants floating this way and that, refilling Nephesh's and Elon's glasses with wine, I knew something big must be coming.

And I had a horrible feeling it had to do with Lucia.

My brothers had already been in the Court when I arrived with her. I had heard Nephesh's noise of surprise when I introduced Lucia. It hadn't escaped me that my eldest sibling was going to have a lot of questions for me before I was able to leave.

If he could get over that last little skirmish we'd had.

But the way he was sloshing his wine down like it was water made me think it wasn't going to go that way.

"My sons, the pride of the Underworld, I'm glad you could meet me today."

"Was there an option not to, Father?" Elon, the second youngest of my family, sat directly across from me. He was in his human form, the hood of his jacket high and over his face. You could only see the shadows and divots of this form. He had suffered the worst in our initial fights with the Drude, taking a painful-looking curse to the face as he attempted to keep the punished souls, the most dangerous in the Underworld, from being corrupted. I had wondered for years if he had ever bothered to heal himself.

It seemed not.

As the keeper of Tartarus, Elon maintained the farthest realm from my own. I saw him the least but felt his pain the most. It hadn't mattered that Kadmiel was the youngest. Elon was the brother who we had always worried after. The keeper of the darkest souls in our world. It was a job no one wanted, yet he continued to do so without recourse.

I flinched inwardly as I remembered the rare occasion one of his dreams had come to my library.

Pain. Despair. Desperation. They had been full of it. Enough to kill a mortal, but only enough to torture the Lord of Punishment. No, I did not envy him.

"No, Elon, of course there wasn't. When I call, you come." Lucifer had kept his human form as well, and I wondered briefly if I should join the majority. Lucia had not seen me in that form since she was old enough to remember. I had only been this to her. I glanced down at where my black-tipped, gray-clawed hands rested on my thighs.

I would show her someday. But not tonight.

"I need to speak to you about the Drude."

I bristled from my chair, my magic seeping through my skin like black ink. "What of it?"

Lucifer casually looked at his fingernails "The creature continues to evade you, do they not?"

I didn't answer. I didn't need to. For a moment, I considered telling them about Paran's worries over a spy in my realm, but my father went on.

"That's what I thought. We are continuing to notice more and more lost souls throughout the Underworld, and while I believed I knew who was doing this, I have a suspicion that the Drude is only a pawn in a larger plan to infiltrate the human world."

I glared at my father. "You believe the Drude is working for someone else?"

"I do."

"Since when?"

Lucifer's eyes, a dark onyx in his human form, flashed red. A testament to his frustration at me. "Perhaps since they were threatened by the return of your soul. It would make sense to use the Drude's power in the dream realm first, since the creature originated there." My father's jaw flexed. "But now the Corrupted are sweeping across the Underworld."

"You think they are tracking Lucia, don't you?" I could feel my brothers' eyes on me.

"She is the first sign your souls may come back to you. And if you are each finally brought into full power, then there is nothing we cannot do."

Nephesh snorted. "Good thing for the Drude that my brother has no idea how to actually extract his soul from her."

I gritted my teeth until they nearly cracked. "We are working on it and have several options. That's part of the reason we came here. Father, we need to know everything about how you and Mother cast the spell."

Lucifer's brow raised. "That was a very, very long time ago, Arafel." There was a warning under his words. One I chose to ignore.

"The devil is in the details, Father."

Elon made a sort of snorting noise from under his hood. When I glanced his direction, he was completely still once more, only the thick red wine in his cup showing any sign he'd moved.

Desperate to give Lucia news, I forced the words past my fangs. "Please, I know you keep everything recorded. Let us have access to the library."

"My library? Don't you have your own?"

"You and I both know those are two different things."

Lucifer took a loud sip of his wine, purposefully drawing out the moment. "Fine, fine. But now, back to why I asked you here." He paused a moment, likely making sure he had our undivided attention.

"Other than the little Drude situation the two of you created," Lucifer pointed between Nephesh and me. "We have seen a higher volume of souls being sent to Tartarus than ever before."

"Perhaps they deserve it," Nephesh said coldly.

"A lifetime of pain and torture? Not likely," Elon said from the chair. "If you think otherwise, Judge, perhaps you need to come down to Tartarus for a while. Perhaps seeing it for yourself will alter your perspective."

"No thank you, brother." Nephesh sniffed reproachfully. "I have no interest in your realm."

"Only in sending the damned into it."

Nephesh's smile was dangerous, his human glamor flickering as his power gathered around him. "We all bear a burden, Elon; some of us bear it more easily."

Elon was standing in an instant, his own brand of power heating the room around us. "Say what you will, Nephesh, but you have no idea what life I live."

"Boys, boys." Lucifer stood. This time the anger on his face was real.

We stilled, and after a long moment, Elon sat again.

"Regardless of what Nephesh is doing or how Elon is punishing, something is lost in between. Souls are wandering free, dangerous souls who are easily corrupted by the Drude and whomever they serve. And it is up to us to contain them. The more souls they have, the more power they wield."

"Do I need to remind you of what happens when we lose more of our power?"

"No, Father," Nephesh said, voice cold. "We live in the reminder of it every day." For the first time, guilt swirled in my belly. This fight, this attempt to again set the Underworld back to rights, was largely based on destiny. On the luck, Lucia might say, that each of us were able to be made whole once more. With only my father and me with that possibility, the future was looking more and more dim. More than ever before, I wished I knew how my brothers' realms fared. I should've been more aware, but these past years, I'd been consumed with protecting Lucia, gifting as much of my power to her as possible.

And now I knew that my family had been suffering while I was distracted. My resolve to unify my soul once more hardened. Lucia and I would find a way, and then I would help my brothers.

Lucifer's eyes flickered toward the door connecting to the dining room. Other guests must be arriving. My father confirmed when he spoke again, his tone jovial. "We should move on to dinner. Our guest and the rest of your brothers will be here soon. Hiram!"

One of the demons, this one my father's favorite, moved from where he'd been posted by the doorway. He wore the crest of my family, a five-pointed star centered over a flame.

"It is time."

Hiram opened the door to the office. His gnarled, over-long fingers wrapped around the heavy obsidian doors and held them wide as each of us passed through into the dining room.

"Sire," Hiram murmured as I stepped past, catching my attention. My father's attendant didn't often have anything to say to me.

"Yes, Hiram?"

His red eyes moved between me and the door that my father was already passing through. "Mind your powers, sire. Your father wants to see how she has affected you. He is looking for a reaction."

I cocked my head. "A reaction? To what?"

Hiram bobbed a short bow and then turned back into my father's office, leaving me standing outside the hall and watching the door settle in the frame. When the key turned on the inside, I knew for sure that whatever time Hiram had to talk was gone.

Grumbling, I moved down the hall and approached the doors. As I got close, I could hear more voices than my brothers and father.

Lucia.

My lips curled, and I threw the heavy door wide as I moved through, fully prepared to ensnare her as soon as I could.

But when my eyes landed on her, every thought disappeared, and I was struck dumb and furious by the woman who stood between Lucifer and Paran, her beautiful face turned to me with a greeting that should've warmed my belly.

Instead, instinct roared through me, my wings slipping from my shoulders to spread wide, my muscles growing and flexing under my shirt until the seams across my arms and back pulled and tore.

He was so close.

They were all too close.

Fury made my blood run hot, and my mind cleared with eerie calm. The killing calm perfectly designed so that I could focus on one thing and one thing only.

Her.

"Arafel?" Her voice was so close now. I had slipped through my shadow, appearing in a breath before her, my fingers spread wide, my hands around her ribs. I held her against me, turning so that I could brace myself against the dining room wall.

I needed to keep my enemies in my sight. They could've hurt her. We had to go.

Back to our home, to our bed. I could protect her there, hold her close, join with her until there was no other male in her eyes, no other thought in her mind but me.

I snarled.

"Well, that's interesting," a voice spoke, drawling and a bit sarcastic. "I knew I put a little too much demon in you all, but it's fascinating to see it manifest."

I growled again, backing up.

"Arafel, what are you doing?" her soft voice whispered from my arms. She was speaking. God below, what the fuck was I doing? My arms loosened, but only a margin.

"Let the girl go, Arafel. You're scaring her." Another male voice spoke this time.

I turned my face to him, a growl deep in my throat. It was Kharon, my brother. I trusted Kharon. I knew he wouldn't take her. Holding the solitary rational thought close to my chest, I loosened my hold a bit more.

"I'm all right. You can let me down." Lucia's quiet voice was like a blade, slicing deftly through the haze that had collected over me.

I lowered her to the floor, hearing the ricochet of her heels hitting stone as my ever-heightened senses surveyed the room.

"Good job, brother. No crushing your soul mate," Kharon spoke again, reminding me again why he and I had remained the closest in recent times. The male may be infuriating, but his voice, his presence was calming. "We aren't here to take her."

"Clearly. If we were, we would've done it days ago."

The sound coming from my throat shocked no one when I whirled around, my wings raised once more in preparation to attack. My other brother, Kadmiel, his human glamor that of a modern-day businessman, glared at me from the door.

"Kadmiel, not now," Kharon hissed.

"What?" My youngest brother spoke again when I moved toward him. "We may all be Lords of the Underworld, Arafel, but even we wouldn't stoop that low. You can calm down."

"Calm down," I echoed. I looked down at Lucia as she wobbled between me and the curled ends of my wings. "I'll calm down when someone tells me what's going on."

"What do you mean?" Kadmiel looked authentically confused.

I gestured at my mate. "The dress."

"Arafel, what are you doing? This is the dress you sent me." Lucia's voice was a hiss.

"I would never."

"What? You don't like it?"

"Of course I like it. I fucking love it. But I thought you might be more merciful to a recently mated male."

Lucia planted her hands on her hips. "I don't even know what that means."

I heard Nephesh's voice from across the room. "There's the problem, Arafel. You didn't explain to her?"

"I was getting to it." I straightened, rational thought returning as realization dawned over me. "Father."

Lucifer was the only one who hadn't moved during the entire situation. He still leaned against the buffet, one finger twirling in the air, a reciprocating ladle stirring the steaming container beside him.

"It was only a little bit of fun. I meant no harm."

"Lying is a sin, Father. Be careful what you say to us." Elon spoke now from the other side of the room. He was the only other one of us who had freed his wings. They stood out against the light-colored walls, the heavy veining visible in his bat-like appearance. Slowly, he retracted them until he was once again the very image of a human man.

But we all knew what lurked under those everyday clothes. And Lucia did too. Perhaps that is why, even in her rage, I could practically taste fear rolling off of her and she stepped closer to me.

"Okay, so I perhaps meant to test you, King of Dreams, to see how capable of protecting her you are." Lucifer stopped stirring the silver dish and moved toward us. "I had no idea that it would spark the primal, demon side of you so significantly. Perhaps it is more than her soul you wish from her."

My body was deflating, my everyday demon form becoming clearer. I could feel the wisps of fabric and thread against my flesh where I had blown out the seams.

"I could've told you that," Kharon mumbled.

Lucifer's dark brows rose. "But would you have?"

I stared around the room, the feeling of Lucia against me slowly calming my racing heart.

"No," Kharon finally admitted on a huff.

"As I expected. Now that the pre-dinner entertainment is over, shall we eat?"

I growled again, but something like a choked laugh sounded from the woman in front of me. My brothers were milling around, finding chairs around a large rectangle table complete with shining gold plates and silverware.

"Lucia?" She turned, and again, I was struck down by her face, that beauty there but also the acceptance. "I'm so sorry."

She wetted her lips, looking quickly over the table. There were two empty chairs closest to us. "I know. And I know you were doing what you thought you needed to."

I waited, sensing there was more.

"But next time, tell me and let me knee him in the balls."

My father's voice slipped over us. "Ah, Lucia, that is not very proper of you."

She turned, raising her chin as my father sank into the chair at the head of the table. "Neither was your dirty trick."

Lucifer folded his hands, looking at her purposefully. "This is the strangest way I've ever heard anyone say thank you. I know you wanted to know how he felt about you—not your soul. You. And now you know."

Lucia huffed but kept her chin raised as we moved to the table. I moved to put a hand on her back but refrained. There was nothing there to keep my skin from hers, the deep, low cut of the back of her dress drawing my attention even now.

Except it wasn't fury I felt anymore. There was only a surging need to possess, to stake my claim over her. And let her claim me. I swallowed, helping scoot her chair in for her.

"Lucia, we must get to know you," Kharon said, sitting diagonally from us. He was grinning at my mate. "What do you like to do for fun?"

Nephesh snorted. I groaned and leaned back in my chair. This was about to be the longest dinner of my life.

24

Arafel

We had made it all the way to dessert before there was any bloodshed. Knowing my family, that was quite an accomplishment. Lucia had handled each of the twists and turns with more grace than I'd ever expected of her.

She sat at a table of demons, some in human form, but Kharon and I remained as we were naturally. His scaled, beautiful skin shimmered against the gold plates. He had been aggressive the other day in the library, but now he was his usual self.

Or closer to it, at least. I could feel the jealousy seeping from him with every breath he took, each time he watched her face with such rapt attention. But then, I understood now. I looked at her that way as well.

"Arafel mentioned you have been reading my old letters," Lucifer spoke from the side, his wine goblet still full. He hadn't touched it all night.

I frowned, watching as her shoulders stiffened. I had not mentioned this to him, and she must have realized that as well.

"I am," Lucia responded, and I watched her tuck her fingers into the napkin on her lap. "The book came to me after I started looking for a way to give Arafel his soul back."

"Interesting." My father appeared bored, but I could feel the conversations around us drawing to a halt, curious about the change of subject. My blood heated again, and my shoulder blades twitched with the need to free my wings and whisk us away from here.

"And have you found anything?" To my surprise, it was Elon who spoke first, shadowed face turned toward us.

"Not much. I had thought that perhaps there would be something in Nephesh's history, since he's the only brother who had previously located his soul. But..." Lucia offered Nephesh a soft smile. "There was nothing there."

"There wouldn't be. I only knew my soul carrier for a few days."

Lucia cocked her head, staring at the handsome veneer my brother wore. "I don't think loss can be measured in days."

Nephesh stilled; Kharon too.

"I'm sorry for your loss, Nephesh," Lucia pushed on. After a long pause, where Nephesh's gaze was riveted onto her, she looked back to Lucifer. "We know that the soul cannot be given through death..."

"We don't know that for sure." I glanced over at Elon, who was swirling the sharp white wine in his glass, words hanging between us.

"I'm fairly sure we do. Neph is standing right there, half a soul still missing."

"Anna was murdered. It is a different type of death." Elon met my eyes boldly, the gold in them shining across the table. "I would know."

"You believe if your human sacrificed themselves that it might work? Then you'd have the other half of your soul back." Kharon's face was serious.

Silence filled the room, and Lucia's hand on the tablecloth drew into a fist. When she finally spoke, her words were smooth, unshaken. "Is that what you didn't want Paran to tell me? That I was expected to be a martyr?"

"You will not be a martyr, I promise you," I said, reaching out to place my hand over hers. Her skin was cool to the touch, unresponsive as I slipped my fingers into hers.

"How?"

"Because I—"

Nephesh set down his wineglass, hard. "Not that it matters anyway. You began to die the moment my brother took you into our world."

Bright, seething anger slipped over my eyes. But I didn't have time to deal with Nephesh yet, not right now. Not when I knew what those words must've meant to Lucia. I turned in my chair, her beautiful blue eyes blinking up at me. There was a small smirk at the corner of her lips.

My heart plummeted. She didn't believe him.

Which meant I'd have to tell her. The one secret I'd held closer than any others. The fear that filled me every second of the day I was away from her. I knew the rest of the family's expressions must have mirrored mine.

"Arafel?" Her face dropped, understanding blooming. She leaned away from me, that mouthwatering dress slipping across her silken skin. "Arafel, what is he talking about?"

I swallowed, claws digging through the tablecloth around our combined fist.

"He's kidding, right?" Her voice was soft, but the pitch rose as my resistance to answering grew apparent.

"He isn't." The words physically hurt to utter aloud.

"What do you mean? I'm dying?"

"All humans are dying," Kharon said softly. "The curse and beauty of mortality."

"Screw our mortality. What does this mean for me?"

I forced my gaze onto her. "Human souls are not designed to be in the Underworld. Not like this, not for so long."

"I'm dying now?"

I nodded, my throat thick.

"Can't you send me home, let me heal or something, and then we can start again?"

"It doesn't work that way."

"He nearly broke my magic bringing you here the first time. My sons can only move through the barrier at the full moons. And there is not another for two weeks." Lucifer's face was serious. "You will be gone by then, your soul left for Kharon to carry on."

"No." Lucia jumped back, her chair screeching on the floor. The hurt in her blue eyes speared through my chest, an ache I could hardly bear. "You knew, and you still brought me there."

"I thought we would find another way." My words were short and tight. "Or that you…"

"That, seeing my imminent end, I would sacrifice myself so that you can have more power." Lucia laughed, but the sound was broken. Like shattered glass, it broke over us. Even Nephesh looked like he regretted his earlier words.

"I thought you brought me here… I thought…"

"I warned you—" I started, but Lucia turned on a dime, her heels sweeping her out of the room and straight down the corridor toward her room.

I sat frozen. After a nod from my father, Hiram broke away to follow her, no doubt to guide her to wherever she wanted to go.

Nephesh shifted, his glamor dropping. "Arafel…" I could hear the regret in his voice, but I didn't care anymore. There was no chance now she would bind herself to me as a mate. Not that I blamed her. And I could never bring myself to hurt her. We were the perfect misalignment. Destined to be together, doomed to forever be apart. Unable to speak, I snapped my fingers, falling through shadow to elsewhere in the castle. I wanted to be alone.

To know what it would feel like for the rest of my existence. It didn't matter what happened to my soul. I didn't need the other half to know it was permanently broken.

***

Lucia

My heart felt like it was pounding straight through my chest. I'd known there was something I was missing; I hadn't expected it to be this. I hadn't expected it to be about him.

He, who had told me I was safe, who had cared for me and loved and kept me for his own.

He had lied.

I ripped the dress off, hurling it into a corner as I stormed around my room, looking for something, anything to wear.

I knew he would be coming here any moment, and I wasn't about to face him bare-ass naked. I needed armor for this conversation. Emotional, physical, anything.

I found my sweatpants and the hoodie the Brotherhood had packed for me. It was my mother's, and the familiar scent of her perfume nearly overwhelmed me as I slipped to the floor. My face was hot, sticky, and I was shocked when I reached up and felt it, only to realize that tears were pouring down my face.

And there I sat, waiting for him for what seemed like hours.

When he finally opened my doors, I didn't dare move, choosing to watch him through a thick haze of frustration and emotional exhaustion. He kneeled by my side, his thick thighs bunching and moving as he hovered over me, large and dark and warm.

I suddenly wanted him gone.

I didn't want to have this conversation. Until we did, maybe I could forget that my entire world was being upended again. That everything I thought I knew was wrong. Again. I didn't want to know.

Not now.

Not ever.

I wanted to go back in time, to our cabin at the edge of the dream realm, where I'd finally found my center, where I'd let myself be free and be with him.

This male beside me was a stranger. A liar. He was ruining the memories I had of the Arafel from the mountains. From my youth. From my dreams.

I turned away, biting my lip hard as a sob eased its way up my throat.

"Sweet Lucia..." I felt more than saw Arafel's hands move in the dark. But if he reached for me, they never landed on my skin. Instead, my flesh covered itself in goose bumps under my hoodie, and I drew my arms even tighter around my knees.

"You knew this whole time, and you never thought to tell me."

He was silent.

"You said you brought me here to protect me."

"I did."

"By bringing me to a place that has already begun to kill me?"

Arafel's heavy sigh ghosted over my skin. "I believed I knew a way to extract my soul from yours. Once that was done, I thought my powers would be able to keep you here."

I glared angrily at my own knees. "So selfish, Arafel. You were using me, when you knew the whole time."

"I believed that if you loved me, when those feelings became stronger, that my soul would allow you to give it back to me. And if it didn't..."

"You would just take it." My voice was bitter, and I knew he could hear the whine in it. "You brought me here, intending to make me fall in love with you, give back your soul, and then if it didn't work...no problem because I was a half-decent human who would choose to give it back to you before I died."

"Lucia, that's not how I meant for anything to go."

"Isn't it?"

"I wanted you to love me, yes, but because I was already so deeply in love with you. And when I realized you were my soul mate, I knew I would find a way to protect you from this."

I scrubbed my face. He had promised to protect me even from himself. He had failed.

"Nephesh... When he found his soul carrier, she was a lovely woman, kind, sweet. She already had children, though her husband had left her. Neph said that what he felt for her was the most powerful draw he'd ever felt."

"How nice," I said. I instantly hated the bratty tone of my voice.

"But," Arafel said, speaking over me and waiting for a moment. "He never loved her, not romantically."

"Okay, so what?"

"He loved her." Arafel's head cocked a little. "Probably similar to what I felt for young Lucia all those years. I adored you, but as I might have adored a friend."

I sucked in a breath. "And now?"

Arafel's intake of breath was sharp, making the silence that fell between us even more deadly as we suffered through it.

"Now, I know I was wrong about everything."

"What do you mean?"

"I was wrong to bring you here. I was wrong to force this bond between us before you knew everything. If I could take it all back, I would... *No.*" Arafel shook his head. "No, I wouldn't change any of it."

I swallowed, wondering if he had heard the words in my head before he had gotten here.

"I am a selfish, dangerous creature, Lucia. But I cannot be sorry you are mine. There will never be a day I regret being your soul mate, even if you decide to never speak to me again."

Silence fell between us, so thick I could barely handle it. "What happens now?"

"We have two weeks, roughly, until you will begin to succumb to the power of the Underworld. Kharon has the best feel for your body's weakness or inability to fight off the pull. He has volunteered to check in on you."

I sniffled. "Does this mean we are going home?"

"Where is home for you?"

Anywhere with you, I would've said only a few hours before. When I'd been ready to follow this man to the edge of insanity and back to give him his soul. Now I knew all I would have to give him was my life.

What a horrific trade it was.

"I meant back to the castle. To your home."

Arafel's horns dipped. "Yes, we will leave in the morning. I don't want to be here any longer than we have to be."

"Good. I'll be ready."

Arafel's body shifted as he stood, and I could hear his footsteps as he moved toward the door. The light from the hall illuminated a demon, the creature from my dreams and nightmares. But this demon was broken, his shoulders sagging, his claws loose.

I tipped up my chin. "Arafel?"

He turned quickly, pale-blue eyes on me. "I don't want to fly home. If you can't take me through the shadows, then ask one of your brothers to do so."

His muscles bulged for a moment, as if the idea of his brothers coming close to me still provoked that primal instinct within him. But his voice was calm and casual when he spoke again.

"Of course."

"Goodnight, Arafel," I said, curling up again, pressing my chin against my knees.

"Goodnight, little soul."

The fabric under my cheek grew damp and cold from my tears, and when others knocked on my door that night, I didn't bother getting up or even moving.

I would stay exactly where I was.

Because if I moved an inch, every instinct inside of me screamed to run to the male I had loved so fiercely.

But that no longer mattered. Love didn't mend souls. Or reunite soul mates. It was a means to an end for him.

And, as it turned out, for me too.

25

Lucia

I wasn't surprised when I woke up to find my things had packed themselves. With an unhappy grunt, I splashed handfuls of cold water on my puffy face and went down to the same dining hall as last night. So far it was the only room in Court I had managed to find on purpose.

I wondered briefly if that was intentional.

I was poking at some oatmeal-looking breakfast makings when Hiram walked in, Lucifer at his back. The two males were deep in conversation, but the language was hard to understand. I wasn't interested in having polite breakfast conversations, so I ignored them.

At least for a few moments.

"Ah, Lucia! How did you sleep?"

I glanced up at Lucifer and briefly wondered how much I could say to him without getting my body cleaved in half. "Fine, thank you." The lie was sharp on my tongue.

"Such a horrible liar, daughter, but I appreciate the effort. Especially after such a ruckus last night." Lucifer sat dramatically in a chair across from me, picking up a cup and holding it aloft for Hiram to fill.

There was no sense denying anything, so I went with it. "Yeah, it sucks to find out you're dying and the male you've been falling in love with wants his soul back." I sighed, tilting my head. "It's a real bummer."

Lucifer clucked his tongue. "I love this side of you. It must be why the magic chose you. You're clearly tough enough to be with one of my sons."

"I'm not with him. I mean… We are…" I ran an angry hand over my braid, tugging on the end as I tried to come up with an answer for what Arafel and I were.

"You intend to love a son of mine and think you won't have a lifetime of fights ahead of you?" Lucifer cocked his head, black eyes gleaming. "I know for a fact how hard it can be to be mated to a powerful entity. But the benefits far outweigh the downsides."

"I'm not mated to Arafel."

"Meh. Not yet." His coy look was enough to set off my usually dormant temper.

"Who are you to give advice? Where is your queen?"

Hiram stilled, his face jerking my direction. I knew in an instant I had gone down a dangerous route. "I'm sorry. I didn't—"

"It's all right." Lucifer's handsome veneer smiled tightly. "You get a pass today. Only one." He stood, his black suit tight against his form. Briefly, I glanced down at the table, noticing his shadow wasn't human any longer. There were immense wings on either side.

"In order to protect our sons, my queen was lost to secrets of the Underworld that even I cannot understand. I long for her each and every day."

"I'm so sorry."

"Don't be sorry. Be brave. You have two weeks to uncover why you're here. I recommend you use them wisely."

I nodded, my throat feeling thick. My oatmeal looked even less appetizing than before. "I understand."

His lips curled in a smirk. "That's more like it. My son is here. I best be on my way; I don't want to set him off again like I did yesterday."

I only nodded again, my head feeling cloudier by the moment.

Lucifer and Hiram disappeared back out the door they had come through, and less than a second later, Arafel came striding through the door I had used. I turned to him, hating how badly I wanted to smile at him, to slip into his lap and let him hold me.

Because I knew what Lucifer had said was right. I had fallen in love with a demon, a creature of war and royalty. There was no way everything would go smoothly. Not for us. I looked him over, noting the lightweight clothing. We wouldn't be flying today. I had asked that of him but wished I hadn't.

Even if things were different now, I would give anything to feel him against me and pretend that I wasn't on a clock ticking down to death—and that he wasn't pursuing me merely because of my soul.

"Good morning." His voice was soft.

I inclined my head. "Good morning. Did you want breakfast?"

"Not today. We'll step through the shadows and be back at the castle in a moment."

Understanding what he needed, I stood, grabbing one bag off the ground. Arafel's hands closed around the others, his dark claws careful as they pushed my things over his shoulder. I moved to his side, and then, when he reached for my hand, I interlaced my fingers with his.

The bolt of attraction, the nearly painful pull of emotion that raced from that contact straight up to my heart, made my breath come short in my lungs.

I gritted my teeth, mentally chanting that it didn't matter.

"Ready?"

"Ready."

And then we were falling back and forward at the same time. The darkness lapped at my legs and hips and finally up and over my face as Arafel's grip on my hand anchored me to his side. I caught a glimpse of a winding silver river and then a dense forested area. And finally, the darkness began to recede and there was solid earth under my feet once more. I panted a little as the rest of our surroundings became clearer. We were in my rooms at the castle. They were both wonderfully familiar and heart wrenching.

I'd lost myself to him in this bedroom.

I'd found myself here.

Fucking lies.

I pulled my hand away, feeling a little frantic to put more distance between us again. I must've been obvious, because Arafel stepped back, hands raised as he placed my things on the floor.

"Thanks." I didn't know why my voice was so shaky. I rubbed at my arms, unsure of what to do. "I'm going to take a bath or something. I'll be reading Lucifer's letters later if you need anything."

Arafel nodded, his jaw clenching. "I have several immediate needs to take care of with the dreams."

"Yeah, of course."

The awkward tension between us pulled, and I turned to dash toward the door. Arafel let out a soft growl, and I could feel the air shift around me right before I felt him press me against the door. His body held mine, one hand around my hips, the other around my breasts, his breath harsh in my ears.

"I can't go on like this."

I blinked, surprised.

"I don't know what to do or what to say to you that I haven't already. I want you to stay. I want things to be as they were before."

His breath was hot against my throat as he dragged his mouth down the column of my neck. Simmering, nearly burning heat lit up my insides, and I didn't stop my body from arching against him. His hands were on me, pulling and yanking and needing, until my leggings were on the ground and he was lifting me, guiding himself inside me.

"Fuck," he growled as his cock slid deep, my body curling to meet him with every thrust. There was nothing sweet between us, only frustration and need building into one cataclysmic moment. My hands and cheek pressed against the door as he pumped into me again and again, my body growing tighter and tighter as the tips of his claws dug into my skin.

"Yes, oh, Arafel, please," I said, my voice desperate. I wasn't sure what I was asking for at first. But he knew, just as he always had. He stepped in, lifting me higher as more of my back slipped against his chest and torso. He was still fully clothed, the friction of his hot body, the clothes he'd frantically pushed aside only made my body clench harder. My orgasm was coming, crashing through my body with the force of an avalanche.

I arched into it and into him, letting his powerful body hold me, use me as I gasped and moaned my way through it.

And when I felt him still, his teeth at my throat, his fingers trembling against my skin, I knew that he'd lost himself in me as well.

In the moments after, there was only the soft panting noises we made as both of us waited for the moment to pass and the irreversible damage of the past few days to come back to the forefront.

I savored those moments, letting my fingers trace over his soft gray skin. He seemed unwilling to part with me too, his body still hard and eager inside me, even though I could feel the evidence of his climax slipping down my legs.

"What happens now?"

His growl wasn't angry or threatening. It was more of a whine than anything. "I don't know."

I let him help me down, his hands holding my legs as he guided each of my feet into my leggings. When I was redressed, I found myself staring up into his eyes. They were glowing blue again; power and pleasure must mix easily in his world. I envied him.

"You may wish you could go back, but it's not your life or emotions you were gambling with."

"Lucia—"

"Leave, Arafel. I want to be alone."

His body was rigid behind me, his breath short and panting. I knew he wanted to say more. Maybe it would even be the right thing to say. But I was done listening. I needed a moment—or four hundred. But I didn't have them.

The clock on my lifetime was ticking loudly.

"Goodbye," I said, tucking myself away from him once more.

He nodded, heavy jaw tight as he moved back to the door. I didn't miss the desperate look in his eyes or the way his claws scored the door as he closed it. And for perhaps the first time, I saw him for what he really might be.

A monster.

On stiff legs, I moved back to the bathroom, cleaning myself up and crawling into the enormous robe waiting on the door there. I couldn't bear to look at the tub where I'd begged for him. Or even the mirror that begged me to see how destroyed my own features were over this.

I knew I would look a mess.

There was nothing a girl loved more than crying at her own reflection, and I simply did not have time for that. There was a lovely soft chair by my fireplace, and I curled up there, my bare legs warm and my belly aching with unhappiness.

Lucifer's letters were getting less organized the further back in time I went. The King of Hell might look the part of a distinguished businessman, but I could practically feel the primal instincts that must still roar through him.

Those instincts had once ruled him and this world. It was fascinating.

I had found a grouping of pages from Lucifer's personal journal, smiling when I noticed that he had denoted the day that Hiram came to work for him. The demonic attendant had once been a disobedient king but begged for another chance when his soul made it to the Underworld. Lucifer crafted him much like he had the rest of his army, by combining a human soul with the power and demands of Hell itself. The result was a demon with human memories and a soul but a body crafted to serve the Underworld.

My mind stilled, catching on something in the back of my thoughts.

Hiram had mentioned he had been alive when the curse had impacted the Lords of the Underworld. He must have known Arafel's mother then.

"Susan?" I whispered the word in the air. I had no idea if the spirit had remained here or had gone back to wherever she stayed in the Underworld when she was attending to me. "Susan, are you still here?"

"Where else would I be?" Susan said, a bit haughtily as she coasted across the room, her body more translucent than I remembered. I wondered if that had anything to do with Arafel's power continuing to wane. Or if it was something else.

I hoped it was something else. Because suddenly the idea of this loving, kind, outrageous soul being gone forever felt like a blade to my heart.

"I just…" I cleared my throat. "Can you tell me about the curse? The one that split the lords' souls?"

Susan's voice was indignant when she said, "I'm not that old, you know."

"I know, but I figure you probably have heard the story more than I have." I shifted, straightening my cramping legs. "I know that it was a spell between Arafel's mother and Lucifer and that it ended up sheering their souls in half, disappearing into the world and binding themselves to human matches."

Susan eyed me, almond-colored eyes curious. "It seems like you know plenty, dear. What am I missing?"

"Who was Arafel's mother? Did you know her?"

"Ah, her. I did not. I heard she was the one who settled Lucifer though. He had been a pagan god for centuries, content to run the afterlife and this world like a half-starved heathen. But then she came, Nicola, bargaining for a living king who held her power captive. No one knows how she managed to break into the Underworld in the first place." Susan sat on the chair opposite, her no-nonsense pantsuit glowing warm in the firelight. "She must've been very powerful. Some say she was the first of her kind, the Witch of Endor, they called her."

"Wow. I don't think I've ever heard of her."

"People are obsessed with witch trials and Halloween, but you have to remember they were a long-established population before all of the hate that came to them. They were powerful but not dangerous. At least not until provoked."

She paused a moment, obviously thinking. "It was her idea to civilize the Underworld, to make use of the creatures and souls that wandered here. She and Lucifer designed the Underworld so that the passage of souls, the magic that every being brings, could be used to sustain our world."

"She sounds brilliant."

Susan nodded. "But all good things come to an end. Lucifer and Nicola had devised a deal to end the slaughter of a great war above. But when the queen went to deliver the message, she was captured and tortured. Horrible thing. Lucifer's hellfire set half the world on fire that day. And even now, he searches for her, or her body, so that he can bring her home." Susan shook her head, and I realized I was clutching the letters in my hands.

"Why doesn't he mention her in any of this?"

Susan cocked her head. "Do you believe this is everything? That Lucifer would surrender information like that, about his greatest weakness, to you?" Her tongue clucked at me, and I grimaced.

"I feel stupid."

"That male is a wise and worthy leader, but he is still the devil, Lucia. He isn't going to give that up. Especially if it has anything to do with his wife."

I stared into the fire. "Yes, he will."

"Why is that?"

"I'm going to make a deal with him."

Susan choked on her next words, shoulders hunching as she covered her mouth. "No, you will not, young lady. I forbid you."

"You forbid me? I have two more weeks to live, Susan. I don't think we have a lot of other options."

Susan's pale face grew more grim, and I realized what I had said.

"Yes, I know. Congrats on keeping your secret." My voice was harsh in the warm glow between us.

"He is my master, Lucia. And I believed he was doing it for the right reasons." Susan stood, her posture stiff and unyielding. "I have other duties to attend to. I suggest you explore all other options before consulting the devil with your little deal."

I didn't know how to respond, so I nodded.

"If you think Lucifer hasn't looked over every inch of those documents already, you're crazier than I believed."

"I know." I swallowed hard. "But I have to try."

Susan sniffed and turned to leave the room. "Call if you need something other than more stories."

She was gone before I could respond, and I hated the swirling frustration and sadness that warred in my belly.

The curse was a result of Lucifer and his queen. If they were the beginning, they also had to be the solution.

26

Arafel

Simeon and Paran sat in front of my desk, Gatam by the window. Each of them was silent as they observed me.
"What?"

"You smell like her," Paran said, his tone casual. But I could see the sharpness in his gaze.

I growled. "Be careful, Paran. That body doesn't regenerate like it used to."

The warrior shrugged and looked over at Gatam, who was smirking at us all. "We thought you were going to try to stay away."

"I was."

"Great success, my lord," Simeon said with a huff.

I wished I could reach across and slam a fist into his handsome smile. But I didn't. Because I deserved whatever retribution I would get for being with Lucia.

"Interesting that you seem to be covered with her scent, but from what I've heard, she left Court in tears."

I could feel their anger at me, the protectiveness of the males I'd entrusted to care for my carrier, my soul mate. I didn't blame them for being upset with me. I was furious with myself. But I couldn't take it back now. And nothing would change our timeline. Let them hate me. All that mattered was that she had two weeks until her body began to fail her, leading to her death.

I didn't know how to send her back through to the living world; my power continued to drain away. The only thing that helped was contact with her. Which was an oxymoron of the cruelest type.

I needed her soul to keep my realm safe. I needed her alive to keep my heart safe.

My head ached, and I dropped it into my steepled hands. "I ruined everything."

"Let's focus on what we do know," Simeon said simply. "Then we will deal with your love life."

I groaned but gestured for him to continue.

"More souls have been slipping through the boundaries between the realms. Kharon has all but abandoned his home to roam the riverbanks to try to keep them inside until they can get to Nephesh. Mazikeen stopped by on her way to Court. Elon has her out hunting deserters of Tartarus."

"Deserters?"

Simeon shrugged. "Escapees. Whatever you want to call them."

A rumble formed deep in my chest. This was so much worse than even I had imagined. The dream realm was important because it formed a barrier between the living and the dead, both physically here in the Underworld and mentally in every soul that visited in their sleep.

I glanced up at the sky, a thunderous gray at the moment. My father's mood must've been poor. I wondered if he'd already heard of Mazikeen's update from Elon.

"How has it affected you, my lord?"

I held up my fist, watching the veins pulse there. "Not as much yet. But it won't be long."

"Kharon believes they will attack the river again. It's the most vulnerable place to steal souls from," Paran said. "I'd like to take a small battalion there to assist in guarding it."

"Agreed. Gatam, will you stay and guard Fel?"

Gatam nodded, flipping his dagger in his hands. The silver flashed in the air, and I found myself staring at it numbly.

"Now...about Lucia." I cleared my throat. "I need to know how to get her safely to the living world."

"What?" Simeon and Paran spoke at the same moment.

Gatam's blade swept through the air one more time.

"I need to find a way to get her home."

"Why? She has to be here; she has to give you your soul back." Paran was blinking at me as if I hadn't stayed up all night thinking this through.

"She doesn't *have* to do anything." I stood at my desk. "She didn't ask for this, nor should she have to suffer or die from it."

"But you're the only one who has found your other half... There's no chance for any of them if you can't make it happen." Simeon's eyes were wide. "Sire, you have to think about this."

"We don't know that. Maybe Lucia was simply the first. Perhaps more will come soon."

Paran's lips curled in dislike. I could taste the lie on my tongue even as I said it. Because I did know. I knew each and every day my brothers were scouring the living world for the chance that the other half of their soul could be found. And after meeting Lucia, finding out that she was not only my carrier but my soul mate, it made sense that they would be even more motivated to find them.

I wished them luck with their fate. Mine was sealed long ago and then reinforced by my selfish actions. Because it didn't matter if I was whole. Even if I had to give her up in order to achieve it, I would find another way to fight the darkness spreading across the Underworld and my realm. Half soul or no. My soul mate came before all else, damn this mess.

"I won't ask again. Find me a way. Another way."

They knew they'd been dismissed, and all three left my office. I felt the loss of their company in an instant. I'd never thought of myself as a lonely male. After all, I was surrounded constantly by the mahrs and other Underworld creatures. I had the Brotherhood as well as my actual brothers. If I were desperate enough, I could venture to Court to be completely surrounded.

But things were different now.

When I met Lucia, I knew she would change my life. I hadn't realized the depth of which she'd already done so. How she'd warped my world to fit her and her presence into it. I folded my hands, thinking about how she had adapted so easily to our way of life. How she had known so instinctively to guide the souls through their dreams. The way she had stared down my father as if he weren't the symbol of her own mortality. And the way she had taken me inside of her, promising things a male like me should never hope for.

Everything was different now. *I* was different now.

I would rather spend the rest of my existence with half a soul before letting her suffer another day of pain. When she did finally come to the Underworld, I wanted her to be a soul well satisfied. She deserved everything that life could offer. It was more than I could handle.

I pulled out a slender book from the drawer in my desk, my fingers sweeping around the heavily damaged edges. I had never shown anyone this, my darkest secret and deepest weakness.

The time for these secrets would come. I slid the book back into its hiding place. It would come to me when I needed it the most.

***

I slipped out of a dream, the bitter taste of fear from its inhabitant fresh on my tongue. I scrubbed a hand over my face, placing the dream book back on my desk and willing it back to the library. As it cleared, I noticed the eerie silence of the room around me.

The library was never completely silent. The mahrs were constantly milling about. I typically found the sounds of books being moved, shelved, even destroyed a pleasure. But this was different. It was wrong.

I stared into the swirling dark, unease growing in my stomach. Pure instinct made me press my wings around my shoulders until they acted as a shield. The feathers were not only for looks. They were slick, powerful, and quite efficient at repelling magical blows.

Gritting my teeth, I conjured a portal to Castle Fel. The darkness wasn't even complete before I could hear the sounds of chaos and bloodshed. I launched myself through the shadows and straight into battle.

Castle Fel was under attack.

The hallways around me were filled with a mixture of mahrs and towering harpies. At first, I stumbled, unsure of how to proceed. They looked to be attacking one another. Mahr versus mahr, and the same with the harpy soldiers.

I growled, deep and low. The Drude had come, the corrupted creatures. I launched into the corridor, my fists and wings spread wide as I roared my fury to the castle. Letting the tether on my power loose, I called to the creatures of the dream realm. To the mahrs and the harpies and my brothers.

I was to make a stand here, and I needed them. Every creature within range returned the call, their eyes glowing the same blue that mine always had.

"To me, creatures of the dreams," I roared, summoning my swords from where they hung in my rooms. They fell through shadow and darkness to appear in my hands. I let my form go, letting my power and fury fill my body until it expanded and grew.

I knew if Lucia were to see me now, she would only see the monster. No longer the male who held her in his sleep. And it no longer mattered.

I sliced through the nearest corrupted mahr as they clamped down on my forearm. Several lower-level demons, possibly from my father's court before the darkness had found them, were screaming orders to the dark creatures.

I flung several attackers from my path, my eyes on a trio of looming souls, their forms dark and made whole. If I could dispatch them, then the lower ranks might scatter. I ran into Gatam as he leapt from a chamber off the main hall. His blade was slick with black blood. I squared up against him, suddenly concerned he'd been turned. But the Brother shot me a devious grin and bounded off, his gaze intent on one of the other leaders skirting the corner of the hall.

I gave him a short salute and then turned, finding a corrupted demon had backed themselves into a nook in the stone walls. I approached him slowly, watching the way his red eyes flickered all over, searching for a way out. A way around me.

"Why did you come here?"

The demon gave me a slow, rattling growl. "The dream realm was the last to be created. It will be the first to fall."

"Not while I still live."

He cackled. "It doesn't matter if you live or not, demon lord. You can no longer protect the realm. You are no longer whole. And after all these centuries, a little human girl was the answer. What irony."

Sidestepping, I manipulate the demon farther from his soldiers. Behind us, I could hear the battle rage on. "How do you know this?"

"She knows everything."

"She? Who sent you?"

"You will have to kill me."

"I will kill you regardless. Tt least do me the favor of sharing something worthy in the meantime."

"Not likely." The demon wrinkled what was left of its nose at me, and I struck, slamming my fist straight through their torso. Their heart, beating on by the blessing of my father and the power of the Underworld, halted.

"Arafel?"

I turned quickly, sword raised once more. Lucia stood there, her eyes wild on me. I hadn't realized how close we might be to her hidden door. Dread struck me hard, making my chest ache as again I was torn between protecting my mate and defending my home.

I had to get her away from here. "Hide, Lucia. You can't be here."

"What's happening? Are you okay?"

"They will kill you given the chance. Go back to your rooms, Lucia. Now!" I articulated the last word with a slash of my sword through a ghostlike ghoul who floated toward us.

"But—"

"Now!"

27

Arafel

I turned, panic slipping into my mind as I noted the hundreds more Corrupted that seemed to pour into the castle from every which way. I cut my way through the crowd; my chest heavy with fury. They had come to my home, desperate to find me. To kill the one person here who might be able to restore my power.

They had known we were back.

I growled deep in my throat. I had a spy in my midst.

"Brother," a voice bellowed, and I turned to see Nephesh standing there. He was in full battle form, his long white hair wild around his face as he cut through the surrounding corrupted souls with a long, curved blade. Red eyes glowing, he was the picture of demonic power as he plowed through the crowd toward me.

"Thank you for coming," I grunted as I joined him. I laid my hand briefly on his shoulder, feeling the bulk of his muscles there.

"I was already here. I followed them from the river."

I sliced through another harpy, who screeched at me. "Kharon?"

Nephesh cut me a sharp look, shaking his head. "I'm not sure. I couldn't find him."

We spun, dancing forward as the horde threatened once more. "Is she safe?"

I took a moment to look at my eldest brother, to watch as he thrust his sword through a mahr, who grasped at his cloak and then turned to face me once more. There was no mockery or anger on his face. A genuine question.

"Not safe enough. I need to find a way to get her home."

Nephesh pivoted to slam his fist into the back of a corrupted mahr who was climbing up one of my soldiers. "The Brotherhood didn't find anything?"

"Not yet. I thought we had more time."

Nephesh's eyes bled red as they found mine again. "There is never enough time, Arafel."

And in that moment, I knew exactly what I had to do. "Help me."

My brother's brow lowered. "I'm right here, fighting beside you."

"Get her safe. If I leave again, I might forever damage the veil between my realm and the living. You heard Father. The magic is weak."

"And what of my realm? How do you want me to manage that without damaging my own?"

I growled at my own stupidity. "I can't take her until the full moon, and by then it will be too late." I bent at the waist, avoiding a spear thrown from above. "I cannot let her die, Nephesh. She is my mate."

"I know, you idiot. Again, what can I do?"

"You have to take Lucia. Take her up the river, past Kharon's pier, and have him ferry her across to the living world."

"Why can't you?"

I looked around us, terror finally sinking its thick claws into my heart. "I'm not strong enough." I raised my eyes back to his. "I'm begging, brother, please."

We stayed like that, frozen, eyes locked, long enough that we were nearly overrun by the horde once more.

Finally, Nephesh inclined his head. "It is done." He jerked his chin toward the invisible door to Lucia's room. "Take a moment. It's not much, but it's what I can give you."

I nodded, turning and dropping my shoulder to thrust my way over a large mahr that lumbered my way, wide, snarling mouth agape.

I moved through her door and took a deep breath on the other side, my heart pounding in my chest as I looked around her room. For a moment, I was afraid she hadn't listened. That she'd run or another corrupted creature found her along the way.

But I heard her now, the slight sniffle that echoed across the room from her closet. I ripped the door off in my hurry to get to her, and as soon as light spilled into the small space, she was standing and leaping toward me, arms outstretched.

"Arafel!"

I breathed her in. "Sweetling, I'm sorry I yelled." I swallowed back the pain and regret that began to sink in. This was goodbye. The final one.

"I'm sorry for many things." I stroked a hand up and down her back. "I'm sorry I didn't understand what you meant to me."

Her fingers tightened around my neck. "Why are you saying this? Arafel, put me down." Lucia struggled against me, but her slender body was no match for mine. And secretly I savored those moments, the last that I may feel as I turned and began to walk through the door. I could feel my brother's energy, dark and haunting, as he moved closer to her door.

The monster inside me wanted to tell the Underworld it could go fuck itself and to whisk her away to the Sleeping Mountains. Back to our cabin.

But there was only this left for me to give her. The one thing I'd always been capable of. I wouldn't fail her now, not after everything we'd shared.

Safety. I could offer her that.

Nephesh stepped through the cloaking magic, his eyes immediately on Lucia. She stilled in my arms, a tremble going down her back.

"What's he doing here?"

My nose was deep in her hair, inhaling the sweetness and sunshine of her scent. The scent of my mate. I savored it, knowing it was the last time. "He's going to take you somewhere safe."

"I'm safe with you."

"No, little soul, you are not. All I can offer you is this chance to be safe, to be free of this." *Of me.*

"I don't want to be free of it."

I chuckled, the sound grave. Nephesh stepped closer, his face blank and emotionless as he observed us. I leaned into the side of her face, passing my lips under her ear so that I could whisper the final words to her.

"Shine bright, little soul. And know that you carry my heart as well as my soul."

I looked up, and Nephesh was there in an instant, powerful arms stealing Lucia away from me as he turned back to the door. Lucia was stunned, her face pale. There was blood on her cheek, rubbed off from when I held her.

She was beautiful. Too beautiful for this world. And I smiled through the pain as Nephesh stepped back into the chaos. Blood pumping, I followed him out, ignoring the rest of the destruction as I forged a path for my sibling and my soul mate. The bodies were falling easily now, my power soaking into my skin as soul after soul of the Corrupted was reclaimed by the Underworld through my blade.

Nephesh paused by the vast open doors, now being held by dream realm demons, all of them loyal to me.

I could see Lucia hanging off of him, resisting the hold he had on her.

With a grimace, he resettled her so she could face me. "We must go."

I reached out, brushing a knuckle along her jawline. Then lower until I could feel something transfer from my hands to hers.

There was a crashing noise behind us. The horde had discovered where we'd gone, and they were climbing the walls. I could hear the cries of my people once more.

"Go!" I shouted at Nephesh. "Get her out of here."

"No! Arafel!" Lucia screamed, her voice growing more and more quiet as I plunged myself back into the thick of fighting. And when I did finally take a chance to glance back at the edge, Nephesh and Lucia were nothing but a distant spot of white wings on the horizon.

She was safe.

I turned back to the bloodshed.

28

Lucia

"Nephesh, you have to put me down."

"No."

"Please, Nephesh, you have to help him."

"I am helping him." The silver-haired male looked down at me, the ends of his unbound hair trailing over the shoulders I still clutched. "He needs you safe. I'm taking you home."

"How? We didn't find a way to give him his soul."

Nephesh's powerful white wings beat against the air around us. "Arafel no longer cares about that."

"Why not?"

He casts an amused, slightly irritated look down at me. "You truly need me to answer for you? You humans are all the same."

"How's that?"

"Afraid. Afraid of what might happen, what won't happen. You spend your entire lives transfixed on this. And when it comes down to the end, to when you end up at my bench, it matters not one bit."

"You think I'm afraid of Arafel?"

"I think you are afraid of what you two could've been."

I leaned into his chest as he swooped lower, my heart hammering with dislike over the heights. I forced myself to keep talking though. Anything to keep my mind off of what we were doing. Or who I was leaving behind.

"He only wanted me because of his soul. If he hadn't been forced to find me..." I broke off, shrugging as much as I dared.

Nephesh grunted a little then banked to the side, not answering. We were directly over the river now, the pale curving current cutting through the green landscape. It wasn't as forested here. The grasses were high and a mixture of green, blondes, and large boulders were sprinkled throughout. Nephesh had his eye on something, his face trained to the ground below us.

It gave me a moment to look, really look at Arafel's oldest brother.

Nephesh's horns were different from Arafel's curling onyx. They were short, iridescent and silver, tapered back from his temples and above his slightly pointed ears. For the first time I noticed the numerous silver rings tucked in the lobes of his ears.

I smiled, surprised by the slightly flashy jewelry in such a serious, straitlaced male. He was heavier than my mate too, with thick muscles. Comparatively, Arafel was finer boned, his features sharp and lean. His predatory, gleaming red eyes were relaxed but no less unsettling as I stared at him. Not for the first time, I wondered about the male who held me. He seemed loyal, kind, even in his own gruff way. I knew from the letter book that losing his soul carrier had changed him.

"Where are we going?" I looked over his shoulder, staring into the swirling gray fog that seemed to be descending all around us.

"I sensed my brother below. We are going to find Kharon."

"And you can...sense him in all of this."

Nephesh's lips lifted in something between a grimace and a smile. "I can sense more about people than you'd ever wish to know."

"Is that why they call you the Judge?"

Nephesh sighed. "Do you always ask so many questions?"

"It's a human thing. Or at least it seems like it is. You demons aren't very engaging."

He grunted and then shifted one more time, taking us lower over the waters. "Yes, I am sometimes referred to as the Judge. It is my duty here in the Underworld to judge whether a soul has deeds for which they should atone or if they deserve the kind of afterlife all humans dream of."

"A land flowing with milk and honey."

This time Nephesh snorted. "I would love to speak with whomever came up with that term. But yes, souls may share a world after death, but it doesn't mean it is all equal."

As I opened my mouth to ask exactly what that meant, Nephesh's wings swept forward, nearly halting us midair.

Before my stomach could catch up, we were falling, spinning like the seed of a dandelion. I bit down on the shriek that threatened as we careened toward the ground. Moments before I was sure we were going to be smashed into a pile of river stones,

Nephesh's wings slashed at the air, pulling us up in time to land us sedately on top of the larger boulder.

He released me in an instant, red eyes looking over my head at the river. "Kharon?"

"Here, brother."

Nephesh and I both turned when Kharon spoke. His voice was thin, worn, and when I saw him, I immediately knew why.

Kharon was approaching the river. His long arms, spread wide, a sarcastic gesture of welcome that fell flat because he was surrounded by a group of souls. I stared, unable to stop myself. They weren't like Susan, who seemed so alive. These souls were skeletal, the shape still human-like but their faces gaunt and shadowy. They floated along, their feet dragging over the grasses and pebbles as they were herded back to the river. As soon as their shadowed forms touched the shore of the river, they transformed, their bodies filling in, their eyes becoming more alive, their features more human-like once again.

"Oh, my," I said, not meaning to speak out loud.

"How many more?" Nephesh was looking past his brother into the foggy field behind him.

"None." Kharon rolled his shoulders, gazing upon the souls as they wandered deeper into the river. "These are the last."

"Why did they run?"

"They were told it was a way out, back to their families." Kharon sat at the water's edge, letting his bare feet, which were far more human-like than Arafel's clawed toes, sink into the water as well. "Several were caught and corrupted before I could get to them. But the rest..." Kharon paused, breathing deep. "The rest are safe again."

"Are you all right?"

Kharon looked up at me, his eyes more serious than I'd ever seen them. "Lucia? Why are you here?" He looked at Nephesh. "And with him?" The demon lord attempted a smirk. "I always told you you'd end up here, but I didn't think you'd bring the Judge with you."

Nephesh made a desperate sound in his throat. "Shut up, ferryman. You're too tired to be this sarcastic."

"Fel was attacked," I answered quietly. "Arafel... He's still there."

Kharon craned his head up to look at us. I didn't meet his gaze though, my own eyes riveted to where the water lapped at his feet; with each rhythmic surge of the Styx, the water moved up his legs higher, slowly coating the soft blue skin.

"Arafel asked me to take her to safety."

Kharon's brows rose even more. "And you brought her here."

Nephesh had the decency to duck his chin. "We mean to hitch a ride back to the living world."

"Hitch a ride?" I said at the same time that Kharon groaned loudly.

"It's the only way. To take her back through the shadows would crumble what little power Arafel has left. And he needs that to fight back the Drude while we find another way."

"The Drude was at Castle Fel?"

Nephesh shook his head. "Not that we saw, but his corrupted were in full force. Hundreds of them, Kharon."

Kharon looked at me, and I could tell he was waiting for my answer too. "There wasn't anything else I could do," I explained to him. "I really wanted to help you, to help all of you. We tried."

The water demon looked up at me, a small smile on his lips. "I know you did. Arafel never did anything partially."

I rubbed at my arms, still curious about the souls who were slowly making their way back into the water. I watched as their heads slowly sank beneath the surface. I couldn't stop the sharp intake of breath, and reached out my hand. "Are they—?"

"They are safe," Kharon said. He reached out a long, graceful arm to his brother, and Nephesh pulled his sibling back to his feet.

"I can't promise you perfection, but let me get home for a minute and regroup." Kharon began walking along the riverbank. "Then we can discuss getting *you* home."

The brothers strode away, Kharon's bare feet and Nephesh's boots silent in the damp ground, while I felt like I stumbled through the soft, sandy loam alongside the Styx.

The brothers were deep in conversation and ignoring me as we trucked along. I was tired, and all I wanted to do was go back to Fel. Back to him. I didn't care about the fight. I didn't really care about anything but seeing with my own eyes that he was all right.

I swallowed back the flush of tears. Then stopped, bending over at the waist to force the air back into my lungs.

"Lucia? Are you all right? We are getting close." Kharon's voice was gentle.

I glared at him and his brother. "Am I all right? Am I all right? No, I'm not all right. Since the moment Arafel came back into my life, I've been dragged all across a world I don't know, with creatures I don't understand, all for it to end up with my heart shattered and a ticking time bomb in my chest. What do you think?"

Kharon elbowed Nephesh. "I can see why Arafel likes her so much."

Nephesh snorted.

"We don't expect you to be all right, little soul. It was meant as—" Kharon waved his arms as though trying to come up with the right words "—a conversation trigger. Nothing else. I'm sorry if I upset you."

I stood there, breathing hard, while the brothers looked at me. "You said we are close?" I felt a hysterical laugh bubble up in my chest. "I want this to be over."

Nephesh's face flashed with surprise before carefully going blank once more. Kharon gestured in front of them, and the fog vanished. There, built over a twist in the river, was a large, stilted building. I blinked at it, wondering if it was real.

It looked like a mixture of the floating houses in Venice and a treehouse, the tall, domed center, surrounded by large, covered porches that led directly out into a dock. Under the house, all around the house, the river flowed, unbothered by the dwelling.

Kharon led us up the door to the porch and to the front door. We moved inside through the open arched door, past a light curtain there, and found a comfortable, sparsely decorated main living area. I could see a dining room table, chairs scattered around it in various sizes, and more arched gateways that clearly indicated there were more rooms to the back of the home.

Kharon went straight in, guiding us to the living space in the front, where enormous open windows let in the soft noises from the river running all around us.

"Your home is lovely."

Kharon grinned at me, white teeth gleaming. "Thanks. I thought a houseboat was a little too on the nose. This is the best of both worlds."

I nodded and moved to the windows, staring out at the direction we'd come.

"He wants you safe, Lucia." Kharon flopped into a heavily cushioned sofa, his loincloth still wet.

"It doesn't feel right. I can't leave him like this."

"You have to," Nephesh grunted as he settled, arms crossed, into a chair by the window. The breeze picked up his silver locks and brushed them back from his face. "Let him go on knowing you are safe. The alternative is..." Nephesh's voice trailed off. "Horrific."

A strange silence fell over the room, and I broke it again. "How are you supposed to get me home? I thought moving through to the living world created flaws in the boundaries?"

"It does."

"So how are we going back?"

Kharon glanced at his brother then to me once more. "You and Nephesh are going to go out the entrance."

I cringed, my throat growing tight. "That doesn't sound right."

"It isn't. And it is one of the last few avenues that souls can move through. If the darkness were to find out about it, it could prove fatal to the entire Underworld."

"So why tell me?"

Kharon rolled his eyes. "Who are you going to tell in the living world? It won't work again for you, until, you know, you do come here as simply a soul."

"Ah." I sniffed hard. "That makes sense."

"I'm going to get the things we need, and then you two can be on your way."

Kharon sprang up off the sofa then moved out of the room, leaving Nephesh and me alone once more.

"I want to go back."

Nephesh sighed. "I know."

Silence fell again, and I let the tears that had been building behind my eyes slip free. "I hate feeling this way. I'm so confused."

Nephesh shifted but remained quiet. At least at first. After the tears dripped from my chin to the floor, tension bloomed between us once more.

"I never explained to anyone what happened with Anna. Not really."

I sniffed, turning to stare at the pale-faced demon. He was so still against the sofa, he could've been carved from granite. "What?"

"Anna. She was the carrier of my soul. The first one we'd ever discovered." Nephesh's throat barely moved, the only sign the words came from him. "She was lovely and kind. A mother to several children, recently widowed. She cried out to me in grief and pain. And so, I went to her, overjoyed I had found the source of my power."

"She offered to give my soul to me. She tried. We both did. For a week, I lived with her and her family in the living world. They took me in, treated me like I was part of their family. I loved her in an instant. Everyone did. But I had no idea then of the dangers humans were to each other, even to such a kind soul as Anna."

"They killed her."

Nephesh gave a jerky nod. "An intoxicated driver. Her whole future was wiped out in a moment. When she needed me most, I was too late."

"I'm so sorry."

The demon lord stood and moved to stand at the window by me. "You know why I'm telling you this?"

"No."

"Because the love, the devastation of losing Anna, was not only because of her soul. There were no romantic feelings between us. It was the recognition of two souls who cared for each other." Nephesh turned to meet my gaze. "It was not what Arafel felt for you. Or you him."

"What?" I sputtered as the cool red eyes surveyed me. "I don't... I mean..."

"I grieved for the loss of a dear friend and the chance to find my other half. But I didn't love Anna the way Arafel loves you." His lips quirked. "Soul mate has many meanings here, and fortunately for you, they all mean a lifetime of devotion."

My heart pounded in my chest. "Nephesh…"

"We should go," Kharon said from behind them, startling me. Nephesh didn't move. Then again, he must've sensed his younger brother coming into the room and had still told me these details.

"Okay," I said over my shoulder then looked back to Nephesh. "Are you coming with us?"

"Only Kadmiel and Elon are allowed to leave so sporadically. The rest of us are bound to the full moon to let us in and out of the Underworld."

Nodding, I reached out and brushed a hand over his. Nephesh's skin was surprisingly warm, and I saw the flicker of surprise on his face as I squeezed his fingers. "Thank you, Nephesh. Keep him safe too, okay?"

The Judge nodded, stepping away from me. Passively, I followed Kharon out onto the porch and down to the docks. Nephesh did the same but took the other direction, back to the riverbank, where his wings spread wide. Red eyes found us once more before he turned back to the direction of Castle Fel and launched himself into the air.

I gasped, still surprised by the power and grace they all seemed to exude. It was easy to accept Arafel. He was different— he was…mine. But his brothers, there was still a level of fear and unknown there that I had never experienced.

"Feathered showoff."

I turned, my smile feeling wobbly as Kharon held out a long necklace to me, the charm at the center glowing with soft blue light.

"What's this?"

"The River knows you are a soul, and it will care for you in the same way. The charm is magicked to protect your physical body." He shot me a crooked grin. "As you've already learned, the Underworld is rough on your human body. The river will only accelerate the impact."

I swallowed, fear making my belly clench.

"Lucia." Kharon's voice was gentle, it seemed to ripple through me. It was soothing, more soothing than I'd ever remembered it. I blinked up at him.

"Is this one of your abilities? Do you soothe your guests?" I gestured in the air, unsure of who to call the souls I'd seen.

"Yes, some of my patrons do find my voice calming."

Nodding, I rubbed my palms on my legs. "I don't mean to be so nervous. It's just that…"

Kharon watched me, blue eyes unusually bright.

"This is it, isn't it? I won't be able to come back. I mean, until I come here for real, and then it won't be like now. It won't be for him."

Kharon smiled sadly. "It's time to go to, Lucia."

I found myself hopping on my feet, my body filled with the flee instinct. But not to home, not to Kharon and his glowing necklace. Back to Arafel. It was where I belonged. A broken noise slipped free, and I knew I was crying again. But this time, instead of soothing me or even offering words, Kharon simply stepped forward, wrapping his arms around my body. I had just enough time to take a deep breath in before he stepped backward, and together, we fell off the dock and straight into the River Styx.

***

Arafel

After the Brotherhood and my soldiers had done away with the majority of the demon leaders, there was nothing keeping the corrupted creatures another moment. They disappeared from Fel in a matter of moments, slipping away into the darkness around us.

The souls we did manage to dispatch were already moving across the realm, their eyes trained on the waterfall. Joining there would take them to Kharon, where they would begin the process of moving through the Underworld and back into the life they were taken from by the darkness.

I was exhausted, my fury from earlier burned off through the combination of fighting and handing off my soul mate to my brother mid-battle.

"The castle is secure, my lord." Simeon fell in step with me as we crossed the inner courtyard and back into the front hall. Everywhere I looked, there were dream realm soldiers lying down, leaning against walls. Thick blood covered the stone floors, and I knew that based on the expressions of the faces of those around me, morale was at an all-time low.

I gritted my teeth. "Any sign of Nephesh returning?"

Simeon stopped, helping a thickly built succubus to the ground, where he continued to wrap a wound on his shoulder. "Nothing yet. But many saw her leaving, my lord."

My physical weariness banked, the fresh pain of Lucia drowning everything else out. And not only that, but the failure of myself as a leader.

I had failed my people. I had failed my soul bound. "They all know."

His hesitation spoke volumes. Finally, a quiet response. "Not all, perhaps, but enough."

I glanced down at my stained clothing. "It doesn't matter anymore. They will all know soon."

"I'm sorry."

His apology cut even deeper. "You didn't do anything wrong. This was my decision."

"Still hurts like a bitch, huh?" Simeon shrugged a little as I blinked at him in surprise. "Some of the new vernacular is quite expressive."

I grunted noncommittally.

The demon I'd cornered and questioned had been correct. The dream realm was the most vital to the living world and therefore had always been the weakest. But now, the darkness was capitalizing on it in every way.

Without the other half of my soul, I wouldn't be able to hold them back forever. Even if every one of my brothers came here to help, we wouldn't be enough to turn them away. They would take more souls, corrupt more of my creatures. And in the end, they would be able to make the jump to the living world and wreak havoc on that one as well.

Simeon must've known I was lost in my own head, because he gave me a long look then wandered away, moving through the hall while he rolled his sleeves up. The gold brand of the Brotherhood shined across his wrist.

I moved through the room, my eyes barely seeing the gore and destruction around me. My feet took me to my rooms, where I found myself desperate to get rid of the layers of grime and blood that chafed my skin. By the time I climbed into the steaming tub of water, I could already sense the dream realm was returning to a precarious but functioning level.

It would only last a little while longer.

But I would hold on to what I could.

***

Lucia

If someone had told me that someday I would be dragged upriver by an enormous pale-blue river demon with webbed toes, I would've said they needed to adjust their medication.

Yet as Kharon dragged me by an invisible tether up and through a bubble-filled current, there was enough pain in my chest and lungs that I knew I wasn't dreaming.

If the pain from leaving Arafel wasn't enough, the way that the air in my lungs fought to escape with every second reminded me how mortal and broken I would be after this.

Before I felt like my chest might explode, it was all over and I was kneeling by an absolutely miniscule goldfish pond. Breathing hard, I gulped in the fresh air, surprised by how strong it tasted on my tongue.

It was different, brighter—overwhelming after the weeks I'd spend in the Underworld.

"Breathe, Lucia. You're safe now."

I stared blankly at the male—no, the man in front of me. He was beautiful, a short crop of deep auburn hair on his head, vibrant green eyes over perfectly bow-shaped lips. He looked like he should be walking a runway in the suit instead of kneeling on the wet dirt and dealing with me.

"Kharon?" I couldn't stop staring.

That pretty face turned to a smirk, one brow lifting. "Not bad, eh?"

I didn't bother to answer, coughing up more of the river that seemed lodged in my throat. Kharon patted my back, his broad hand gentle as I fisted my fingers in the damp grass. "Where are we?"

Kharon glanced around us then turned back to me. "Weber Park. It's a few blocks away from where the Brotherhood picked you up."

I nodded. "Did anyone see us?"

"I'm very good at my job, Lucia, even the parts of it I do not do often. You are safe here. No one followed us in or out of the Underworld."

"I'm sorry. I don't mean to doubt. I just... I just want him safe."

Kharon sighed and helped me to my feet. "Then let me get you home so I can go help and be able to look my brother in the eye when I tell him that I kept my promise. That Nephesh did as well."

I nodded and began to walk. It was an easy walk, and it passed in comfortable silence. The jaunty step of Kharon at my side was so at odds with the dread that filled me each time my worn soles touched the earth.

Things were too bright to my gaze, and it felt like the morning after a night with too many margaritas. Kharon didn't seem to be suffering in the same way, so I pretended to be okay. Step after step, I closed the gap between the life I had grown so attached to and the life I thought I had wanted back.

And when we stood together at my apartment's doorway, I had nearly convinced myself I was going to be okay. But then Kharon leaned in, his lips brushing over my forehead.

"Since my brother is too stupid to say it," Kharon said against my hair, "he will miss you. Always, if my hunch is correct. But he would never be able to live with himself letting you die on his watch."

Tears were burning a trail down my face.

His fingers brushed the tears away. "So live, Lucia Walker, and love every second. He'll be watching."

"Kharon—"

But he was stepping away, his handsome smile slowly fading as he got farther away. I didn't bother chasing him. I wouldn't catch him, nor would I know what I would do if I did. I couldn't go back to Arafel.

This was what I had left.

I let myself into the apartment I barely recognized, the sharp smell of must and mold making me flinch. I left the door open wide as I moved through, staring around at the familiar yet unfamiliar things all around me.

I hated it instantly.

But there was nothing left to do but walk straight back to my bedroom, pull the sheets back, crawl in, and pretend I didn't just leave my heart in Hell.

29

Lucia

It had been weeks since I left the Underworld, the days passing in a blur of night and day. At first, I wasn't sure if it was me or the city itself that felt too big, too bold. As if my skin wouldn't be able to hold a second more of the exposure around me. And so I mostly stayed in, my lights off, my eyes on the television or my phone as I stared unseeing at the screens.

Had this life been what I wanted once upon a time?

It felt all wrong. And as I approached the start of a new term, I could barely open the textbooks that arrived. In fact, as soon as they did, I piled them neatly on my coffee table and then walked out into the dim evening light.

It was this time of day that reminded me the most of him. Perhaps it was Lucifer's nearly constant mood changes, but the Underworld had always had a certain type of glow. A perpetual golden hour that had stretched for days.

This reminded me of that. My feet slapped the pavement through the soles of my shoes as I slowly made my way down the street. I knew there were Brotherhood members watching me. I didn't know who they were, but I sensed them. Arafel couldn't very well leave his soul wandering the living world with no protection. They were with me all the time. But no sign of Simeon or Paran or even Gatam.

I didn't know whether I was relieved or devastated by that. I knew that if it were them, then I would have already begged them to take me back. Before, when they rescued me, they had said that the three of them together might have been powerful enough to take me there. There was a full moon this week, and the boundaries between the worlds would be thinnest.

But my plan always died off there. What would happen then? Would my time here in the living world buy me more time once again? Or would my body pick up right where it had left off? Would I return to the realm of dreams only to inevitably sacrifice myself to a lost cause? It seemed a lot like it.

My aimless wandering had taken me down a few blocks, and the slowly darkening sky was bringing the lights and signs all around me to life. I flinched a little as a large sign flashed on above me.

Blinking, I looked up, my heart leaping out my throat as I slowly read the words.

"Huggins Auto Sales," I whispered. The sidewalk around me was deserted, and on a better day I would've been relieved no one else was around to hear me. Today I didn't care.

My feet were moving before my brain could register how bad of an idea this was. The glass door was heavy in my hands, a pleasant bell tolling above as I stepped into the small lobby.

"I'll be right with you!" a voice called from the back.

I didn't bother to respond. And when a tall, well-dressed man walked around the corner, I recognized his smile.

"Theo," I breathed.

He cocked his head as he stopped in front of me, hand extended. "I'm sorry, have we met?"

"I, uh…"

Theo's gaze flickered over me. "You look familiar though."

"I, uh…" I scrambled for an idea, any idea. "I knew your grandfather." I gestured around the lobby. "He was always talking about your place. And since I was out, I wanted to see it for myself."

You knew Grandpa? That's amazing." He had captured my hand and pumped it vigorously up and down. "Come in!"

I coughed, laughing a little at his enthusiasm, but let him guide me inside his cramped office.

"How did you know Grandpa?"

Surprisingly, the lies rolled right off my tongue, a partial truth, a partial lie. "My mother and I lived just down the road. We'd see him out and about."

Theo beamed. "He was always out there checking in on his coffee shops and his crosswords."

We laughed together, the weight on my chest lessening. Then out of nowhere, my eyes fogged, vision blurring as my emotions hurtled through my chest.

"Oh no," I whispered, pressing a hand to my chest, "I'm so sorry. I never—" My words cut off as I felt the first hot streak of tears escape.

"Are you okay? Uh... um..."

"Lucia," I supplied with a choked noise. "And yes, I'm so sorry."

"It's okay, honey." Theo sat back in his chair, pinning me with understanding eyes. After a moment, he scooted the tissues on his desk closer to me.

I picked one up, dabbing at my throbbing eyes. "I never cry."

Theo let out a breathy laugh as more tears slipped out. "You seem like you have a lot on our mind."

"My mother died a few weeks ago, and then..." I stared down at my hands in my lap. "I lost someone very special."

When Theo spoke again, the words were slow, measured. "When I lost my grandpa, I thought my entire world would come to an end."

I chuckled wetly.

"But you know what?"

I risked looking up, the tears I'd been hiding a steady stream. "He really wasn't gone. I carried a little bit of him with me." Theo patted his chest. "Right here."

My hand rose instinctively, pressing between my ribs, where I'd always believed Arafel's and my soul were intwined. I sniffled.

"I think we carry a little bit of everyone in our life, all the good, the bad...the special and ordinary. And in return they carry ours."

Mind blurry, I blinked at Theo. "You believe that."

"I do. My grandpa always said that whoever came into your life changed you, became a part of you. Your mother is a part of you—your special person, a part of you. And they carry a part of you too."

I froze in his hardback chair. "What?"

Theo laughed. "Don't take my word for it. This isn't church, miss. It's an autobody shop."

"I know, but...what did you say?"

"I think it goes both ways, especially with the people you love most. You give to them, they give to you, and together, you are better for it."

"Oh my God."

Theo's face scrunched. "I'm confused..."

"He doesn't need his back; I've never given him mine." Heart thundering, I lurched to my feet. *Arafel, Arafel, Arafel,* my mind chanted as I stood there. How had we missed such a simple solution? It wasn't his soul that he needed to be complete. He needed mine. Part of mine, another half, exactly like his mother had said.

True power lay in the ability to give to others.

"Lucia, you aren't making very much sense."

I had to get back to the Underworld.

"I'm so sorry. I have to go." I was running to the door before the words were out of my mouth. And a few heartbeats later, I was down the street, my keys jingling as I stuffed the house key into the lock and fell into my apartment.

There I stood, my back against the door as I stared around my living room.

Could it really be that easy?

We knew I couldn't give him his soul back. We'd tried. And if I were to die, like poor Anna, it wouldn't go back to its owner.

It was because I wasn't supposed to give him his soul back. I pressed a hand against my chest. Arafel's soul was where it was supposed to be. Where it was always supposed to have been.

I needed to give him part of mine.

I smiled a little then, thinking about the time he had said my soul was bright, full of light. And if I was correct, then the King of Dreams was destined to have a part of it inside of him forever.

But I had to get it to him.

"Well, crap." I had absolutely no idea how to do that. I couldn't open my front door and yell for the Brotherhood to come help me. And even if I could get that far and managed to not get mauled by a corrupted soul or something, I still wasn't sure they were even strong enough to get me back to the Underworld.

Staring around the room, my eyes fell on the small book Kharon had pressed into my hands the day he left. The pages were full of words I couldn't read or understand. I'd given up on reading it early on.

It was a dream book. I ran my fingers down the spine, caressing the thick leather. Slowly, the letters moved, forming and reforming in front of my eyes, exactly like they had in the Underworld.

It was Arafel's book.

My skin broke out in goosebumps as I stared down at the book, but my decision was already made for me. I thought back to Theo's dream. To the beach with Simeon.

I had been able to affect those dreams, like Arafel could.

Because I had half of his soul inside of me. I was made to not only carry his soul, but to house his powers.

I was made for him.

I smiled to myself. Now I just had to find a way back to him. And I could do that all on my own. Starting here.

I looked around the apartment, my eyes falling on all the things I would be leaving behind. The pile of shoes by the door. A grocery list still stuck to the fridge from before I'd left. The framed photos lining the walls.

Pausing, I stepped to the closest shelf and picked up a photo of my mom and me at high school graduation. She was beaming, a beautiful face staring down at me, even as I stared at the camera.

My heart clenched, and tears formed at the backs of my eyes. That was how it had always been, her with her eyes so firmly on me. I sniffed back the emotion, letting it seep into my bones and my soul, letting it become part of me once more.

She was part of me, now more than ever.

"Let's go, Mom."

The back of the frame was easy to take apart, and with as much care as I could muster, I slipped the photo out and stashed it in the pocket of my jacket. Then, shaking my head to clear any remaining fears, I focused on the book in front of me. Its cover was warm and soft in my hands, and I noted the irony of the deep-gray leather. It was nearly identical to Arafel's skin. I wondered if he'd done that on purpose.

"Let's go ask him in person," I said to myself.

I opened to the first page, my gaze falling immediately to the illustration in front of me. It looked to be Arafel sitting at his desk, enormous black wings folded at his back as he leaned over something on his desk.

My lips curled, and I didn't even bother to close my eyes as I leaned in, falling into the book with such easy precision, I barely had time to register the apartment I left behind in a blur. Then I was back, the scent of the Underworld, of the familiar warmth that filled me with the sight of him, making me whole.

Arafel was working away, his expression unreadable as I moved toward him.

I wasn't sure if he could see me or not, but I could see every bit of him.

"Arafel?"

But he didn't move, not even a breath as I approached him. I was only a few inches from touching his shoulder when a female voice sliced through the air.

"There you are," it said.

I leapt to the side, my heart pounding as I stared at the woman walking in the door. Her dark-brown hair was loose, trailing down over her shoulder, and the thin-strapped nightgown hung loose on a slender frame.

She moved around Arafel, her arms winding under his arms until she was pressed between him and the desk. Arafel's face changed, bright-blue eyes staring down at the woman with complete devotion.

"Little soul, I thought you had gone to sleep hours ago."

My heart thumped.

It was me. Almost, at least. There were changes I could see, even from where I lurked against the corner. This version of me had longer hair, and there was something in the comfort of her movement that I knew I didn't possess.

At least not yet.

This was Arafel's dream, I reminded myself. He'd said they could be anything, fantasies for the future, memories of the past, even fears or hopes. This had to be some kind of fantasy, and based on the way his hands were running down the other Lucia's arms, I didn't think that it was going to be a fear or nightmare type of dream.

"It's hard to sleep these days."

Arafel's brow furrowed them. "Sweetling, I'm sorry. Let me…"

Dream Lucia laughed, her voice bright and happy as it echoed off the walls. "You can't help me with everything."

"I can try." Arafel leaned down, his lips brushing over her cheekbones. "Tell me what I can do."

My skin was hot and flushed as I watched the pair of them. But it was more than that, because it was real life, my fantasies and memories from the time with Arafel all wrapped up into one. Was this how the King of Dreams was in his own dreams?

I had no idea what to do now that I was there. In the dreams I had visited in the Underworld, Arafel had affected the inhabitants simply by being there. I had seen his hands move, his eyes observing. But nothing physical.

It wasn't like I could run over and grab Arafel's shoulder. Could I?

I eyed the pair on the desk as Arafel lovingly set the strap of Dream Lucia's nightgown back on her shoulder. I felt like an intruder, which was insane. But I thought maybe if I waited, I would be able to see what I needed to. There had to be a reason I was here.

Arafel helped Dream Lucia off the desk, his dark claws slipping through her hair for a moment. "You need your rest."

I scoffed, the exact same sound coming from Dream Lucia's lips as well. But then she moved, curling around Arafel, so that I had a side view of her for the very first time. It was me, but there was so much more, and it all stemmed from the hand she had pressed against her belly.

The perfectly round, early in the process, baby belly that she was sporting. The nightgown had hidden it earlier, and maybe even then I wouldn't have known to look.

But now I couldn't stop.

This was what Arafel dreamed of. Of me, and him, and desks, and offices, and babies. A future as a family.

Something like grief choked me, pushing and pulling at me as I stumbled back into the shadows of his office as Arafel swept a hand over his baby and guided the dream me out of the room.

And then I was falling, straight back to myself in the living world. Gasping, I stared down at the book once more. Then put it down beside me.

I was massively overwhelmed and immediately sought out my kitchen for a glass of water and whatever salty snack I could drag back onto the couch with me. It ended up being a tin of potato chips, and I sat there, chomping away at them as I stared down at that book.

Arafel's dreams included me and a family and a life.

If I went back, that's what I would have.

A family.

A life.

He had told me once that he'd taken hundreds of years to perfect his magic. Even demon born and powerful as he was. Perhaps all I needed was practice.

Licking the crumbs off my fingers, I unfolded myself and went to pick up the book. I hadn't exactly nailed this on my first try. But then, I had rarely succeeded at anything the first time. When had I let that stop me?

"I'm the queen of the dream realm. My mate needs me. I can do this," I announced to the empty apartment, grimacing a little as I realized how crazy I sounded.

Then I flipped the page and let Arafel's dreams take me away.

30

Lucia

By the next morning, I'd slept only a few hours, but I had made more progress than I could've ever imagined. In the last of Arafel's dreams, a strange, fury-filled nightmare about Elon burying him alive in a strange underground place alongside the River Styx, I had managed to not only attract their attention briefly, but I had managed to kick a stone out of my path.

It wasn't what I wanted, but it was something.

And as I passed out, fully, dressed in my bed, I had only one thing on my mind. I was going to do this. I carried the soul of a demon lord. And I had to get back to him.

After rest, a scalding shower, and more carbohydrates, I set up shop back at my desk, flipping to the next page in the book. From the illustration before me, of Arafel and myself standing on an embankment outside of the Castle Fel, I hoped it was simple.

I slipped into the dream easily now, my practice from the past day helping me navigate to this. To my surprise, I settled directly on the terrace behind dream me. And when Dream Lucia stepped back, I had nowhere else to go.

We simply merged.

The feeling was horrible at first, like being caught in clothing two sizes too small for you. But when Arafel's bright gaze snapped to ours, I realized that he didn't know the difference. He just saw the same Lucia as before, his dream version of me.

I could talk to him, my mind screamed, mentally clamoring at the dream of Lucia's form as I attempted to make her open her mouth.

"Speak," I begged, my body stiff and unyielding as Dream Lucia stepped away from Arafel. I could feel her spreading her arms wide, a smile on her lips.

"Now? You want to go now?"

"Just to the cabin and back," stupid freaking Dream Lucia said, a playful lilt in her voice. "Come on. I know you are going to be too busy tomorrow. I need to practice."

"You need to tell him, idiot!" I yelled internally as Dream Lucia took no notice of my request and began to walk backward from Arafel.

"Very well, then, but you know what happens if you lose."

Dream Lucia quirked a brow, her hands reaching back to see if her braids were contained. "Oh, I remember what happens if I win too."

Arafel growled, the rumble deep and low in his chest. And for one incredible moment, I felt myself getting jealous. "This isn't real; this isn't real," I said to myself, shocked when Dream Lucia moved to the wall and, with Arafel's hands on her hips guiding her, stepped up to look down over the vast, sharp edge of Castle Fel.

What the hell were we about to do?

I scrambled, attempting to get my mind to step back, to step back out of Lucia or even out of this dream. Anything to avoid the sheer fall right before me.

But nothing worked. Lucia took a deep breath in and then released it softly. As she did, there was a sharp snap along my shoulder blades, a combination of pain and pleasure that left me gasping. Dream Lucia shimmied her shoulders, and I saw them, the most beautiful pair of white wings. They were mine. I knew them as one knows their own hands. And as Lucia bent her knees, I was forced to stop looking, to stop staring at them as they folded back, tight to our body, and together we fell straight off the wall of Castle Fel.

I stumbled out of that dream like a drunk on St. Patrick's. I had wings? That actually made sense. Arafel had wings. It would be no surprise I would have wings too. I took several deep breaths, trying to forget about how it had felt to free fall off the side of a mountainside castle.

I had reached the part of Arafel's dreams where he had begun to fantasize about what he wanted to do with me if I had stayed. Maybe if I had fought back against him and Nephesh that day, then I would know.

But I hadn't.

Tears stung, and I blinked them back.

This had been a major development though. For the first time, I had been inside of the dream, really inside of it, living it alongside him. I couldn't make her talk, but maybe next time, maybe if I could grow my powers a little more, then there was hope.

I sighed. The book had to be the key. There was a reason, however far buried in my mind, that I had called this book to me. My fingers traced the notes I had tucked in between the pages from all those days searching for a solution.

At the bottom of the page, in my own scrawling print, I'd written in heavy ink: Oaths are sealed in blood.

I'd looked at these notes before. After all, my theory was that I had to somehow pledge my soul to Arafel while avoiding any of the traps that the Underworld was so well known for. Oaths could be a key. Kudd had said in passing that this was how the creatures of the Underworld claimed their mates publicly. Once united, the pair would be unbreakable, bound together until death.

Arafel's mother had been a witch, a human like me, and yet she'd lived there with Lucifer for hundreds of years. At least that's what I assumed. The Underworld hadn't been built in a single lifetime. No way. I tapped my fingers on the countertop, unsure of what I was missing. With a sigh, I opened my phone, casually searching for the Witch of Endor.

The screen was filled in an instant with images of a dark, cloaked figure, a woman who had been at the beck and call of kings for generations. She had many names, but Lucifer had called her beloved, or Nicola. I smiled sadly at the memory.

Maybe after all of this, there would be a way to find her again. To reunite Arafel's entire family.

But first, I had to find a way home to Arafel. Something in the recess of my mind was triggered, and I stared down at the book again. *"Where you go, I go."*

I remembered Arafel's fanged smile as our eyes met. My heart was pounding. He'd said it, that night at Hell. He'd said "Deal" when I promised that.

I lurched to my feet. I didn't need a new oath to find Arafel. I already had one in place. My hands urgently opened to the last page in Arafel's book of dreams. It was empty, smooth and creamy.

The past, present, and future were all a part of our dreams. And I was his.

I closed my eyes, breathing in the smell of leather and aged paper, and let myself fall in.

Instantly things were different. The dream was more vivid than before, its unclear edges in sharp contrast. And this time I moved through it with confidence. This was where I was supposed to be. Castle Fel was my home. It had been in my heart since the beginning.

Carefully, I walked to the front door and touched the handles there. I could feel the cool gold, the metal a searing reminder of the reach I had now.

Taking ahold of the door handle, I swept it open, the cool air brisk and bright on my tongue. I could feel it. I could taste it.

I forced my feet into the hard stone floor and closed my eyes.

"Where you go, I go."

The deal I had made in Hell, the one I hadn't even thought twice about. My secret cheat code to getting back to him. The world twisted for a minute under me, and I clamped my eyes shut.

When I opened them once more, it was there, really there. Everything around me was so familiar and dear that tears slipped into my eyes, making my gaze watery.

"Lucia?"

I turned with a gasp. Simeon stood there by the corner, his eyes wide and surprised. "How did you do that?"

Relief warred with worry when I didn't see a familiar gray shadow. "Where's Arafel?"

Simeon moved faster than I could've imagined, his grip on my wrist tight. "You have to get out of here. It's not safe."

"No, I have to stay here." I wrenched away from his grip. "I belong here, as Arafel's soul bound, and..." I swallowed hard. "I'm his mate; take me to him now."

"Lucia." Simeon's face was dirty, a grimace foreign to the expression blooming as he glared at me.

"Now," I snapped, and the ground under my feet cracked.

"You're here."

Simeon let go of me, stepping away with his hands raised. "Why?"

I rushed to him, my eyes looking him over desperately. I knew that he healed fast, but the battle, those corrupted souls, they must've hurt him. But the Arafel before me had no injuries, just a shocked expression that did nothing to get rid of the blur of nerves in my belly.

"I had to come back. Arafel, I know what to do."

"You have to go; you don't have much time."

"Shut up. For once in your life, let me save you."

Arafel's bright-blue eyes moved over me, his expression warming as the time passed. "You're really here."

"What?"

The hand on my chin tightened, and I didn't dare break his stare. Slowly, Arafel's lips curled ever so slightly. "Only my Lucia would ever dare to speak to me like that."

And then we were gone, the shadows leaping from Arafel's skin as they enveloped us both. When I blinked again, we were in his rooms, the familiarity of it sinking into my skin. But as soon as we were there, Arafel released me, stepping away and back.

"Why did you come back?" His chin lifted. "*How* did you come back?"

I tried to ignore the pain that stabbed through me at his line of questioning. All the relief and pleasure that had lashed on his face when I first appeared was gone. Replaced by a weariness, a worry that I hated. His hands turned to fists.

I pushed past my initial concern; he would understand soon. He would know. "I know what to do. I know how to help the dream realm, your brothers, everyone."

"You were supposed to stay gone."

"Arafel—"

"Do you know how hard it was to send you in the first place? To watch Nephesh carry you away, knowing I could never see you again?" His voice was nearly a wail, cutting me to the quick.

"I didn't mean—" I started, but he cut me off.

"And then you came here, a task that is impossible. And have the audacity to stare up at me with those beautiful eyes and tell me you came back to save me." He swallowed. "Why?"

I stared, unsure of what to do. Arafel was standing so close now, I could see the flecks of dirt on the side of his face. He must've been flying or fighting before I got here. It was now or never. My heart hammered in my ears.

"Because I love you."

Arafel's face fell, a blue glow snapping from his eyes. "What?"

"It's why I came back. It's why I'm here." I pressed a hand against his torso, feeling the bunch and move of his muscles. "You've been saving me since the day I was born. Let me save you." My lips quivered. "Just this once. Then you can go back to saving me."

Arafel's breath was short and sharp. "You know how to give me back my soul?"

I shook my head, braids flopping over my shoulders. "I don't."

"You said—"

"I told you I know how to save you and this realm." I blinked, watching Arafel's blue eyes flicker bright. "It's not *your* soul you need."

Arafel tilted his head.

"It's mine."

31

Arafel

It was hard to focus on her words when every part of me screamed to grab Lucia, to heave her up against my body and tuck us away somewhere dark, where it would be just us. Forever. Or at least as long as my realm had left. I would give it all for her.

"Yours?" I didn't understand. "Your soul?"

Beautiful face determined, she nodded. "Yes. I'm going to give it to you."

She couldn't. I wouldn't let her. Her soul—it was beautiful, bright, unblemished by my darkness. I refused to ruin it with my lifetime of blood and war and pain. "Lucia, it's not that easy. For all we know, that will kill you. I refuse to take the risk."

"It won't."

"And you know that because?"

She gnawed at her lips. "I was remembering the stories, from Susan, from Hiram, even from your father. I believe your mother wanted to split her soul. She wanted able to go back and forth from the living world and the Underworld easily. The first witch wasn't a warrior. She was a healer, a matron, a protector of humankind."

She shook her head slowly.

"But your father didn't understand. He was desperate to have her all the time and refused to give her half of his soul." She laughed a little. "That part I assumed after meeting your father. He doesn't seem to like to share."

I grunted, intrigued. "You think my mother set up a fail-safe."

"With her death, she sheered your souls in half. Half to go to a mortal human, a mortal woman, probably someone with connections to her coven. Half to remain with you. That way you would be safe no matter what."

"She had to know that it would make us weak." My mother was a distant memory now.

"I mean, maybe, but can you imagine a better way for a mother to ensure her sons would never be alone?"

I blinked down at her, letting my guard down a little. My hand rose and snapped her hair ties. A satisfied sigh left my chest as her braids unraveled and I could sink my claws into the waves of her hair.

"But we still don't know how to do this. My mother was a witch. The spell would've been easy for her."

"The Underworld runs on deals, on oaths. And I was chosen for a reason." Lucia's lips quirked. "I was made for you, Arafel."

I had known that since I had met her, but I had given her time, afraid of what rushing her might bring. Only to lose her completely. I could still lose her now. Treading carefully, I brought a strand of her hair to my nose, inhaling the scent of my beloved, my mate. "What does that mean?"

"Only I can make this deal with you, to swap my soul in exchange for something."

"And what do you want?" My claws traced the line of her face, etching every cell of it into my memory.

She captured my hand with hers, pressing it flat against her cheek. "What I've always wanted. A home, a life filled with love and adventure and knowledge."

"With me?"

"With my monster." The words hung between us, the silence nearly painful. I tightened my grip in her hair, and she responded only by leaning her chin back until she was looking up into my face completely.

"Oaths are sealed in blood. But must be willingly given." She tilted her chin to the side, watching me closely. "You're Lucifer's son. Tell me how."

"It is a contract, written and signed in your blood. It is how the demons keep each other accountable. How my father makes his deals with mortals."

Blue eyes of steel met mine. "Show me how."

"What if it hurts you?"

"Having my soul torn in half? I'm fully prepared for it to hurt. It cannot possibly hurt as much as going to the place I called home for almost twenty years, only to realize I had missed out on the one person who was my perfect match."

I growled, my body rigid. I hated hearing she was in pain, but the idea of her going home and being in pain because of me was inexcusable. "I know it hurt, but I can't let you do this. I sent you home to keep you safe."

"I'm tired of safe." Silently, I stared. Chest heaving, she squared up against me. "You are offering me everything I've ever wanted. Sacrifice is part of life, and pain is too. Don't let the pain of the moment take away from the beauty of the action." Lucia sniffled. "Losing my mother? Moving time after time, never understanding who I was? That was pain. But I'm done letting it take away from the joy in those memories."

Lucia reached her hands up, soft pads running over the edge of my jaw. "Let me do this."

I had seen my mother and father do a spell like this before, when they had bound themselves together. It hadn't been a soul, but that connection... It had been the strongest thing I'd seen. It was the best shot I had.

I released Lucia to reach over my back and drag my shirt forward. I wasn't prepared for the gasp or surprise or horror on Lucia's face when my body came into view. I glanced down, once again surprised by the array of half-healed cuts and bruises that peppered my body.

"You..." She swallowed loudly, her fingers dropping to lightly trace a deep-purple bruise against my ribs. I tried not to flinch. "You're not healing."

"My powers are needed elsewhere."

Lucia was shaking her head, dark locks falling forward. "I didn't know."

"I didn't want you to know. I wanted you safe. I could live out the remainder of my existence hunting these corrupted souls if I knew you were safe."

A single tear slipped from her eyes. I wanted it to be the last. Her voice was a soft brush or breath against my skin. "Safe isn't living, Arafel."

"I know." My head fell back. As always, I was helpless to deny her anything. Even this.

"Tell me what to do."

I took her hand in mine, turning it over so I could run my claws carefully down the silken lines of her palm. Her body twitched, and I wasn't sure if it was fear or pleasure. But it didn't matter now. Making it so she had only her pointer finger out, I tucked the rest into a fist and raised the exposed finger to my lips.

Lucia's brows lowered and a suspicious look slipped over her face as I popped the tip of her finger in my mouth. I held it there, tasting the simple joy of her for a moment, before swiping my tongue across the digit.

As I suspected, Lucia's mouth dropped. "Arafel, what are—?"

Her voice dropped off in an instant as my fangs grew long and sharp against the pad of her finger. I tasted the copper tang of her blood and knew that she was bleeding. Guilt stole my words, but when Lucia slowly took her hand back from me, she seemed transfixed by the tiny cut. And by the rivet of bright-red blood that circled around her finger.

"Blood has power," she murmured.

"Your blood more than others, little soul."

Her lips curled for a moment before she took a long, rattling breath in. Raising the bleeding finger high, she pressed it against my sternum.

I quickly grasped her wrist with mine.

"Repeat after me."

Luca nodded, eyes wide and black on mine. Something in them was swirling and bright, different than the eyes I'd looked into for so many years. We were waking something up. Something deep inside her.

"I, Lucia Walker…"

"I, Lucia Walker," she repeated dutifully.

My magic tingled in my body, crawling under my skin, gathering in force. "Offer me, Arafel, Lord of the Underworld, half of my soul."

"Offer you, Arafel, Lord of the Underworld, half of my soul."

I urged her to continue repeating. The power of the deal spreading over my body. "In exchange for a lifetime of devotion and love."

Her eyebrows lowered, and I gave her a small nod.

"In exchange for a lifetime of devotion and love."

"Or until the stars fade to dust."

"Or until the stars fade to dust," she finished, her lips quivering.

"Names have great power here, Lucia." That was all I said and all I could say. Bright light, similar to how my brothers and I glowed, filled her gaze. That beautiful light filled the space between us as she raised her hands to my chest once again. With a flick of her wrist, Lucia was writing on me, her bloody finger the instrument of delivery as she scrawled out her name across my chest, directly atop where my heart beat loudly only for her.

Every crest of the letters, every swirl I felt in my core. My soul mate had come home. She had come to save us. She had come to save *me*.

And as I watched her, I knew that this was only the beginning. Because when my mother had chosen Lucia for my soul, she had chosen the only being in the world made to be mine. And I was made for her. No matter what came next, I would face it beside her, hand in hand. Our souls a tangle of light and darkness.

I smiled as the blue light from Lucia's eyes expanded. Even as my eyes slid shut, I could feel the power there, bright and beautiful.

Lucia gasped, the noise a combination of pain and joy, and then together, we fell into darkness.

***

"My son."

My throat burned. "Mother?"

The flickering glow before me wasn't shaped like a human or like the beauty my mother had always been when she was alive. But still, there was a familiar quality here, a power that reminded me so much of my mother that I knew it had to be her.

That low, feminine voice spoke again. "I'm glad you found your way back to us, Arafel."

"I was never gone."

"You were. Bearing the empty half of a soul is more than any one person should be able to weather. When your father and I split your souls to protect you, we had no idea it would leave so much room for evil to creep inside." The flicking glow before me grew small. "I did it to protect you."

"I know." My chest was aching. It hurt badly, and I wished I could press my hand against it. But they wouldn't move. They remained cemented to my sides, useless. "Where are you, Mother? Father has been looking for you."

Silence filled the space. Briefly, I wondered if I'd lost contact. "He knew where to find me."

"Who?"

"The darkness."

"What? He has you? Where are you?"

"He made sure I could not come to your aid. It was enough of a struggle to slip free and plant Lucia in your path." The voice grew soft. "I will release more as soon as I can. You need your souls, all of them, in order to fight him off. In order to protect the Underworld."

"Mother—wait…"

"Goodbye, Arafel. Tell Nephesh I will see him soon."

***

"Arafel!" The pain in my chest was blinding as I reared up, nearly smashing Gatam as he kneeled beside me. Paran was on my other side.

Paran clasped my forearm, grounding me as my consciousness settled back in my body. "Gods below, I thought we had lost you for sure."

I pressed a hand against my chest, the swirling, driving pressure of my new soul making everything sharp to my eyes.

"Lucia?"

"She's fine. Susan is getting her up." Paran gestured above me, and I twisted to see my mate in a similar position, her hand pressed to her heart as she stared blearily around the room.

"What happened? You and Lucia disappeared, and then a few minutes later we heard this noise." Paran swallowed. "It sounded like all of Hell was coming loose. And then the crashing from below. We came straight here to find you both unconscious on the ground, my lord."

I turned to look at her. "Lucia? Are you all right?"

"Did it work?" she choked out, her eyes still swimming with tears.

I blinked. It had to have, because now, at my core, instead of the usual rhythmic beat of my power, I felt so much more. I felt the gentle swell and fall of emotions not my own. The give and take of power trying to settle into a new form.

My mate. She was truly a part of me now.

I rolled to my knees, letting Gatam heave me to my feet while Paran went to help Susan get Lucia up. We stood looking at each other, staring.

"Your chest?" she said, stepping close. I glanced down at my unflawed, healed body and noticed something new. Where she had placed her hand against me, signing the contract to give her soul to fill in the missing half of mine, the blood that sealed the deal was now permanently inked into my skin.

I pressed a finger against the letters, feeling the soft hum of the magic there, a seal that could not be broken.

"Marked for life, mate," I said to her and watched as her eyes flickered instantly to mine.

"Forever," she murmured back.

Simeon came through the door then, his chest heaving. "My lord, you have to see."

32

Lucia

Together we followed Simeon up the stairs to the rooftop, where I'd once been so afraid. But unlike then, when I stepped close to the edge, I just felt the slight edge of fear before a warm confidence swept over me. The same feeling I got as Arafel's wings slipped free of his glamor and wrapped around me. I loved the soft little flickers of his feathers against my cheek as I turned to look out over the Sleeping Mountains and the dream realm.

My jaw loosened and I knew a noise must've escaped me. But it wouldn't have been heard, not in this instant or the next thousand, because all around us where the cries and cheers of the Castle Fel soldiers and dream warriors who were beholding the change before us.

Every branch, tree, strand of grass was a bright, vivid, healthy green, and at the edge of the river, as it stole through the land, I could see the glow of the blue light across its surface. It shimmered like glass and glitter strung together, so inhumanly beautiful that it stole my breath the instant I saw it.

Arafel was staring out at his realm, shock on his beloved face.

"Your magic," I finally choked out. "It's back."

Slowly, he turned to me, his other wing coming in to curl around us and hide us from view. "*Our* magic has brought the dream realm back." His forehead dropped to mine. "You brought light back, Lucia."

"You brought me back, Arafel, time after time. A little light for the Underworld is the least I could offer."

Arafel's eyes glowed a brilliant blue color, darkening for an instant when my eyes mimicked his exactly. Then a wide smile curled his mouth.

"What next, soul mate?"

I gripped his chin, watching the way his lips parted. Pushing to my tiptoes, I waited a breath away from his mouth before finally answering. "I want to learn to fly."

And then I leaned in to kiss him, tasting the laughter and joy on my mate's lips.

There was nothing left to fear. I knew he wouldn't let me fall.

Epilogue

Arafel

Lucia and I walked along the edge of my territory, the River Styx at our sides. Kharon hadn't been by in the weeks since I was able to pour power back into my realm, but I knew where he was. Busy of course, managing my father as well as Elon.

Busier at the moment because Nephesh had all but disappeared. I had a suspicion about where he might have gone, but I couldn't be sure.

I wasn't about to tell my father I thought my sibling had gone to hide out in the living world to find his mate.

I glanced down at the slender fingers between my own. I didn't believe Father would understand. Not this part.

"Where do you want to start today?"

"I'm not sure." Lucia looked around, her blunt white teeth biting on the bottom lip like she always did when she was nervous. My fingers twitched with the need to soothe that lip free, to taste it with my own.

"Why are you nervous? You did very well last time."

"I landed on a cliff."

Happiness and humor made my chest ache as I looked at my beloved. "And I got you right back down."

She threw me a desperate look and stopped. The grass here was waist high to her, and I knew she was thinking it would be a soft landing if her flying lesson did not go well. She didn't need to worry about that though. I would never let her hit the ground.

"Here's good."

I nodded. "Do you remember what to do?"

"Think like a demon."

I laughed. "Think like a feather on the wind, feeling the currents, let them take you, instead of fighting with them."

"Easy for you to say."

I shrugged but didn't bother answering. We had had this fight a hundred times since she had returned to the Underworld. And while I greatly enjoyed getting my little mate all worked up, I wasn't about to do it now, not when she wanted to focus on flying.

I licked my lips. There would be time later to see how worked up I could get her.

Lucia took a breath, her beautiful white wings unfolding from her back easily now. She didn't wear them often but was convinced having them would make her feel more empowered at Castle Fel. And I was loathe to do anything that didn't make her happy. I would coach her until the day she was perfectly happy with her abilities.

I enjoyed the time alone with her.

We had been hosting a great variety of guests since my soul was returned to me. My power had sent shock waves through the Underworld, and everyone except for my father and Kharon had been beating down my door for assistance with their realms.

I was trying to do all I could.

But the magic still had limits. The soul bind between my mate and me was new. I wasn't about to break or damage her by testing it too early. Still, I did what I could.

"Here I go," Lucia whispered to herself, but I heard her easily. My own wings unfolded, and the light breeze blew over them like a caress.

Albeit awkwardly, Lucia bent her knees, spreading her wings, and leaped up, sending the grass and dust from the ground below her swirling as she flapped into the air. She had a better start than our last lesson, and the pride I felt in seeing her hover happily above the grassy landscape nearly made my chest burst open.

Mine, I thought happily, watching her laugh into the air, mine to love.

With a twist of her wings, she began to move around in the air, little curves and circles as she found her way through the soft currents.

"You're doing so well," I said to her, my face in a smile.

"I know! This is amazing." Lucia held her arms out, coming back to a hover a few yards in front of me. "Suck on that, Nephesh."

My brow rose. My eldest brother had, of course, insisted no human, even my soul mate, had the ability to fly properly. I wasn't sure he had meant it or not, but Lucia had been bound and determined to show up the white-winged demon.

"Please don't say that to him. He will be so confused."

"He won't be the only one."

I growled low, spinning and throwing my wings wide as a voice spoke from behind me.

"Kadmiel, what are you doing here?" My youngest sibling was in his human glamor, a sure sign he had been in the living world. His golden eyes flickered over me and up to where I knew Lucia still hung in the air.

"I was brought a message this morning." His voice lowered. "From the seraphim."

"What?"

"They are asking me why my brother is hanging around Miami, making all of their angels nervous."

I deadpanned, "Nephesh is in Florida?"

Kadmiel's face dropped in an instant. "No, you idiot. Kharon is." His eyes narrowed at Lucia and me again. "What is going on here?"

I sighed, stepping forward. "I think it's time to probably tell you what Mom told me."

Kadmiel shrugged out of my embrace. "No more fluffing things up, Arafel. What's going on?"

Lucia landed behind me, a little off balance, but I let her manage it on her own. "They must've found their souls!" she said excitedly, coming to stand beside me.

Kadmiel's face didn't change at all.

"You're kidding. Both of them?"

"He doesn't kid," Lucia said loudly then turned to Kadmiel. "If your brother is in Florida, it's because he's found his soul. Give him some time. Buy him some with the seraph—whatever you said."

Kadmiel looked at me pointedly. "You haven't told her about the seraphim yet."

"I'm getting to it."

"Arafel..." Lucia's brow quirked my way.

I glared at my little brother. "Buy them some time. I'll speak with Father about it."

"Whatever you'd like," Kadmiel said, stepping away from the pair of us. "But if the angels show up down here, it's your funeral at Court, not mine."

The End

Want a steamy bonus scene from after Lucia and Arafel find their happily ever after? You can get it from my website: www.maggiewhitebooks.com.

The Lords of the Underworld series continues on in book two, Nephesh's story, Judge of Saints and Sinners.

There are thousands of books published every day. I'm so honored you chose one of mine to share your time with. Without our readers, authors are merely daydreamers and story-spinners. You are what makes this all real.

To my mother for her unwavering support. You can never know what it means to have you on my team every single day. And to my kids, who interrupted this book a thousand times to ask me to play, please never stop. Being your mom is the best part of my life.

Here's your peek at the next great Underworld romance...

Judge of Saints and Sinners

The heir to hell. A soul torn between good and evil.

Together they hold the scale of judgement in the Underworld, and each other's last chance at love.

Nephesh was born into chaos. The first son of hell, the child of a powerful human witch, and a fallen angel. He waged wars beside his father, together carving out the world that became Hell's domain. But no matter how strong he was, Nephesh still couldn't save the human carrying his soul. He'd lost her and any chance at saving the Underworld. It was then that Nephesh decided, the next time he found his soul, if he were ever so lucky, he would do everything he could to keep it safe, and take it back.

Justine has been cursed since the day she lost her parents. A shadow follows her, a darkness she can't escape. She will do whatever it takes to survive, the marks up on her soul the only currency in a world who never accepted outliers. But when Justine find an injured man on the streets, something tells her to save him. Ultimately inserting herself in a war hundreds of years in the making.

When darkness creeps in on her world, Nephesh is the only one Justine can turn to.

Can Justine really promise her soul to a demon in exchange for the life she thought she wanted, knowing that it would never have him in it?

Judge of Saints and Sinners is the second book in the Lords of the Underworld series. This story follows the first son of Lucifer, Nephesh's journey to reclaim his realm. It contains mature language and themes.

You can read *Judge of Saints and Sinners* now on Amazon. Signed paperbacks, hardbacks and special editions available on www.maggiewhitebooks.com